PRAISE FOR THE
CHARLOTTE HOLMES SERIES

Also in the Charlotte Holmes series

A Study in Charlotte

The Case for Jamie

THE
LAST
OF
August

A Charlotte Holmes novel

THE LAST OF August

A Charlotte Holmes novel

BRITTANY CAVALLARO

KATHERINE TEGEN BOOKS
An Imprint of HarperCollins Publishers

Katherine Tegen Books is an imprint of HarperCollins Publishers.

The Last of August
Copyright © 2017 by Brittany Cavallaro
All rights reserved. Printed in the United States of America.
No part of this book may be used or reproduced in any manner whatsoever
without written permission except in the case of brief quotations embodied in
critical articles and reviews. For information address HarperCollins Children's Books, a
division of HarperCollins Publishers, 195 Broadway, New York, NY 10007.
www.epicreads.com

ISBN 978-0-06-239895-6

17 18 19 20 21   PC/LSCH   10 9 8 7 6 5 4 3 2 1
❖
First paperback edition, 2018

For Emily and me, in Berlin

HOLMES

(for Jamie, because he insisted)

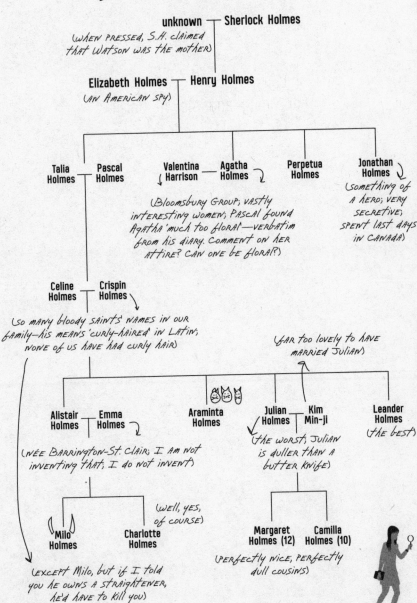

unknown ─┬─ Sherlock Holmes

(when pressed, S.H. claimed that Watson was the mother)

Elizabeth Holmes ─ Henry Holmes

(an American spy)

Talia Holmes ─ Pascal Holmes   Valentina Harrison ─ Agatha Holmes   Perpetua Holmes   Jonathan Holmes

(Bloomsbury Group; vastly interesting women; Pascal found Agatha 'much too floral'—verbatim from his diary. Comment on her attire? Can one be floral?)

(something of a hero; very secretive; spent last days in Canada)

Celine Holmes ─ Crispin Holmes

(So many bloody saints' names in our family—his means 'curly-haired' in Latin; none of us have had curly hair)

(far too lovely to have married Julian)

Alistair Holmes ─ Emma Holmes   Araminta Holmes   Julian Holmes ─ Kim Min-ji   Leander Holmes

(the best)

(née Barrington-St. Clair; I am not inventing that; I do not invent)

(the worst; Julian is duller than a butter knife)

Milo Holmes   Charlotte Holmes

(well, yes, of course)

(except Milo, but if I told you he owns a straightener, he'd have to kill you)

Margaret Holmes (12)   Camilla Holmes (10)

(perfectly nice, perfectly dull cousins)

MORIARTY

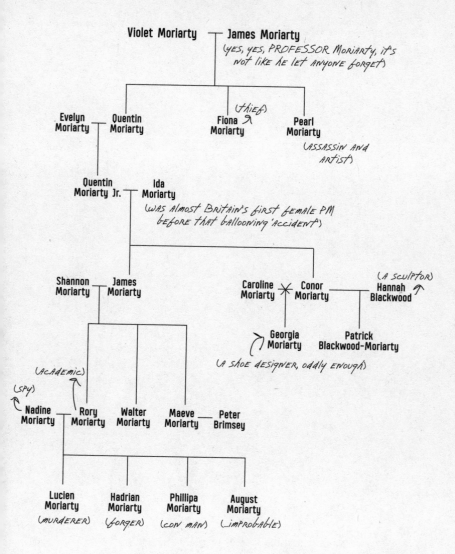

Violet Moriarty — James Moriarty
(yes, yes, PROFESSOR Moriarty, it's not like he let anyone forget)

Evelyn Moriarty | Quentin Moriarty | Fiona Moriarty *(thief)* | Pearl Moriarty *(assassin and artist)*

Quentin Moriarty Jr. — Ida Moriarty
(was almost Britain's first female PM before that ballooning 'accident')

Shannon Moriarty — James Moriarty

Caroline Moriarty ✕ Conor Moriarty — Hannah Blackwood *(a sculptor)*

Georgia Moriarty *(a shoe designer, oddly enough)*

Patrick Blackwood-Moriarty

(spy) Nadine Moriarty — Rory Moriarty *(academic)* — Walter Moriarty — Maeve Moriarty — Peter Brimsey

Lucien Moriarty *(murderer)* | Hadrian Moriarty *(forger)* | Phillipa Moriarty *(con man)* | August Moriarty *(...improbable)*

There you have them. Please tell me you don't have any plans to frame these.
—C.H.

"Do you know what love is? I'll tell you:
it is whatever you can still betray."
THE LOOKING GLASS WAR, JOHN LE CARRÉ

one

It was late December in the south of England, and though it was only three in the afternoon, the sky outside Charlotte Holmes's bedroom window was as black and full as it would've been in the Arctic Circle. I'd forgotten about this, somehow, during my months in Connecticut away at Sherringford School, even though I'd grown up with one leg on either side of the Atlantic. When I thought of winter, I thought of those reasonable New England nights that arrived punctually just after dinner, disappearing into morning blue by the time you'd stretched awake in bed. British winter nights were different. They came on in October with a shotgun and held you hostage for the next six months.

It would have been better, all told, if I'd visited Holmes

for the first time in the summer. Her family lived in Sussex, a county that hugged England's southern coast, and from the top floor of the house they'd built you could see the sea. Or you could if you happened to own a pair of night-vision goggles and a vivid imagination. England's December darkness would have put me into a mood all by itself, but Holmes's family manor was stuck up on a hill like a fortress. I kept waiting for lightning to break the sky above it or for some poor, tortured mutant to come stumbling out of its cellar, mad scientist in hot pursuit.

The inside didn't do much to dispel the feeling that I was in a horror movie. But a different kind of horror movie—some art-house Scandinavian deal. Long dark uncomfortable couches that weren't designed to be sat on. White walls hung with white abstract paintings. A baby grand lurking in a corner. In short, the kind of place that vampires lived in. Really well-mannered vampires. And everywhere, silence.

Holmes's rooms in the basement were the messy, living heart of that cold house. Her bedroom had dark walls and industrial shelving and books, books everywhere, organized alphabetically on shelves or tossed on the floor with their pages flung open. In the room beside, a chemistry table crowded with beakers and burners. Succulent plants, twisted and knobbled in their little pots, that she fed a mixture of vinegar and almond milk each morning from an eyedropper. ("It's an experiment," Holmes told me when I protested. "I'm trying to kill them. *Nothing* kills them.") The floors were scattered with papers and coins and busted cigarettes, and still, in all the endless clutter, there wasn't a single speck of dust or dirt. It was what I'd come to expect from her, except for maybe her stash of chocolate biscuits and the entire hardbound *Encyclopedia Britannica*, which she kept in the low bookshelf that served as her nightstand. Apparently Holmes liked to pore over it on her bed, cigarette in hand. Today was volume C, the entry "Czechoslovakia," and for some unknowable reason, she'd insisted on reading the whole of it out loud to me while I paced back and forth in front of her.

Well. There might have been a reason. It was a way to avoid our talking about anything real.

While she spoke, I tried to avoid looking at the Sherlock Holmes novels she'd stacked on top of volumes D and E. They were her father's, filched from his study. We'd lost her own copies in a bomb blast this fall, along with her chemical experiments, my favorite scarf, and a good deal of my trust in the human race. Those Sherlock Holmes stories reminded me of the girl she was when we met, the girl I'd so badly wanted to know.

In the last few days, we'd somehow managed to retreat backwards from our easy friendship, back to that old territory of distrust and unknowability. The thought made me sick, made me want to climb the walls. It made me want to lay it all out at her feet so we could begin to fix it.

I didn't do that. Instead, in the grand tradition of our friendship, I picked a fight about something completely different.

"Where is it?" I asked her. "Why can't you just tell me where it is?"

"It wasn't until 1918 that Czechoslovakia liberated itself from the Russo-Hungarian Empire and became the country as we knew it in the twentieth century." She ashed her Lucky Strike on the coverlet. "Then, a series of events that transpired in the 1940s—"

"Holmes." I waved a hand in front of her face. "Holmes. I asked you about Milo's suit."

She batted me away. "During which the state did not precisely exist as it had before—"

"The suit that definitely won't fit me. That costs more than my father's house. The suit that you're making me wear."

"Until that particular territory was ceded to the then–Soviet Union in 1945." She squinted down at the volume, cigarette dangling from her fingers. "I can't make out the next bit. I must have spilled something on this page the last time I read it."

"So you reread this entry a lot. A little Eastern Europe before bed. Just as good as Nancy Drew."

"As who?"

"No one. Look," I said, growing impatient, "I understand your wanting me to 'dress for dinner,' and that you can say those words with a straight face because you grew up with this level of unbearable suffocating poshness, and I don't know, maybe you *like* that it makes me uncomfortable—"

She blinked at me, a bit stung. Every word out of my mouth today was crueler than I wanted it to be. "Okay, fine," I said, backtracking, "so I'm having a very American panic attack, but your brother's rooms are locked down more tightly than the Pentagon—"

4

"Please. Milo has better security than that," she said. "Do you need the access code? I can text him for it. He changes it remotely every two days."

"The code to his childhood bedroom. He changes it. From Berlin."

"Well, he's the head of a mercenary company." She reached for her phone. "Can't have anyone finding Mr. Wiggles. Plush bunnies need the same protection as state secrets, you know."

I laughed, and she smiled back at me, and for a moment I forgot we weren't getting along.

"Holmes," I said, the way I'd done so often in the past— out of reflex, as punctuation, with nothing I really planned to say after.

She let the moment hang longer than was usual. When she finally said "Watson," it was with hesitation.

I thought of the questions I wanted to ask her. All the horrible things I could say instead. But all I said was, "Why are you reading to me about Czechoslovakia?"

Her smile tightened. "Because my father is having the Czech ambassador to dinner tonight along with the newest Louvre curator, and I thought we might as well be prepared, because I rather doubt you know anything about Eastern Europe without my guidance, and we want to prove to my mother that you're not an idiot. Oh," she said, as her phone pinged, "Milo's changed the code to 666, just for us. Charming. Go on and fetch your suit, but be quick. We still need to discuss the Velvet Revolution of 1989."

At that moment, I wanted to take up arms myself. Curators?

Ambassadors? Her mother thinking I was stupid? I was, as usual, in over my head.

To be fair, my own father had insinuated that this would be a difficult trip, though I don't think he'd predicted the particulars. When, a few days after the Bryony Downs affair wrapped up, I told him my plans—we'd spend the break at my place first, then hers—he'd begun by saying that my mother would hate the idea, which was ineffective as a warning because it was so obvious. My mother hated the Holmeses, and the Moriartys, and mysteries. I'm sure she hated tweed capes just on principle. But after what had happened this fall, the thing she hated most was Charlotte Holmes herself.

"Well," my father had said, "if you insist on going to stay with them, I'm sure you'll have a very . . . nice time. The house is lovely." He'd paused, clearly searching for something else to say. "And Holmes's parents are . . . ah. Well. You know, I heard they had six bathrooms in that house. Six!"

This was foreboding. "Leander will be there," I'd said, a bit desperate for something to look forward to. Holmes's uncle was my father's former flatmate and longtime best friend.

"Yes! Leander. Very good. Leander will surely act as a buffer between you and . . . anything you need a buffer for. Excellent." Then he'd trotted out something about my stepmother needing him in the kitchen and hung up, leaving me with a whole new host of doubts about Christmas.

As soon as Holmes had brought up the idea of us spending the break together, I'd begun imagining us somewhere like my mother's apartment in London. Sweaters, and cocoa, maybe watching a *Doctor Who* special by the fire. Holmes in some bobbly knit hat, dismembering a chocolate orange. We were, in fact, already sprawled out on my living room couch when Holmes told me to stop avoiding the subject and just ask my mother if I could go down to Sussex. I'd been actively avoiding that conversation. "Be diplomatic," Holmes had said, then paused. "By that I mean, plan out what you want to say, and then don't say it."

It was no use. Holmes and my father had predicted her reaction more or less exactly. When I told her our plans, she began shouting so loudly about Lucien Moriarty that the usually unflappable Holmes backed herself bodily into a corner.

"You almost *died*," my mother concluded. "The Moriartys almost *killed you.* And you want to spend Christmas in their enemy's stronghold?"

"Their stronghold? What do you think this is, Batman?" I started laughing. Across the room, Holmes buried her head in her hands. "Mum. I'll be fine. I'm almost an adult, I can decide what to do with my holiday. You know, I told Dad not to tell you about that whole near-death thing. I said that you'd over-react, and I was right."

There was a long pause, and then the shouting got somewhat louder.

When she capitulated—which she finally did, with extreme prejudice—it came with a price. Our last few days in London were miserable. My mother sniped at me for everything from the cleanliness of the living room to the way my English accent had returned, with a vengeance, on my return to London. *It's like that girl even took away your voice,* she told me. Maybe I had pushed my mother a little too far to begin with; she certainly wasn't happy I'd brought Holmes to visit in the first place. I think it would've been a relief to both of them had she stayed behind, but I had a point I wanted to make—I was tired of my mother's disdain for someone she'd never met. Someone who was important to me. For my sake, my mother should be able to accept my best friend for the brilliant, thrilling girl she was.

That worked out about as well as you'd expect.

Holmes and I spent a lot of time out of the house.

I took her to my favorite bookstore, where I loaded her up with Ian Rankin novels and she bullied me into buying a book on European snails. I took her to the chip shop on the corner, where she distracted me by giving a detailed-and-probably-bullshit account of her brother's sex life (drones, cameras, his rooftop pool) while she ate all my fried fish and left her own plate untouched. I took her for a walk along the Thames, where I showed her how to skip a stone and she nearly punctured a hole in a passing pontoon boat. We went to my favorite curry place. Twice. In one day. She'd gotten this look on her face when she took her first bite of their pakora, this blissful, lids-lowered look, and two hours later I decided I needed to see it again. It was so good to see her happy that it made up for the embarrassment I felt that night, when I found her instructing my sister, Shelby, on the best way to bleach out bloodstains, using the curry dribble on my shirt as a test case.

In short, it was both the best three days I'd ever had, my

mother notwithstanding, and a fairly standard week with Charlotte Holmes. My sister, unused to this phenomenon, was completely overcome. Shelby had taken to trailing Holmes like a shadow, dressing in all black and straightening her hair, dragging her away to show off things in her room. I didn't know exactly what *things* were, but from the lilting, earnest music coming from under the door, I had a feeling that their soundtrack was L.A.D., Shelby's boy band du jour. My guess was that Shelby was showing off her paintings. My mother had told me that my sister had taken up art with a passion while I'd been away, but that so far, she'd been too shy to show anyone what she'd made.

Not that I would have known what to say to her about it. I didn't know a whole lot about art. I knew what I liked, what made me feel something—portraits, usually. I liked things that felt secret. Scenes set in a dark room. Mysterious books and bottles, or a girl with her face turned away. When asked, I trotted out Rembrandt's *Anatomy Lesson* as my favorite work of art, though to be honest, I'd lost the ability to call it up clearly in my head. I tended to spend too much time with my favorite things, loved them too hard until I wore them down. After a while, they became more like a shorthand for who I was and less like things I actually enjoyed.

"Shelby wanted my advice, and I know enough to give her my opinion," Holmes was saying. I'd asked if she'd been talking to my sister about her art. It was our last night in London; we were leaving for Sussex the next afternoon. My mother had turned my bedroom into a study, so we were where we'd been all week—on a pair of hideaway mattresses in the living room, our bags stacked behind us like a barricade. The sky outside was beginning to lighten. One tradeoff of being friends with Holmes was sleep. As in, you never did again.

"Enough?" I asked.

"My father thought it was an important part of my education. I can go on endlessly about color and composition, thanks to him and"—she scowled—"my old tutor, Professor Demarchelier."

I propped myself up on one arm. "Do you . . . make art?" It struck me, then, how little I knew about her, how all the facts of her life before this September had come to me either secondhand or in bits and reluctant pieces. She'd had a cat named Mouse. Her mother was a chemist. But I had no idea what her first bought book had been, or if she'd ever wanted to be a marine biologist, or even what she was like when she wasn't wanted for murder. She played the violin, of course, and so I imagine she'd tried out other kinds of art as well. I tried to imagine what a Holmes painting would look like. *A girl in a dark room*, I thought, *with her face turned away*, but as I watched her, she tilted her face toward me.

"I don't have the skill, and I don't invest my time in things I'm rubbish at. But I *am* a fair critic. Your sister is quite good. A nice sense of composition, an interesting use of color. See? There you go. Art talk. Her range is limited, though. I saw about thirty paintings of your neighbor's dog."

"Woof is usually sleeping in their backyard." I smiled at her. "Makes him an easy subject."

"We could take her to the Tate Modern. Tomorrow morning, before we go. If you wanted." She stretched her arms out above her head. In the darkness, her skin looked like cream in a pitcher. I jerked my eyes back up to her face. It was late, and when it was late, I had these kinds of slippages.

I had them all the time, if I was being honest. At four in the morning, I could admit to that.

"The Tate," I said, pulling myself together. Her offer had sounded genuine. "Sure. If you actually want to. You've been really nice to Shelby already. I think you've heard enough L.A.D. for a lifetime."

"I love L.A.D.," she said, deadpan.

"You like ABBA," I reminded her. "So I don't actually know if that's a joke. Next I'm going to find out that you wear a fanny pack in the summer. Or that you had a poster of Harry Styles in your room when you were eleven."

Holmes hesitated.

"You did *not*."

"It was *Prince* Harry, actually," she said, folding her arms, "and he was a very good dresser. I have an appreciation for fine tailoring. Anyway, I was eleven years old, and lonely, and if you don't stop smirking at me, I will come over there and—"

"Yes, I'm sure it was his *fine tailoring* you appreciated, and not his—"

She hit me with her pillow.

"To think," I said through a mouthful of goose down. "You're a Holmes. Your family's famous. You could have maybe made it happen. *Princess* Charlotte, and the bad-boy spare.

God knows you're pretty enough to pull it off. I can see it now—you in a tiara, doing that screwing-in-a-lightbulb wave in the back of some convertible."

"Watson."

"You would have had to make *speeches*. To orphans, and general assemblies. You'd have to have your photo taken with puppies."

"Watson."

"What? You know I'm teasing. The way you grew up is just beyond me." I was rambling, I knew it, but I was too tired to put the brakes on. "You've seen our flat. It's a glorified closet. You've seen how my mother gets all weird and tight-lipped when you talk about your family. I think she worries that I'm going to go to the Sussex Downs and get sucked in by the decadent, mysterious Holmeses and never come back. And you smile politely and bite back whatever you actually think of her, and my sister, and where we live. Which, let's face it, has probably taken a ton of effort on your part, because you're not particularly nice. You don't have to be. You're fancy, Charlotte Holmes. Repeat after me. *I'm fancy, and Jamie Watson's a peasant.*"

"Sometimes I think you don't give me enough credit," she said instead.

"What?" I sat up. "I just . . . look, okay, maybe I'm feeling a little punchy. It's late. But I don't want you to feel like you have to act a certain way, or impress anyone. We're impressed already. You don't have to act like you like my mum, or my sister, or where I live—"

"I like your flat."

"It's the size of your lab at school—"

"I like your flat because you grew up here," she said, looking at me steadily, "and I like eating your dinner because it's yours, which makes it better than mine. And I like your sister because she's smart, and she worships you, which means she is *very* smart. You talk about her like she's a child, I've noticed, but the fact that she's attempting to explore her nascent sexuality by listening to a lot of droopy-voiced boy sopranos isn't something you should tease her for. It's certainly safer than the alternative."

The conversation had taken a turn I hadn't expected. Though maybe I should have seen it coming from the moment the words "you're pretty" slipped out of my mouth.

She'd pushed herself up to face me. Her sheets were twisted around her legs, her hair rumpled, and she looked like she was in some French film about illicit sex. Which was not something I should be thinking. I ran through a familiar list in my head, the least erotic things I could think of: Grandma, my seventh birthday party, *The Lion King*. . . .

"The alternative?" I repeated.

"It's rather better to dip in a toe before you get dragged underwater."

"We don't need to talk about this—"

"I'm so sorry if I'm making you *uncomfortable*."

"I was going to say if you don't want to. How did we even get here?"

"You were trashing your upbringing. I was defending it. I

13

like it here, Jamie. We're going to my parents' house next, and it won't be like this. I won't be like this."

"Like what, exactly?"

"Stop being dense," she snapped. "It doesn't suit you at all."

For the record, I wasn't being dense. I was trying, repeatedly, to give her an out. I knew she was skirting right around the edges of something we didn't ever talk about. She was raped. We were framed for that rapist's murder. Whatever feelings she had for me were caught up in that trauma, and so whatever feelings I had for her were on ice for the time being. While I might, on occasion, spiral into some stupid reverie about how beautiful she was, I'd never voiced those thoughts. While I'd given her openings to talk to me about the two of us, I'd never pushed her. The closest we'd come were these elliptical conversations at dawn, where we circled around the subject until I said something wrong and she shut down completely. For hours after, she wouldn't even look at me.

"I was just trying to say that I won't go there if you don't want me to," I said, and by *there*, I meant *Sussex*, and *Lee Dobson, who I routinely fantasize about digging up and killing again*, and *talking about the two of us, which frankly, I am not equipped to do*, and *even though your hair keeps brushing your collarbone and you lick your lips when you're nervous, I'm not thinking about you like that, I'm not, I swear to God I'm not.*

The best and worst thing about Holmes was that she heard everything I didn't say along with everything I did.

"Jamie." It was a sad whisper, or maybe it was too quiet for me to tell. To my complete shock, she reached out and took my hand, bringing my palm up to her lips.

This? This had never happened before.

I could feel her hot breath, the brush of her mouth. I bit back a sound at the back of my throat and kept myself still, terrified I might scare her away or worse, that this might break apart the both of us.

She ran a finger down my chest. "Is this what you want?" she asked me, and with that, my willpower broke completely.

I couldn't answer, not with words. Instead, I dropped my hands down to her waist, intending to kiss her the way I'd wanted for months—a deep, searching kiss, one hand tangled in her hair, her pressed up against me like I was the only other person in the world.

But when I touched her, she recoiled. A rush of fear went across her face. I watched as that fear turn to rage, and then to something like despair.

We stared at each other for an impossible moment. Without a word, she pulled away and lay down on her mattress, her back to me. Beyond her, the bruised colors of dawn spread out across the window.

"Charlotte," I said quietly, reaching out to touch her shoulder. She shook off my hand. I couldn't blame her for that. But it twisted something in my chest.

For the first time, I realized that maybe my presence was more of a curse than a comfort.

two

THIS WASN'T THE FIRST TIME SOMETHING HAD HAPPENED between us.

We'd kissed. Once. It had been brief, a brush of a thing. I'd been sort of dying at the time, so the kiss might've come from pity; we were at the end of our murder investigation, so it might have come from a misplaced sense of relief. Either way, I hadn't really seen it as a promise of things to come. She'd said as much. Even if she did want something romantic with me, it wasn't hard to see she was working through a metric ton of psychic damage. Like I said, I had no intentions of pushing her. I didn't know if I *wanted* to push past this, if I'd shatter the strange, fragile thing that we'd spun between us, if we'd be worse off. After last night, it seemed like we would be.

We didn't go to the Tate that next morning. We didn't sneak out for breakfast on a couple hours' sleep, as we'd done in the days before. We packed in silence, Holmes pale in her dressing gown and socks, and after we said good-bye to my mother and my teary little sister, we walked to the station in silence. We rode to Sussex in a private compartment, her face turned resolutely to the window. I pretended to read my novel, and then stopped pretending. I wasn't fooling her, or anyone.

When we finally got off the train at Eastbourne, a black car was waiting for us at the curb.

Holmes turned to me, hands stuffed in her pockets. "This will be fine," she murmured. "You'll be there, so it'll be fine."

"It would probably help the whole 'fine' thing if we were, you know, talking to each other." I tried not to sound as hurt as I felt.

She looked surprised. "I always want to talk to you," she said. "But I know you. You always want to make things better, and I don't know how us talking to each other right now will do anything but make it worse."

As the driver came around to take our luggage, she patted my shoulder in her absent way and stepped down to say hello. I stood there holding my suitcase, furious at her for deciding on silence as a way to handle this. For making every decision. She treated me like I was her pet, I thought, and it came over me in waves, the kind of world-splitting *lostness* I hadn't felt in months.

It was that same feeling that had gotten me into the whole mess that was Charlotte-Holmes-and-Jamie-Watson to begin with, and I wasn't so far gone as to not appreciate the irony.

HER PARENTS WEREN'T WAITING FOR US WHEN WE GOT TO the house, which was fine by me. I didn't think I could manage to be friendly to them, or anyone. A housekeeper met us instead, a neat, quiet woman my mother's age. She took our coats and showed us down to Holmes's rooms, and it was dark by the time we finished the lunch she brought down to us on a tray.

That night, after my impromptu lesson on European history, that same housekeeper produced a wooden box for me to stand on while she hemmed Milo's too-long pants, a length of measuring tape draped over her shoulders. She'd been the only person in Holmes's room when I returned with my suit. As I stood awkwardly, trying not to fidget, I tried to imagine where Holmes was hiding. Maybe shooting pool in a billiards room, or feeling her way blindfolded through some family obstacle course, the way Holmeses were rumored to train their kids. Maybe she was eating chocolate biscuits in the closet.

"Finished," the housekeeper said finally. She stood up to survey her work with some satisfaction. "You look very handsome, Master Jamie. The open collar suits you."

"Oh God," I said, tugging on my cuffs. "Please don't call me that. Do you know where H— where Charlotte is?"

"Upstairs, I imagine."

"There's a lot of upstairs here." I had a vision of myself

wandering aimlessly through their house in a borrowed suit. Speaking of obstacle courses. "Second floor? Third? Fourth? Uh . . . is there a fourth?"

"Try her father's study," she said, holding the door open. "Third floor, east wing."

I think it might have taken less time for me to get from London to Sussex, but I found his study at last, at the end of a mullioned hall hung with portraits. This wing felt older, darker than the rest of the house. The paintings glowered down at me. In one, Holmes's father and his siblings were clustered around a table piled high with books. Alistair Holmes looked just like his daughter, serious and withdrawn, hands folded before him. The one with the rakish smile was clearly Leander, I thought. I wondered if he'd arrived yet, and hoped he had.

"Come in, already," said a muffled voice from behind the study door, though I hadn't knocked. Of course they knew I was there. There were secrets in this house, it was clear, but I wasn't going to be able to keep any of my own.

I reached for the handle, then stopped. I hadn't noticed this final portrait. Beside me, Sherlock Holmes sat with pursed lips and a magnifying glass clutched in one hand, clearly annoyed by the whole enterprise of being painted, at having to do his best impression of himself for someone else's benefit. Dr. Watson, my great-great-great-grandfather, stood behind him. He rested a reassuring hand on his friend's shoulder.

I could've taken it as a sign that everything would be okay. But I looked at that hand for a long minute and wondered how many times Sherlock Holmes had tried to shake it off.

Watsons, I thought, *generations of masochists*, and pushed open the door.

The room was dimly lit. It took my eyes a moment to adjust. A massive desk stood in its center, and behind it, bookshelves spread out like wings. Sitting in front of all that collected knowledge was Alistair Holmes, his canny eyes fixed on me.

I liked him immediately, though I knew I shouldn't. By all accounts, he'd driven his daughter half to death with his training and expectations. But he knew me. I could tell by the cataloguing look on his face, one I'd seen on Charlotte Holmes time and time again. He saw me for what I was, a flustered middle-class boy in a borrowed suit, and yet he didn't judge. Honestly, I didn't think he cared about my social class one way or another. After the emotional turmoil of the last few days, it was nice to encounter a little impassivity.

"Jamie," he said in a surprising tenor. "Please, sit. It's a pleasure to finally meet you."

"You too." I perched in the armchair across from him. "Thanks so much for letting me stay with you."

He waved a hand. "Of course. You've made my daughter very happy."

"Thanks," I said, though it wasn't entirely true. I'd made her happy, or I thought I had. I'd also made her miserable. I'd held her while our hideout burned. I'd collapsed at her feet, too weak to stand, while Lucien Moriarty taunted her through Bryony Downs's pink sparkly phone. *This was a practice round. I wanted to see what was important to you. I wanted to see how much this foolish boy trusted you. I threaten him, and you kiss him. Cue strings. Cue the applause.* And now I'd driven her to hide somewhere in her massive house by the sea, while her father made the kind of small talk with me that she'd always found abhorrent.

"Did you like that last painting in the hall, of our shared ancestors? I heard you stop to look at it."

"You look a lot like Sherlock Holmes. Like the pictures I've seen of him, anyway," I said. He nodded, and I found myself wanting to push past all the pleasantries and get to something real. "It made me think about how things have ended up. I mean, Charlotte and I are running around together. We've solved a murder case and found a Moriarty on the other end of it. It's almost like history is repeating itself."

"There are plenty of family businesses in the world," he said, steepling his long fingers under his chin. "Men pass on their cobbler shops to their sons. Lawyers send their daughters away to school and then give them a place at the firm. We may have certain affinities that we pass down to our children, through genetic inheritance or through the way we teach them to think, but I don't think it's entirely out of our control. It's not like we're Sisyphus's scions, forever pushing his boulder up the hill. Look at your father."

"He's in sales," I said, trying to keep up with his train of thought.

Holmes's father lifted an eyebrow. "And the woman who painted that portrait you were admiring in the hall was Professor Moriarty's daughter, and she presented it to our family as an apology for her father's actions. The past's actions may echo, but you shouldn't take it to mean that we're predestined. Your father may like solving mysteries, but ever since he moved to the States, he's seemed to be happier as a spectator. I imagined it helped him to be away from Leander's influence. My brother is an actual agent of chaos."

"Do you know when he's getting in? Leander?"

"Tonight or tomorrow," he said, checking his watch. "One can never really be exact, with him. The world must reshape itself around his desires. He's much like Charlotte in that way. Not content to observe, not even content to mete out justice. Working for the benefit of others has never been their primary goal."

I leaned forward, despite myself. Alistair Holmes was like a relic from a long-ago time—his formal language and determined stare. It was hypnotic, almost, and I didn't resist the spell he cast. "Then what do you think Charlotte and Leander's goals are?"

"To assert themselves on the world, or so I've always thought." He shrugged. "They aren't content to act behind the scenes. They always manage to be caught up in the play itself. In that way, I suppose they're both more like Sherlock than any of the rest of us. He was always the would-be magician of the family. Do you know, I toiled away at the Ministry of Defense for years—I was the architect of some small international conflicts—and yet I rarely stepped out from behind my desk. I was content to move theoretical armies in a theoretical battleground, and let others make those ideas real. My son Milo does similar work. In many ways, for good or ill, he's made himself from that mold."

"But is that the best way?" I heard myself ask. I hadn't meant to challenge him; it'd just slipped out. "Don't you think it's better to see the consequences of your actions firsthand, so that you can learn from them and make smarter decisions in the future?"

"You're a thoughtful boy," he said, though I wasn't sure if he meant it. "Do you think I should have insisted that Charlotte stay and watch the fallout from *her* actions, after that debacle with August Moriarty, instead of sending her away for a fresh start?"

"I—"

"There are many ways of taking responsibility. We don't always have to pay for our sins with our blood, or by sacrificing our futures. But I hear Charlotte down the hall, so we should change the subject." He squinted at me. "You know, you aren't what I imagined."

"What did you expect?" I asked, feeling self-conscious all of a sudden. I wasn't built for these sorts of deep-sea conversations, all murky ocean floor.

"Something rather less than you are." He stood and walked to the window, looking over the dark hills that rolled down to the water. "It's a shame."

"What is?" I asked, but Holmes was rapping sharply on the study door.

"Mother is going to kill me," she said when I opened it. "We should all be downstairs five minutes ago. Hello, Dad."

"Lottie," he said, without turning around. "I'll be there

soon. Why don't you show Jamie down to the dining room?"

"Of course." She tucked her hand into my arm in a matter-of-fact way. Were we still fighting? Had we been fighting in the first place? I was exhausted by this train of thought, and anyway, it didn't matter, not in her family's sprawling house in the dead of winter. I was getting the sense that, without Holmes as my translator, I wasn't going to make it through this week alive.

"You look very nice," I told her, because she did—floor-length dress, dark lips, her hair tied up in a knot.

"I know," she sighed. "Isn't it awful? Let's get this over with."

EMMA HOLMES WASN'T SPEAKING TO ME. SHE WASN'T really speaking to anyone. Her left hand glittered with rings, and she was using it to rub the back of her neck. The other was busy with her wineglass. This wouldn't be a problem except that if their dining room was a continent (it was the size of one), I was sitting somewhere in Siberia.

I'd been placed between Holmes's mother and the silent, sullen daughter of the Czech ambassador, a girl named Eliska who gave me a once-over and sent a pleading look up into the ceiling. Either she could sniff out my lack of a trust fund, or she'd been hoping for a taller, buffer Jamie Watson, one who looked a little more like a volunteer fireman and less like a volunteer librarian. Either way, I'd been left to make small talk with Holmes's mother while Eliska sighed over her food.

Holmes—my Holmes, if she was that—wasn't any help. She'd cut up all the food on her plate and was now busily rearranging it, but I could tell from the distant look in her eyes that she was preoccupied with the conversation at the other end of the table. The only conversation, actually, something about the going prices for Picasso sketches. Alistair Holmes was correcting the weaselly-looking museum curator. Of course he knew more about art than someone who worked at the Louvre. I couldn't muster the energy to be surprised.

In fact, I couldn't muster much energy at all. I kept waiting for the threat in this place to be made real, something I could see or hear, something I could counter. I'd expected a colder welcome. Holmeses falling over themselves to put me in my intellectual place. Maybe an actual flaming hoop. What I'd gotten instead was some very nice food and one cryptic conversation with Holmes's father. I thought back to the warning she'd given me before we'd arrived, and I couldn't make heads or tails of it.

"Sherringford? What a horrid school," Alistair was saying. "Yes, it's been something of a disappointment, but we had no doubt that Charlotte acquitted herself well, despite the circumstances."

Charlotte's smile was small and cold.

"I'm sorry to be so quiet, James," her mother said to me in a low voice. "I've been having a rough go of it recently. In and out of hospital. I hope you're enjoying your dinner."

"It's great, thanks. I'm sorry you're not feeling well."

At that, Holmes's attention snapped back to me. "Mother," she said, scraping her fork against her plate. "You really could ask Jamie some of the standard questions. It's not a difficult script to remember. How does he like school. Does he have any sisters. Et cetera."

Her mother flushed. "Of course. Did you have a nice stay in London? Lottie loves it there."

"We had a lot of fun," I told her, giving her daughter a dirty look. Her mother seemed to be doing her best. I felt bad for her, all dressed up in this ridiculous room when she clearly wished she was back in bed. "Walked along the Thames. Saw a lot of bookshops. Nothing too demanding."

"I always think it's nice to take a break after a difficult semester. From what I've heard, yours was especially so."

I laughed. "An understatement, actually."

Her mother nodded, eyes half-focused. "And remind me. Why was it, again, that you and my daughter were immediately suspected for that boy's murder? I understand that he attacked her. But why on earth were *you* involved?"

"I didn't volunteer to be a suspect, if that's what you're asking." I tried to keep my tone light.

"Well, the reason *I'd* been given was that you'd been nursing some ridiculous crush on my daughter, but I still don't understand how that demanded your involvement."

It was as if I'd been hit across the face. "What? I—"

Charlotte continued rearranging her food. Her expression hadn't changed.

"It's a simple question," her mother said in that quiet voice. "A more complicated one would be, why are you still shadowing her if those circumstances have resolved themselves? I don't see why she has any use of you now."

"I'm fairly sure she likes me." I enunciated my words. Not out of spite—I was terrified that I would stutter. "We're friends, spending time together over the winter holiday. It's not a new concept."

"Ah." There was a wealth of meaning in that syllable: doubt, derision, a healthy dose of scorn. "And yet she doesn't have friends. It hardly hurts that you're handsome, or that you're from reduced circumstances. I imagine you'd follow her anywhere. That combination must be *catnip* for a girl like our Lottie. A ready-made acolyte. But what could possibly be in it for you?"

Had we been anywhere else, with anyone else, Holmes would have barreled into this conversation like an armored tank. I knew how to defend myself, but I was so used to her quick, fearless wit that, in its absence, I found myself speechless.

And it was absent. Holmes herself was absent. Her eyes had gone dark and faraway, her fork still tracing patterns on her plate. How long had this been broiling under Emma Holmes's skin? Or was it something concocted on the spot, a punishment for Charlotte mouthing off to her mother?

Emma Holmes turned her lantern eyes to me. "If you're planning something. If you're in someone's employ. If you demand things from her that she cannot give—"

"You don't have to—" Finally, her daughter spoke. Only to be cut right off.

"If you hurt her, I will ruin you. That's all." Emma Holmes raised her voice to the rest of the table. "And on that subject,

Walter, why don't you tell us about the exhibit you're working on? I thought I heard the name Picasso tossed around."

It wasn't meant as punishment. It was love for her daughter, and it was terrifying.

I watched as a shudder ground through Charlotte's shoulders. No wonder she never had an appetite, if mealtimes had always been as tumultuous as this.

Down the table, the curator was dabbing his mouth with his napkin. "Picasso, yes. Alistair was just telling me about your private collection. You house it in London? I'd love to see it. Picasso was quite prolific, as you know, and gave away so many sketches as gifts that new pieces are always coming to light."

Holmes's mother waved a hand. I recognized the gesture from her daughter. "Call my secretary," she said. "I'm sure she can arrange a tour of our holdings."

At that, I excused myself. I needed to do that clichéd movie thing where I splashed cold water on my face. To my surprise, Eliska dropped her napkin on her chair and followed me down the hall.

"Jamie, yes?" she asked in accented English. When I nodded, she peered over her shoulder to make sure we were alone. "Jamie, this is . . . bullshit."

"That sounds about right."

She stalked into the bathroom to check her reflection in the mirror. "My mother, she tells me we go to Britain for a year. Not too long to miss my friends back in Prague. I will make new ones. But everyone is a thousand years old, or stupid, or silent."

"Not everyone here is like that," I found myself saying. "I'm not. Charlotte Holmes isn't. Usually."

With a finger, Eliska wiped off a bit of stray lipstick. "Maybe somewhere else, she is better. But I go to these family dinners in these big houses and the teenagers are silent. The food is very good. At my home, the food is terrible and the teenagers are much more fun." She looked at me over her shoulder, considering. "My mother and I go back in one week. She has a new job in the government. If you are in Prague, come see me. I feel—how should I say?—sorry for you."

"I always appreciate a good pity invite," I countered, but my heart wasn't in it. Eliska could tell. She flashed me a smile and left.

When I got back to the table, Emma Holmes had already gone up to bed. Dessert had been served, an architectural piece of cheesecake the size of my thumbnail, and Alistair Holmes was asking his daughter a series of softball questions about Sherringford. *What have you learned in your chemistry tutorial? Do you like your instructor? How do you think you'll apply those skills to your deductive work?* Holmes answered in monosyllables.

After a minute, I found I couldn't listen to the questions anymore. I couldn't, not when Charlotte Holmes was pulling one of her magic tricks right across from me. She wasn't pulling a rabbit out of a theoretical hat or transforming herself into a stranger. This time, without moving a single muscle, she was disappearing completely into her high-backed velvet chair.

I DIDN'T RECOGNIZE HER. NOT HERE. NOT IN THIS HOUSE.
I didn't recognize *me*.

Maybe this is what happened when you built a friendship on a foundation of mutual disaster. It collapsed the second things righted themselves, left you desperate for the next earthquake. I knew, deep down, there was more to it than this. But I wanted an easy solution. It was awful to wish for a murder case to fall at your feet, and I found myself wanting it anyway.

Holmes left dinner without saying anything to me. When I caught up to her, she'd already locked her bedroom door. I knocked for a solid five minutes without any reply. For a long, pointless moment, I stood there in the hall. Upstairs, I heard the edges of a male voice, shouting. *They can't do that to us. They can't take that from us*—and then a door, slamming.

"We can't have that," a voice said behind me. I jumped. It was the housekeeper, who'd found me waiting in the hall like some pathetic dog. She showed me to my room. From her kind, impersonal manner, I got the idea that she must have been used to finding strays around.

I spent that night in a giant bed across from a set of giant windows that rattled every time the wind whipped by. "Spent the night" was the right term—it'd be a lie to say I slept there. I couldn't sleep at all. I knew now that I wasn't the only one who wished for awful things. Every time I closed my eyes I saw a slump-shouldered Holmes willing herself into nonexistence across the dinner table. It kept me up because I knew that if she made up her mind, she was determined enough to follow through, to take a handful of pills and lock the world out. I'd seen her do it once already, under my father's porch. I couldn't watch it happen again.

Back then, I'd stopped her. I didn't think I could now. Now, I was the last person she wanted to comfort her, because I was a guy, and her best friend, and maybe I wanted to be more than that, and with every passing hour she added another brick to the wall she was building between us.

At two, I got up and shut the curtains. At three thirty, I opened them again. The moon hung in the sky like a lantern, so bright that I pulled the pillow over my head. I slept, then, and dreamt that I was awake, still staring out across the Sussex countryside.

At four, I woke but thought I was still dreaming. Holmes was perched at the end of my bed. Actually, she was perched on top of my feet, effectively pinning me in place. It might have been sexy, except she was wearing a giant T-shirt that read CHEMISTRY IS FOR LOVERS, so it was insane, and her face looked like she'd been crying, so it was terrifying.

Completely unbidden, my father's list of rules for dealing with Holmeses began scrolling through my head. *#28: If you're upset, Holmes is the last person you should ask to make you feel better, unless you want to be chided for having feelings. #29: If Holmes is upset, hide all firearms and install a new lock on your door.* I swore and scrabbled to push myself up on my elbows.

"Stop," she said, in a graveyard tone. "Just shut up, will you, and listen to me for a minute."

But I was too wound up to do that. "Oh, are we talking now? Because I thought we were just going to let your crazy family *eviscerate* us at the dinner table and then abandon each other there without saying a word. Or maybe I could try to kiss you again, so that I could get another round of the silent treatment—"

"Watson—"

"Will you just stop with the theatrics? They're not fun anymore. This is not a game. This isn't the nineteenth goddamn century. My name is *Jamie*, and I don't need you to act like we're part of some *story*, I just need you to act like you like me. Do you even like me anymore?" I was embarrassed to hear my voice cracking. "Or am I just some . . . some prop for the life you wish you had? Because I don't know if you've noticed, but we're back in real life now. Lucien Moriarty's in Thailand, Bryony Downs is in a black box somewhere, and our biggest threat is having to eat breakfast with your batshit mother tomorrow morning, so I'd appreciate a little acknowledgment of reality."

She raised an eyebrow. "Actually, the housekeeper will bring us in a tray."

"I hate you," I said, with feeling. "I hate you so much."

"Are we finished with this little production? Or do you need to rend your clothes first?"

"No. I like these pants."

"Fine. Fine," she said again, and took a slow breath. "I want things from you, intellectually, that I don't want physically. That is to say, I could want you like—like that, but I can't. I . . . want things I don't want." I could feel her shift her weight. "And maybe I just want them because I think that *you* want them from me, and I'm afraid you'll up and go if you don't get them. I have no idea. Either way, if it wasn't bad enough to know that I've lost control over my own reactions, I also know that I'm hurting you. Which, honestly, isn't my main concern right now, because it can't be. But I feel badly about that. You're feeling badly about that. Every time you look at me, you flinch. And I'm fairly sure my mother has interpreted *that* as you having secret nefarious plans toward me, and then when she tore you apart at dinner, I was happy, because I'm *frustrated* with you and I'm not allowed to express it. Watson, this is boring, all this wheel-spinning, and there's no way out I can see unless we turn each other loose. But that isn't an option for me."

"It isn't for me either," I said.

"I know." Her mouth twisted. "So I suppose that means we'll be sharing this prison."

"I knew we'd end up in one eventually." The moon hid behind a cloud, and the room was washed dark. I waited for her to say something. I waited a long time, and she watched me watching her. We were each other's mirrors, always.

But the air between us wasn't charged the way it had been. It wasn't suffocating anymore, either.

"So what now?" I asked. "You get a therapist, and I go back to London?"

"I loathe psychology."

"Well, right now, I think you might need it."

To my surprise, she flopped down next to me, her dark hair spilling over her eyes. "Watson, how do you feel about an experiment?"

"Not terrific, actually."

"Stop. It's not a difficult one," she said, her face buried in a pillow.

"Fine. Shoot."

"I need you to touch my head."

Gingerly, I poked her scalp with my finger.

"No," she snarled, and grabbed my hand, fitting it against her forehead as though I was taking her temperature. "Like that."

"Why am I doing this?"

"You're demonstrating nonsexual touch. It's akin to how a parent would touch a child. When you were ill last semester, I felt fine climbing into your bed, because I knew that nothing could happen. Look, I'm not recoiling. I don't want to hit you." She sounded pleased. "Really, I should be recording my findings."

"Wait," I said. "You wanted to hit me the other night?"

Holmes lifted her head from the pillow. "I want to hit everything all the time."

"I'm sorry."

"I should join the rugby team," she said nervously. Stalling. "I, um. I want you to . . . touch my face. Like you would have, the other night, had we kept going."

I eyed her for a long minute. "I want to help you do—whatever it is we're doing. But I don't want to be your guinea pig."

"I don't want you to be one. I want you to understand."

For some reason, it felt dangerous to breathe, and so I didn't. I held myself as still as I could, except for my hand running down her soft, shining hair to her cheek. Her skin was pale in the dark, but as I traced my thumb along her cheekbone, she flushed the barest pink. I bit my lip, and her mouth opened, and without thinking about it, really, I let one finger brush against her mouth, and then her hands slid up my chest, pulling against my T-shirt and then pulling at the collar, pulling me down toward her until I could feel myself pressing her down into the mattress, and my nose dug into her neck and she laughed, she exhaled and her breath was soft and a little sharp, and I tangled my fingers in her hair, the way I'd wanted to for months now, all of this I'd wanted for so long, and she angled her head as though she was about to kiss me—

Then she dug her elbow into my stomach and heaved me off her.

"Shit," she said as I gasped for air. She swore again, fluently, and pulled the pillow down over her face.

"That was a terrible idea." I needed to throw up. I needed a cold shower. Maybe I would take a cold shower and throw up in the tub. That sounded great, actually. I staggered to my feet.

She nodded. I could tell because the pillow was moving up and down. "Come back," she said.

I dragged my hands through my hair. "God. Why?"

"Just—"

"Holmes—are you okay? Like, really, actually okay?" It was such a dumb question, but I couldn't think of another way to ask it.

"Don't you think it's sort of backward, that you're the one always asking me that and not my family?"

"Honestly? All the time."

We stared at each other.

"They think this sort of thing shouldn't've happened to me at all," she whispered. "Not to someone as . . . capable as me."

"This isn't your fault," I said fiercely. "God. Has no one told you it's not your fault? Of all the fucked-up families in all the world—"

"It was never said, as such. It was implied."

"Like that makes it any better." I stared at the ground. "I know this isn't your favorite subject, but have you thought about—"

"Talk therapy isn't a panacea. Neither are drugs. Neither is wishing it away." When I glanced up at her, she was wearing a sad little smile. "Watson. Come back."

"Why? No, give me an actual answer."

With a groan, she pulled the pillow down against her chest. "Because, contrary to how I just reacted, I don't actually want you to leave." She looked at me with baleful eyes. "I also don't want to . . . do that again. I just want to go to sleep, and if I'm correct, it'll be much easier for us to continue talking to each other the way we normally do if we don't have to first go through tomorrow's formalities."

Gingerly, I sat down. "I still think that makes little to no sense."

"I'm fine with that." She yawned. "It's dawn, Watson. Go to sleep."

I eased myself back in under the covers, careful to leave a few inches between the two of us. *Leave room for the Holy*

Spirit, I thought semihysterically. I hadn't been to church since I was a kid, but maybe the nuns had gotten it right.

"Are you measuring the space between us?"

"No, I—"

"It's not funny," she said but it was dawn, and we were exhausted, and I could tell she was trying not to laugh.

"What we need is a good murder," I said, not caring how horrible I sounded. "Or a kidnapping. Something fun, you know, to keep our minds off all this."

"All this? Do you mean sex?"

"Whatever."

"Lena keeps texting me. She wants to fly out from India and take us *shopping.*"

"That's not a distraction. That's a reason to throw myself into the ocean. I need an explosion or something."

"You're a sixteen-year-old boy," she said. "I think we'll probably need a serial killer."

Leander Holmes would turn up the next day. Three days later, he would disappear. And for weeks and weeks after, I'd wonder if, by wishing, we'd brought everything that happened after that onto ourselves.

three

I WOKE TO CHARLOTTE BESIDE ME AND SOMEONE ELSE flinging back the curtains.

Even with the sudden brightness, even knowing there was a stranger in my room, I couldn't make myself look. It felt like I'd gotten less than five minutes of sleep—maybe five minutes in the last five months—and my body was finally drawing the line.

"Go away," I mumbled, and rolled over.

The lamp flicked on. "Charlotte," a low, lazy voice said, "when I gave you that T-shirt, I didn't intend for you to interpret it literally."

At that, I cracked an eye open, but the man speaking was too backlit to see.

"I don't think you intended for me to ever wear it, either," Holmes was saying beside me, but she sounded pleased. Somehow, she didn't look tired at all; on the contrary, she was sitting up, her knees tucked under her shirt, stretching out the words CHEMISTRY IS FOR LOVERS. "It really is the worst Christmas present I've ever gotten, and that's saying something."

"Worse than the time that Milo bought you a Barbie?" the figure tutted. "I really must be a monster. Come on, goose. Introduce me to your boyfriend, unless you want to continue pretending he's invisible, in which case I'll play along."

Holmes paused. "No lecture?"

Leander—because it had to be Leander—laughed. "You've done worse things, and anyway, it's fairly clear you aren't actually having sex. This may be indelicate, but those sheets aren't hardly wrinkled enough. So I'm not quite sure what I should be lecturing you on."

That was it. I was going to pass a law against people making deductions before lunch.

As I sat up, rubbing at my eyes, Leander crossed to the other side of the bed. I finally got a good look at him. We'd met once before, at my seventh birthday party. He'd brought me a pet rabbit. All I remembered was a tall man with broad shoulders who'd spent most of the party laughing with my father in a corner.

That impression held true, though the man standing in front of me was impeccably well dressed, given the hour. (The clock beside me read 7:15, because the world was trying to kill me.) He was wearing a blazer, and his shoes were shined up like mirrors. Below his slicked-back hair, his eyes were wrinkled with smile lines. He held out a hand to shake.

"Jamie Watson," he said. "Do you know, you look just like your father did when I met him. Which is making all of this quite a bit stranger for me, so could you please get out of the bed you're sharing with my niece?"

I scrambled to my feet. "We're not—I'm not—it's very nice to meet you." Behind me, Holmes was snickering, and I rounded on her. "Come on, really? Some backup would be nice."

"Do you want me to give him the details, then?"

"Do you want me to give you a shovel so you can keep on digging me this hole?"

"Please," she shot back. "I'd rather watch. You're doing such a nice job of it, after all."

Something was wrong. Our usual banter sounded meaner, pettier than usual. I stopped, not sure what to say.

Leander saved me. "Children," he said, pulling the door open. "Stop bickering, or I won't make you breakfast."

The kitchen was cavernous, all metal and marble and glass. The housekeeper was already hard at work, rolling out a blanket of dough on the counter. I don't know why it surprised me. Clearly Holmes's parents weren't making their own meals, if last night's formal dinner was any indication.

"Hello, Sarah," Leander said, pressing a kiss to her cheek. "How late were you up last night, cleaning up after that soiree? I'll take over. We'll send breakfast to your room." He gave her a look I recognized too well, a criminally charming smile straight out of the *Charlotte Holmes Is Conning You* playbook.

The housekeeper laughed, and blushed, and finally gave up her apron to his waiting hands before she left.

At the counter, Holmes propped her head on her fists. "You're much more efficient at that than I am."

Leander didn't answer for a moment, selecting a saucepan from the hanging copper rack. Holmes's eyes followed his hands. "You do know that it works best if you mean what you're saying," he said. "Fried eggs?"

"I'm not hungry." She leaned forward. "You have some fascinating bruises on your wrists."

"I do," he said, as if she'd commented on the weather. "Jamie? Bacon? Biscuits?"

"God, yes. Is there a kettle here somewhere? I need tea."

He pointed with his spatula, and the two of us got down to making a breakfast fit for an army. The whole time, Holmes sat with narrowed eyes, taking him apart.

"Go on then," Leander said finally. "Let's hear if the deductions you're making are correct."

Holmes didn't waste any time. "Your shoes are hastily laced—the right's done up in a different pattern than the left—and your blazer wrinkled at the elbows. And I know you're aware of that; you're as aware as I am of these things, which means that either you're trying to send a message to someone or you are actually too worn out and tired to care that you're pressed to something less than perfection, which means that things have been *very* hard for you lately. Your hair was just cut by someone in Germany. Don't give me that look, it's far more avant-garde than your usual, and Milo mentioned seeing you recently. Berlin, then. If you were to take the pomade out, it'd fall just like one of Jamie's emo singers. Oh, stop glaring, both of you. I happen to know that Uncle Leander has been going to the same barber in Eastbourne since his teens." Impatiently, she pulled at her own hair. "You're hiding a limp, you've developed some terrific neck-beard, and—have you been *kissing* someone?"

The kettle began to whistle loudly enough that neither of them heard me laugh.

Leander made a tsking motion with his spatula. "Charlotte." He was the only one in her family, I noticed, not to call her by her nickname. "Darling girl, I won't tell you a single thing unless you agree to eat."

"Fine." A smile crept across her face. "Hateful man."

After Leander brought a tray up to the housekeeper's room, we settled in around the counter, and I snuck another look at Holmes's uncle. She was right; he did look tired, the kind of tired I remembered from late last fall, where I felt like I wasn't allowed the vulnerability of sleep. That, coupled with the trace of worry behind his showman's smile, and I wondered just where he'd been before Sussex.

"Germany," he said, picking the thought out of my head. "Charlotte was right on that count. Their government asked me to uncover a forgery ring that may or may not be churning out work by a German painter from the thirties. I've been in rather deep cover, and for a long time. It's a delicate business. You're winning the trust of some dangerous people, *and* you need to know how to talk to skittish art students ripping off Rembrandts to make a living." Unexpectedly, he grinned. "It's quite fun, honestly. Like playing Whac-a-Mole, only with guns and a wig."

Holmes tugged at the cuff of his shirt, exposing the bruise beneath. "Yes. Fun."

"Eat your bacon, or I won't explain." He pushed her plate toward her. "Like I said, I've not been involved with the most genteel crowd these past few months. And honestly I didn't really want to take this case to begin with. As interesting as it is, it involves *so* much legwork, and my legs are happiest on my ottoman. I like a pretty little puzzle as much as the next man, but this . . . well, and then I had lunch with your father, Jamie, and he persuaded me to take it. Like old times, he said, when we were sleuthing together in Edinburgh. He has a family now, so he's less mobile than I am, but I've been sending him daily emails, and he's helping me put it together from afar."

"Really?" I asked, bemused. "He's helpful?" My father was excitable, irresponsible, a little touched in the head. I had some trouble imagining him as an analytical genius.

Leander raised an eyebrow. "Do you really think I would involve him if he wasn't?"

I raised my eyebrow right back. My father might be helpful, sure, or he might just be the audience for Leander's magic show. With Holmeses, you never really knew where you stood.

Next to me, mine was ripping up her biscuit. "Yes, but the bruises. And the kissing."

"Deep cover," her uncle said in a dramatic voice. "Deep, deep cover."

She wrinkled her nose. "Then why are you here, in England? Not that I'm not happy to see you."

Leander stood and gathered our plates. "Because your father has contacts I can't gain access to through my illegitimate means. And because I wanted to get a good look at Jamie, here, since the two of you are now attached at the hip. Morning *and* night, apparently."

Holmes shrugged, her shoulders thin under her shirt, and she brought a sliver of biscuit to her mouth. I watched her, the line of her arm, how her lips still looked bee-stung from the night before. Or was I imagining that detail, coloring it in because I needed to make it a story, to see cause and effect where there wasn't any?

She'd almost kissed me. I'd wanted her to. Everything was fine.

"If it matters at all," Leander said from the sink, rolling up his sleeves, "I approve."

Holmes smiled at him, and I smiled at him, because neither of us knew what to say.

It was like the night before existed in some other universe. A lone hour in a sea of awkwardness where we could talk to each other the way we used to, and now that it was over, we were adrift again.

THE NEXT FEW DAYS PASSED SLOWLY, AS MOST PUNISH-ments do. During the day, I read the Faulkner novel I'd brought in a sunny alcove off the servants' quarters. Those rooms stood mostly empty now, so I didn't have to worry about being found. Which was a relief. I'd run out of things to say to Holmes's parents fairly quickly. Even if I found her mother terrifying, I didn't hate her. She was ill and worried about her daughter.

Then Alistair told us that Emma's condition had begun to deteriorate. She stopped eating meals with us. One night before dinner, I found Leander giving directions to nursing staff as they hauled a hospital bed in through the front door.

"I thought she had fibromyalgia," Holmes murmured over my shoulder. "Fibromyalgia doesn't require a live-in team. I thought—I thought she was getting better."

I managed not to jump. She'd taken to doing that, to ghost-ing at the edges of whatever room I was in, and then, as soon as I noticed her, giving an excuse and running away. So I didn't say anything, didn't try to comfort her, just watched Leander grimace as the orderly crashed the bed into the doorframe.

Upstairs, a man's raised voice said, *But the offshore accounts—no, I refuse.* Was it Alistair's? A door slammed.

It didn't matter. By the time I turned to her, Holmes was already gone.

I found Leander later in the living room. "Living room" might have been too friendly a name for what it was—a black sofa; a low, expensive-looking table; a cowhide rug beneath them. I'd been prowling the halls, looking for my absent best friend, and found her uncle and mother instead.

I was surprised. A hospital bed had just come through the front door, and I'd expected that she'd be in it. But no—she was on her back on the sofa, the heels of her hands pressed against her forehead, while Leander loomed over her.

"This is the last favor I'll do for you," he was saying, in a low, furious voice. "For the rest of our lives. This is the last one. I want you to understand that. No school tuition. No bailouts. You could have asked me for anything, but this—"

She dragged her hands down her face. "I know what the word 'last' means, Leander," she said, and in that moment, she sounded exactly like her daughter.

"So when?" he asked. "When will you need me?"

"You'll know," Emma said. "We're almost there." At that, she stood, swaying on her feet. Like all the soft parts of her had shriveled away, leaving a dusty, exhausted shell.

Leander noticed it, too, reaching out a hand to steady her, but she held up a hand in warning. With slow, labored steps, she left the room.

"Hello, Jamie," Leander said, his back still to me.

"How did you know it was me?" I said lightly. "You all need a different party trick. I almost expect that one now."

"Sit," he said, and motioned me over to the sofa. "Where's Charlotte?"

I shrugged.

"I thought it might be like that," he said.

"Is everything okay with Mrs. Holmes?" I asked, in an attempt to change the subject.

"No," he said. "That's obvious, though. Tell me—I've been in touch with your father, of course, but I'd like to hear it from you—how's your family doing? How is your darling little sister? Is she still into Your Little Sparkle Ponies, or whatever they're called? James misses her something awful."

"Shelby's good," I said. "She's past the sparkle ponies and on to painting portraits of dogs. Starting to look at secondary schools near our flat."

Leander smiled at me. "James was making noises about having her sent to Sherringford. It might be nice to have you both in the same place. Do Sunday dinners. Go mini-golfing on the weekend. Or to the roller rink. Roller rinking is a family activity, right?"

"Uh, right." Though I was pretty sure it was called roller-skating, and that I'd rather die before doing it. "I heard you say 'no school tuition,' though. We can't afford to send Shelby to Sherringford. Not on our own. And it's no secret anymore that you're footing my bill."

His smile faded. "That doesn't apply to your family. It never would. I'd stand by your father through anything, Jamie, because I know he'd never ask me to . . . It doesn't matter. Listen, don't ever think you'll be a casualty in this war. You won't be. I'll make sure of it."

An invisible war with invisible blood. Or not invisible—just not our own, not yet. Lee Dobson had been a casualty already, and I'd come knife's-edge close to becoming one myself. "How did this even start?" I asked him. It was a question that had been nagging me for weeks. "Like, why did the

Holmeses hire August Moriarty anyway? I know it was a publicity stunt or whatever, but if you all hated each other so much, why would Holmes's parents take that risk?"

"It's not a short story, you know."

I laughed. "I mean, I don't know how I'll fit it into my busy schedule of being avoided." And it was true. What else was I going to do this afternoon? I might as well fill in some of the blanks that Holmes wouldn't help me with.

"Fine," he said, "but if you're going to make me tell it, we're going to need some tea."

Ten minutes and one pot of Earl Grey later, we were settled back onto the sofa.

Somewhere in the distance, I heard the rush of the sea. "You're familiar with Sherlock Holmes's run-ins with Professor Moriarty, aren't you? Sherlock took down a number of 'notorious' men, but Moriarty was the one at the top. A right bastard. Every other criminal in England paid him protection money. He orchestrated their actions, knit them together into a web. And Holmes was able to deduce the spider from that web." Absently, he rubbed at his temple. "Stop me if you've heard this before."

"I've heard it before," I said, blowing on my tea. Half the world had heard it before. Sherlock Holmes squaring off against the professor; Holmes and Dr. Watson's flight to Switzerland to escape him; my great-great-great-grandfather on a hill overlooking a waterfall, wondering if his best friend and partner had died in its depths. Both Holmes and Moriarty had disappeared that day, Moriarty for good, and the man who'd come back to Baker Street had done so only years later, after eradicating the last of the crime lord's agents.

Or so the story went.

"When I was a child, I never understood the fixation on Moriarty," Leander was saying. "He's never mentioned in the good doctor's stories, not until 'The Final Problem,' where it's like he was invented to explain all these fabulously strange crimes that Sherlock had investigated. Then he's gone again. And you know, growing up, our relationship with that family was fairly civil. A bit apologetic, really. They didn't have the best reputation—being cursed with an infamous last name will do that to you—but sins of the father, and so on. *They* weren't the Napoleons of crime. I said as much to my father."

"How did that go?"

Leander ran a hand over his slicked-back hair. "Poorly," he admitted. "He told me that there's a criminal strain in their blood. We might have been at peace when this August business started, but we'd spent the majority of the twentieth century tangling with them, one way or another."

"We did?" I said, then corrected myself. "You did?" From what I understood, the Watsons mostly spent the twentieth century losing their spectacular fortune at cards.

"Forgive me if I get the dates wrong," Leander said, sipping his tea, "but. 1918. Fiona Moriarty, dressed as a man, secures a position as a guard at Sing Sing. The costume, as I understand it, involved flour bags tied around her waist for bulk. Apparently it was splendid. After spending two months beating up the most hardened criminals in the world and, one assumes, gathering data, she quits her job. Two weeks later, she gets herself arrested for robbing a bank in broad daylight, disguised as a *different* man, and is thrown behind bars. Within the night, she has escorted twenty prisoners out of Sing Sing through a tunnel she'd spent the last ten days digging. A tunnel that went under the Hudson River."

I let out a low whistle. "Did she get away with it?"

He grinned. "Tunnels have two openings, don't they? My great-grandfather had built a bonfire at the exit. Those poor prisoners all ran yelling back to their cells. Thought they'd found their freedom . . . found lots of smoke, instead. And she was put behind bars herself. Her scheme had been clever, you know. A good five of those prisoners were her father's lieutenants. Men who had helped raise her. Who, after her father's death, escaped to America looking to avoid the long arm of Sherlock Holmes." Leander raised an eyebrow. "Sentiment. It always gets you in the end."

He had on his quoting voice for that part. "You can't believe that," I said.

"She certainly did, by the end of it. The funny thing is that Fiona was *loaded.* She had enough money to bribe the local judges. To bribe the police force. To bribe the Tammany Hall mobsters. And she tried, but none of them would touch her money. Too afraid of the consequences, on our end. Ultimately, one of them wrote his old friend Henry Holmes, who got on the next ship for America, just in time to uncover her scheme and put a stop to it."

"And that wasn't the end of it, I guess."

"No. It goes on like that. 1930. Bank vault heist. Glasgow. All the culprits caught, but the jewels missing. Guess who shows up in society wearing a million pounds' worth of rubies?" He laughed at my expression. "Jamie, you've been in America too long. Pounds *sterling*. The currency. Apparently one of their hired cons had delivered the rubies to them through the sewer, using a pulley system. Quentin Moriarty claimed his wife's jewels came from an inheritance, but Jonathan Holmes disproved that through a pair of rats, a scalpel, and a lady's handkerchief. 1944, and the Moriartys are raiding the museums of Europe during the second World War; 1968, and they're chairing the Nobel Prize Committee; 1972, and my older sister Araminta was asked to decode a series of messages that used Francis Bacon's substitution cipher. They were being used to negotiate the sale of nuclear warheads. To *Walter Moriarty*. What on earth would a Moriarty do with a warhead? Sell it again, probably, and at a profit. He went to trial. Two jurors developed rare forms of cancer. The judge's wife went missing. All quiet. All out of the news. And then someone killed all three of Araminta's cats."

"Jesus," I said. "That's awful."

"Walter Moriarty was out of jail sixteen weeks later. A travesty. And still—you must remember this—the family wasn't all bad." He refilled his cup. "Really there was only one bad apple in a generation. The rest . . . well. I knew a Patrick Moriarty when I was younger. We ran into each other at a party at Oxford, got drunk enough to duck into a corner and compare notes. We got to talking about the bad blood between our families—though it was nothing like it is now—and he said that the fundamental difference between us was that Holmeses were heartless optimists, and they were hedonist pessimists."

"Heartless optimists?" My Holmes didn't seem particularly optimistic. "Meaning?"

"Do you know that old image of Lady Justice? All done up with the blindfold and the scales. Made of shiny copper, not to be touched. I've thought of us that way. In order to pass judgment on other men, you remove yourself from them. Not all Holmeses are detectives, you know. Far from it. Mostly we end up in government. Some scientists, some lawyers. One really dry stick of a cousin sells insurance. But when we do detective work, we tend to work outside the law. We have our own resources. And, at times, when the law won't prosecute, we are our own jury. To wield that kind of power . . . it makes sense that you wouldn't let yourself be blinded by your emotions. Would it really help you to put a man away to know he'd leave behind a starving child? And, to top it all off, it's not in our natures to be effusive. We're mostly brains, you know. The body's just something to get us from place to place. But over time, we calcified. Went brittle, staring at ourselves for so long. Maybe it made us better at our jobs. Because you don't do this kind of work unless you think it'll really make a difference, really make the world better. And you don't think you can make the world better unless you are a *tremendous* egomaniac."

"And the Moriartys?"

Leander considered me over his teacup. "They have gobs of money, and a family name that made them pariahs, and quite a few of them grow up to be geniuses. So they feel entitled to the best parts of the world. Extrapolate from there, my dear Watson. But it wasn't really until this current crop that there were so many marvelously depraved specimens all at once. I miss the ones like Patrick," he said with a laugh. "He grew up to be a hedge fund manager. We're talking minor evil. Ran a couple Ponzi schemes. This lot . . . well, August was a nice kid, much nicer than Patrick could ever be. August was patient with Charlotte. Smart as a whip. When Emma and Alistair hired him, it was because Alistair was about two seconds from being the eye of a media hurricane, and we needed to build up some public goodwill. We hadn't had a run-in with the Moriartys in twenty years. Memories fade. It seemed like a good idea at the time."

"That'll be written on a few tombstones before this is over," I said.

"You have quite the mordant sense of humor." His eyes went faraway. "Still, I wonder if you're right. The cycle's beginning all over again."

"And my family?" I asked him. "We didn't play a role in any of this?" I sounded like a child, I knew I did, but I'd been raised on the Sherlock Holmes stories. My father styled himself an ex-detective. I'd imagined that we'd been in the thick of it all this time, right beside the Holmeses, fighting the good fight.

"Not in a long while," Leander said. "Too many of us were automatons, maybe. Too distant. Our families were friendly, to be sure, but not friends. Not in pairs. Not until I met your father. Until you met Charlotte."

I sighed. I couldn't help it.

He leaned forward to clap me on the shoulder. "You're a good influence on her. Just give her a bit of space. I don't think she's ever had a friend before you."

So I gave her some space.

My Faulkner novel in the mornings, and silence in the afternoons as I wandered through their library, pulling down the books I wanted to read and wouldn't, because they were all first editions, gilt leaf and delicate pages, things meant to be looked at and never opened. I was afraid I'd ruin them. I was afraid for so many pathetic reasons, scared that, in a few weeks, I'd be back at school and without Holmes's friendship, that the dread that prickled the back of my neck was the sensation of loss before it came. I was so messed up that I couldn't shake the feeling even at our dinners, sitting next to Leander, who had taken Emma Holmes's place beside me. In an attempt to cheer me up, he told me ribald, ridiculous stories about my father that always seemed to end with one of them bailing the other out of jail.

"I never really bothered to get a *license*, you see, and the police don't love working with amateurs." He grinned to himself. "The clients did, though. Rather avidly. Remind me to tell you the one about your father and the redheaded lady lion tamer."

"Please," I said, "please, please don't."

Where was Holmes? There, and not there. Silent as a crow

on a power line. Her father was speaking in German to that night's dinner guest, a sculptor from Frankfurt who didn't speak English. There was a whole roster of them, these dinner guests, one or two every night, and as soon as the meal was over, Leander and Alistair would slip away with them to the study and shut the door. It was interminable, waiting for them to stand up and leave so that we could too.

Then that day's spell was broken, and Holmes and I would go back to my room, and suddenly we would be able to talk again.

The first night, she stood, straightened her skirt, and cast a long look at me before she swept out of the room and down the hall. I followed her as though I were in a dream, losing her around a corner in the house's long and winding corridors. But I knew where she'd be. There, in the guest room, at the end of my bed, she was easing the heels off her feet. She dangled one from a finger as she looked up at me, biting her lip, and it should have been ridiculous, but instead it made something in my chest burn.

"Hi," I said, dry-mouthed.

"Hi," she said, and picked up an encyclopedia that had been invisible on the dark floor. "What do you know of the Bhagavad Gita?"

Nothing.

I knew nothing about a seven-hundred-verse Sanskrit epic or why I was supposed to care at midnight on a Tuesday in her parents' house when, the night before, she'd slipped into my bed like an apparition and pulled me down on top of her. She stayed up telling me its history until I fell asleep in a harmless ball.

The next night, she told me about *1001 Arabian Nights*.

No Holmes in the morning; more darkness when I opened the curtains. More Faulkner in the window seat while Holmes's cat Mouse glared up at me from my feet. I wondered if she was watching me out of its eyes. I wondered if I was in a feedback loop, an experiment, a never-ending bad dream. When I wandered down the halls, I could hear her playing her violin, and yet she wasn't in her cluttered basement, she wasn't in the parlor. She was nowhere. The arpeggios she played came up as if from the house's foundation.

I wandered the house like some Victorian ghost. When I passed the hall hung with paintings, the one that led to Alistair's study, I could clearly hear him say, *He won't call here again*, could hear Leander reply, *You won't have to leave this place. I won't let it happen*. Money, always, was the subtext here, money at stake and the family home, and though I only heard bits and pieces, I couldn't put it all together. I was surrounded by wealth. By power. Why all the whispered arguments? Is this how you kept your prizes once you'd won them?

I found myself looking up train schedules. When could I go back to London? Christmas was only a week away, and Shelby was getting an easel from our mother. I wanted to watch her open it. I could go to London, I thought. I could call Lena and see if she was with Tom, my Sherringford roommate and her boyfriend. It would be a relief to see them. We'd play poker. Get roaring drunk. *He might be my only friend, anymore,* I found myself thinking, *the boy who spied on me for money all this fall,* and then I knew I needed to break something right that second.

That was how I ended up down by the Holmeses' man-made lake. It was four o'clock in the afternoon, so it was pitch-dark, and I didn't trust myself to find the ocean. Did it even exist, or was it just a sound, something unreal in the distance, threatening with its weight? It didn't matter. I didn't need it. All I needed were the giant rocks half-buried by this pond, my fingernails to pull them up from the mud, my arms to hurl them away from me into the black water.

When Leander found me, I'd taken a hatchet from the toolshed and started looking for something else to do.

"Jamie," he said. He was smart to say it from a distance.

"Leander," I said. "Not now." There was enough deadfall under the trees to do the job. I started kicking it into a pile, looking for the biggest, thickest branches, the ones that would put up a fight.

"What are you doing?"

I stole a glance at him. He'd stuffed his hands in his pockets, and his roguish smile was nowhere to be seen. "I'm expressing my anger in a healthy way," I said to him, the air quotes visible. "So leave me the hell alone."

He didn't. He took a step closer. "I can get you a sawbuck from the shed."

"No."

"Or a coat."

"Fuck off."

Another step. "I could get you a bigger ax?"

At that, I stopped. "Yeah, okay."

We worked in silence, cutting the brush off the thicker branches, weeding out the pieces with knots. There wasn't a stand anywhere near the house, so I braced my first piece on the ground, piling up rocks to keep it upright. Then I lifted the ax above my head and brought it down, hard.

I couldn't see my hands in front of my face, couldn't hear anything but the blood in my head. Leander set the next piece up, and I split that, too, and the next, and the next, feeling the hot pull in my shoulders build until it broke down into incredible, brain-numbing exhaustion. I stopped to catch my breath. I had bleeding blisters on both hands. I felt, for the first time in days, like myself, and I let that feeling wash over me for a minute before it too disappeared.

"Well," Leander said, brushing off his clothes, "it's too bad they only have gas fireplaces in that house, or you'd be quite the hero."

I sat down on the woodpile. "I don't need to be a hero."

"I know," he said. "Sometimes, though, it's easier to be one than to be a person."

Together, we looked up to the looming house on the hill.

"I thought Sherlock Holmes kept bees," I said. *I could open all the apiary doors. I could funnel them into that massive, awful dining room and let them build honeycombs down the walls.* "I don't see any bees."

"His cottage is my sister Araminta's now. It's down the

lane," he said. "I don't go all that often. She doesn't much like visitors."

I lifted an arm experimentally, then stretched it. "I guess you got all the friendly genes in the family."

"Alistair has his small share, along with the family home." There was a trace of bitterness in his voice. "But yes, you're right. I have friends. I throw parties. I, shockingly, leave my house on occasion. And, if my deductions are correct, I'm the only Holmes in recent memory to fall in love."

I opened my mouth to ask about Charlotte Holmes's parents, then thought better of it. If the two of them were in love, it seemed like it was beside the point.

"Are you still with him?" I paused. "It was a him, right?"

Leander sighed, and sat down next to me. The woodpile shifted under our combined weight. "What is it that you want from Charlotte?"

"I—"

He held up a finger. "Don't give me 'boyfriend' or 'best friend' or any of those other vagaries. Those terms are too loosely defined. Be specific."

I wasn't going to say either of those things; I was about to tell him to stay out of our business. But it wasn't *our* business, anymore.

"She makes me better. I make her better. But right now we're making each other worse. I want to go back to how it was before." It sounded simple when I said it like that.

"Can I give you some advice?" Leander asked, and his voice was like the night around us, cloaked and sad. "A girl like her wasn't ever a girl—and still, she is one. And you? You're going to get yourself hurt either way."

Speaking of vagaries. "What do you mean?"

"Jamie," he said, "the only way out is through."

I was too exhausted to talk it through further, so I changed the subject. "Have you been learning anything? From your contacts, I mean. Anything useful to take back to Germany?"

His eyes narrowed. "Of a sort. I learned that I need to have a word with Hadrian Moriarty. But then, I imagine I'm not alone in that."

Hadrian Moriarty was an art collector, a high-class swindler, and, as I'd learned this fall, a frequent and valued guest on European morning talk shows. I wasn't surprised to hear he was involved in an art scandal.

"And everything's okay? I heard someone yelling about leaving." I looked down. "I know it's not my business."

"It's not," Leander said, but he patted me on the shoulder. "After all that hard work, you'll sleep well tonight. Though I suggest you do it alone, and that you lock your door. And then put a chair against it."

"Wait." I paused. "You and that guy. Are you two still together? You never said."

"No." He touched my shoulder briefly and stood to go. "We never were. He didn't—he's married, now. Or was. And is again."

I was beginning to put together a puzzle of my own.

Because history ran in circles, and my own life especially so, if Leander had been in love with my father. I thought of that list he'd made. *#74. Whatever happens between you and Holmes, remember it is not your fault and likely could not have been prevented, no matter your efforts.* I watched Leander Holmes walk up the hill to the house, and then I buried my head in my hands.

I LOCKED MY DOOR. I PUT A CHAIR AGAINST IT. I WENT TO bed alone, and woke up to find Charlotte Holmes curled up in a small, dark ball on my floor.

"Watson," she said sleepily, lifting her head from the carpet. "You kept getting texts. So I tossed your phone out the window."

The window in question was still open. A cold wind was driving through it. To my credit—to my everlasting credit—I didn't wrap her in blankets, or scream, or demand answers, or douse the room in gasoline.

At least we were on the ground floor.

As coolly as I could, I got up, stepped over her, and pulled my phone from a rosebush. "Eight texts," I said. "From my father. About Leander."

"Oh." Holmes sat up, rubbing her arms. "Can you close that? It's freezing."

I shut the window with a snap. "Apparently your uncle wasn't in touch yesterday. Which wouldn't be a big deal, except my father's gotten an email from him every night for the last four months. He wants us to check in, make sure he's okay."

I tried, unsuccessfully, to keep myself from remembering Leander's forlorn voice. My *father*. My father, who was perpetually rumpled, pleased with himself. My father who bumbled through two countries, a dead-end job, a number of awful mystery stories he wrote out longhand and then read to me, dramatically, on the phone, doing all the voices. How anyone could love him that way was the real mystery.

Holmes's gaze flicked over me, assessing. "You saw him last."

"I did?"

"Leander. He wasn't at dinner. Neither were you."

I'd taken two pieces of bread from the kitchen and gone to my room, unable to face a room full of scrutinizing eyes. "I guess I wasn't."

"No, the two of you were—" She peered at my hands. "Chopping wood? Really, Watson?"

"It was an outlet," I said. She was shivering, so I pulled the duvet from the bed to put around her shoulders.

"Oh, I'm sorry," she snapped, tossing it off. "I forgot that if we don't talk about your feelings every few hours, you devolve into a hipster lumberjack. Never mind how *I'm* feeling."

"Yes, in fact, never mind how you're feeling. Because it's so easy to talk to you while you're hiding from me all day, playing your violin in invisible closets, barricading your door and pretending you're not there. I'm a marvel of sensitivity compared to you. You're the one who picks a lock and kicks out a chair to *sleep on my floor.*"

"I did not," she said. "I climbed in through that window."

The chair was, in fact, still under the doorknob. "Why? Can you even tell me *why* you came in here last night?"

"I wanted to see you. I didn't want to talk to you. So I waited until you were sleeping." She said it like I was a moron. "How is that hard to understand?"

"Come on, weirdo," I said, but my voice came out strained. Despite her blithe words, her eyes were full of something that looked too much like pain, and I hated that I had caused it. I was causing it now, just standing here. "Let's go find your uncle. He's probably sweet-talking the gardener, or teaching the neighborhood squirrels to sing."

He wasn't in the garden. He wasn't in the kitchen, or the parlor, or the room with the pool table that everyone, horribly, referred to as the "billiards room." The marble floors were cold under my feet, and so I walked quickly after Holmes, who had wrapped herself in a long, trailing robe the color of dust.

"He might've gone to run errands in Eastbourne," I said as we approached the front hall.

With a sigh, she gestured to the window overlooking the grounds. "Of course he hasn't. It rained last night, and there aren't any fresh tire tracks in the drive. We might as well ask my father. There's more than one way to leave the house, and Leander might've been in a hurry. We don't know everything he's found out while he's been here." She took off again, this time up the stairs to her father's study.

"Everything? You've been listening in?" I asked, hurrying to catch up.

"Of course I've been listening. What else is there to do in this miserable house?"

"You weren't avoiding me? You were *eavesdropping*?"

She thought about that one. "I might have been doing both."

"Whatever. Keep going."

"From what I can tell, Leander's been gathering information to bolster the persona he's adopted in Germany. Which cartels have which connections, which low-rent artists are known to forge on the side, who has connections to other cities and which ones. He's tracking two forgers in particular, a Gretchen, and someone named Nathaniel." She frowned. "Though maybe that's his current boyfriend. Or both? That would be fascinating."

"Holmes. Leander? Disappearing?"

"Right. Well, I kept hearing that name through the vent, but not with enough context to figure out exactly who he was to my uncle."

"The vent?"

Holmes swept around a corner. "The vent that leads from my closet up to my father's study." It made me remember her eerie, omnipresent violin, the way the sound had come from nowhere. It must have been snaking up through the air ducts as Holmes played in her closet. I imagined her in a nest of clothes on the floor, her head tipped back against the wall, playing a sonata with her eyes shut. "Still, none of this tells us anything we need to know at the moment. Ergo, my father."

"Holmes," I said. I did *not* want to deal with her parents if I didn't have to. "Wait. Did he leave you a note? Have you checked your phone? He could already have explained it all."

Frowning, she dug her phone out of the pocket of her

robe. "I have a new message," she said. "Five minutes ago. An unknown number."

We stopped in the hallway, and she played it on speaker. "Lottie, I'm fine," Leander said, all bluff cheerfulness. "I'll see you soon."

She stared down at it, unbelieving. She played it again.

"Lottie," it said. "I'm fine. I'll see you soon."

"That isn't from his number," I said, peering at her screen. "Whose number is that?"

Holmes immediately hit the Call Back button.

The number you have dialed is disconnected. She tried again. Again. Then she flicked back to the message—"Lottie, I"—and before he could say the rest of it, she put the phone away. I could hear the tinny voice playing out of her pocket.

"That isn't what he calls me," she said. "He never— I need to see my father."

In the hall that led to the study, the long line of paintings glowered down at us. I was just about to ask Holmes if she'd overheard anything else when the door at the end of the hall opened.

"Lottie," Alistair said, blocking the doorway. "What are you doing up here?"

"Have you seen Uncle Leander?" she asked him, twisting her hands. "He was supposed to take Jamie and me to town for the day."

I wondered how, exactly, one lied to a Holmes; I'd never successfully done it myself. Could you actually pull it off if you were one, too?

From the withering look Alistair gave his daughter, I decided you couldn't.

"He left last night. One of his contacts in Germany was growing suspicious of his continued absence." He waved an errant hand. "Of course, he said he loves you, wishes you well, et cetera."

There was a rustle, and Holmes's father flung an arm across the door. "Mum?" Holmes asked, trying to step around him. "Is she in there? I thought she'd be in her room."

"Don't," he said. "She's having a very bad day."

"But I—" And she ducked under his outstretched arm and into his study.

The hospital bed was nowhere to be found. I hadn't seen Emma Holmes in days and had assumed she'd been in her room, but here she was, flung out on the sofa like she'd fallen there. Her ash-blond hair hung limply around her face, and she was wearing a robe not unlike her daughter's, thrown over a set of pajamas that looked wrinkled and sour. As I opened my mouth, she held up a hand. I glanced over at Holmes, who stiffened.

This house was nothing like my family's flat, where you tripped over each other on your way to the bathroom. Here, you could go weeks and see only pale marble floors, floating staircases, invisible plastic chairs. You could start to believe you were the only person in the world.

"What are your plans for Christmas?" her mother asked abruptly. Her voice came out in a harsh whisper.

"I—"

"I'm speaking to my daughter." But she was looking at Alistair, and with anger. It must have been terrible to be this way, prone and weak, when you were used to commanding the room.

Alistair cleared his throat. "Lottie, your brother has just expressed an interest in you staying in Berlin for the holiday."

"Oh," Holmes said, stuffing her hands in her pockets. I could hear the machinery in her brain grinding to life. "Has he."

"Don't exhaust your mother," he said. "We can have a rational conversation about this."

"She *has to go.*" Emma struggled up to her elbows, like a scuttling crab. Her breathing was labored.

"She doesn't," Alistair murmured. He made no motion to help her. "I'd rather have Lottie here. We never see her."

Holmes looked horrified, but her voice was calm. "Milo hasn't spoken to you in weeks," she said. "You haven't had that twitch you get, on the side of your mouth, after you talk to him."

"I've been ill," her mother said, as if it wasn't obvious. "That's enough to change anyone's tells."

"Yes," her daughter said, plowing ahead. "But the doctor you brought in—Dr. Michaels, from Highgate Hospital— doesn't specialize in fibromyalgia. She specializes in—"

"Poisons," her mother said.

At that, Alistair turned on his heel and retreated into the hall, snapping the door shut behind him.

Poisons?

"She also specializes in nanotechnology," Holmes was murmuring, but it was clear her brain had run ahead of her emotions. Then: "Oh, *God*, Mum. Poison? But I hadn't noticed any signs, I should have—I never wanted—"

Her mother's eyes burned. "You might have thought of that before you interfered with Lucien Moriarty."

Dizzily, I leaned against the wall. I still dreamt about it, what had happened to me that fall. The poison spring. The fever. The hallucinations. It hadn't been a poisoning so much as a purposeful infection, but Bryony Downs had still made me into a pale, helpless wreck. I couldn't imagine what Emma Holmes was feeling.

"Where is Leander?" Holmes asked, squaring her shoulders. "Why on earth would he go without telling me good-bye?"

I braced myself for the reaction. But the fire had already gone out in her mother's eyes, and her face was gray again. You could see the veins in her forehead. I remembered the photograph I'd seen of her, all turned out in a black suit, her lips a dark, dark red, power crackling off her like a cut wire. I couldn't square it with the exhausted woman in front of me. *Poisoned,* I thought. *My God.* She must've taken a leave of absence from work. What had Holmes said she'd done again? Wasn't she a scientist?

"That isn't the issue at hand," Emma Holmes said. She shut her eyes to concentrate on the words.

"You're telling me that Leander has snuck out like a fugitive, apparently days after you've been poisoned, and there's nothing to worry about?" She turned to the study door. "That this was all part of the plan? What on earth is happening?"

"We've tracked the poisoning back to the day you arrived; it was an isolated event, and we're taking precautions. We're controlling what we eat, what we breathe. We're culling the staff. We'll figure it out soon enough. But for now . . . Lottie, for your safety, there is no way you and Jamie can continue to stay here. I've transferred funds into your account for the trip. Go see your brother. Get out of this house." With that, she lifted a hand as if to touch her daughter, but Holmes ignored it. Her back had gone straight and still. Her eyes narrowed.

"You need to believe it's for your own good," her mother said.

"For my own good," Holmes said. "For your own good, maybe, but not mine. Never mine. You're a chemist; you'll have this under control by tomorrow. If I'm going—"

"You're going."

"Then I'm going to find my uncle, because if I'm correct, he's in extreme danger."

Emma looked at me. "You'll go with her," she said with despairing eyes. It wasn't a command so much as an entreaty. A peace offering to her daughter.

Everyone in this house seemed to exist in opposition to themselves, anger and love and loyalty and fear all layered over each other into an incomprehensible blur. I opened my mouth to tell her no, that my mother would kill me, that I wasn't her daughter's valet or bodyguard. That out of everyone I knew, Charlotte Holmes could take care of herself, and if she couldn't, I was the last person she'd let help her.

Blindly, Holmes reached out to clasp my hand in hers.

"I will," I heard myself say. "Of course I will."

four

I DECIDED THAT I HAD PRETTY GOOD LEVERAGE TO USE TO strike a deal with my father. Because if I didn't, my mother would hunt me down and kill me for running off to Europe without parental supervision.

"Leander left," I told my father, shifting the phone into my other hand. "Holmes's dad said he took off in the middle of the night. One of his contacts was getting antsy, I guess."

As I spoke, I kept an eye on Holmes next to me in the backseat. She was wearing head-to-toe black: collared shirt, trim pants, a pair of black wingtip boots that I sort of wanted for myself. Between her knees, she balanced her small black suitcase with its giant silver clasps. Her straight hair was tucked behind her ears, and I watched her tapping furiously away at her phone, lips pursed. She looked dangerous, delicate. She looked like a whisper made real.

She looked like she had a new case to solve. I didn't know how I felt about that.

The phone line crackled. "So you're going to Berlin. To look for him." There was a plea in my father's voice. I couldn't think of the last time that so many adults had asked me favors all in a row, like I was someone to be bargained with and not just ordered around. It had been, to put it mildly, a strange week.

A strange year.

"I'm going to Berlin," I said, "because Emma Holmes has been poisoned by Lucien Moriarty. Apparently."

Holmes lifted an eyebrow at that, but said nothing. On her phone, I watched a text pop up from Milo. *I ran that number. Leander was calling you from a burner. It makes sense, you know. He was undercover.*

Find out where it came from. Where was it bought, and by whom?

I was having to stretch my neck fairly far at this point. With an exasperated sigh, she put the phone between us so I could read.

You're more interested in this than your parents' situation? Poisoning? Honestly, why on earth have they told you about this and not me?

Because I'm the smart, well-adjusted child, she wrote back. *Less likely to seek revenge.*

Are you, now.

Tell me, have you already hauled Lucien out of Thailand

and begun pulling out his teeth?

Not yet. For now, I'm assigning a security force to the Sussex house.

Yes, good, but within reason.

Naturally. You're not upset about Mother, are you? Milo asked.

Holmes hesitated before typing a response. *No. Of course not. The situation is under control.*

"Apparently she's been poisoned," my father was saying. "Jesus, Jamie. Way to bury the lede. It's not that I haven't seen this sort of thing before with them—but listen, the Holmeses have always taken care of themselves. Still, while you're out there, do you mind casting out some feelers for Leander? Milo surely knows something. His spies have spies. I'd do it myself, but I have no idea how to contact him directly."

"Of course," I said, and prepared to strike my deal. "I'll do that if you agree to tell Mom why I won't be in London for Christmas. And if you make sure she doesn't come out here looking for me."

He let out a long breath. "Is that what you'd like for your present? Me, roasting on a spit?"

"You could always fly to Germany and look for Leander yourself," I told him, which was unfair, because I was sure that's exactly what he wanted to do. My half brothers were both still tiny, though, and there was no way that my father would leave them over Christmas, not even to search for his missing best friend.

I heard my father snort. "You *are* a piece of work," he said.

"Yes, fine, I will tell your mother if you'll follow up with Milo. I'm sure he can spare a few bodies to look for his uncle."

I can tell you that Leander isn't in the city, the text on Holmes's screen read. *At least not as himself.*

He wouldn't be, Holmes wrote back. *I need whatever contacts you have in Kreuzberg and Friedrichshain. Isn't there some mangy art school out there?*

Hold on.

"I have no idea what you're on about," I hissed at her. "I thought we were going to Berlin. Where's Kreuzberg?"

"In Berlin," Holmes said, as though it were obvious.

"Jamie?" my father asked.

"Can you send along those emails? I'm sure they'll be useful."

He hesitated. "I'd rather not," he said finally, "but if you need any particular information, I can pass it along."

"Why won't you just send them?"

"If Charlotte had written you every day for months, Jamie, can you honestly tell me you'd forward them all to your father without a second thought?"

"Of course I would." Of course I wouldn't. But there wasn't time to argue; the airport was looming in the distance. "Look, I have to go."

"You need to promise me that you won't look for Leander yourself. He's created a complicated scenario, and I don't want you mucking it up. Promise me."

Not, *it isn't safe.* Not, *I don't want you in danger.* He just didn't want me blowing Leander's cover. It was nice to know that, as usual, he had his priorities straight.

"I promise we won't go chasing after him," I said, not meaning a word. "How about that?"

"We're at the airport, miss," the driver called, and beside me, Holmes burst out into horrified laughter at her phone.

I found you a guide, the screen read. *But I'm afraid neither of you will approve.*

"No." Because I was now remembering exactly *who* worked for Milo Holmes. "No. Absolutely not." Then I spat out a few other things that I'd heard on a dark Brixton street from the mouth of a man being curb-stomped.

"Jamie?" my father asked. "What on earth is going on?"

I hung up. I couldn't stop staring at Holmes's goddamn screen, which now read: *Tell Watson to watch his language, will you? He's blistering my poor wiretapper's ears.*

DESPITE BEING SHUTTLED BACK AND FORTH BETWEEN ENG-land and America for most of my remembered life—or maybe because of it—I'd never traveled all that much otherwise. Our family vacations had always been underwhelming. Growing up in Connecticut meant that I'd made the one mandatory trip down to New York City with my family, but in our case, we ate in chain restaurants and saw a Broadway show about roller-blading tigers. (For that, as for most things, I blame my father.) After I moved to London, I went on vacation exactly once: my mother rented a camper van and took me and my sister to Abbey Wood. It was in the south of the city, barely a mile from our house. It rained all four days we were there. My sister and

I had to share a fold-out bed, and I woke up on that last morning with her elbow physically inside of my mouth.

It was, in short, nothing like going to Berlin with Charlotte Holmes.

Greystone was headquartered in Mitte, a neighborhood in the northeast of the city. Milo had begun it as a tech company specializing in surveillance; he expanded his operations when it became clear that there were certain things humans couldn't do. All I knew was that his employees—his soldiers and spies—were the main independent force on the ground in Iraq, and that once, Milo had ordered his personal bodyguards to frisk everyone at Holmes's eighth grade graduation.

Holmes ran me through this, and more, in the cab from the airport, though I knew the bulk of it already. I wasn't sure if she'd assumed I had a bad memory or if she was chattering on because she was nervous. She had good reason to be. In the next ten minutes, we'd be face-to-face with someone whose brother spent this past fall exploring fun and creative ways to have us killed, someone who'd faked his own death to escape that family (and prison), someone Charlotte Holmes had loved so much, she'd tried to have imprisoned because he didn't love her back. August Moriarty had a PhD in pure maths, a Prince Charming smile, and a brother named Hadrian who'd probably taught him everything he knew about wheeling and dealing stolen paintings. Who else would Milo possibly tap to guide us through the city?

I wanted my ax back. Or Milo's head on a pike.

The city was bare of snow and warmer than London, and

I realized I didn't really know a lot about where we were. Anything I did know about Berlin was rooted in world history textbooks and movies about the Second World War. I knew about the Nazis, and I knew that Germany made the best cars, that their language had compound words for emotions I didn't know had names. My mother liked to refer to *schadenfreude*, joy at the misery of others, whenever she laughed at the traffic report on the radio. *Who would be silly enough to own a car in London,* she'd say. We took the tube like proper Londoners, or like what she thought proper Londoners should be.

The Berlin I saw now reminded me a little of London, in that the buildings we saw all seemed to be on their second lives. A grocery store we passed had the façade of an old museum. A post office had been turned into a gallery, the old Deutsche Bundespost sign faded above a window that displayed sculptures of . . . ears. I spotted a painted lamppost looming on the brick wall behind a real one. Everywhere there was art, on the buildings, on the billboards, creeping down the brick walls onto the streets in murals that read KILL CAPITALISM and BELIEVE EVERYTHING and KEEP YOUR EYES OPEN. The words were all in English—lingua franca, I guessed, though I remembered hearing that the city was full of émigré artists, drawn by the cheap rent and the community. What struck me the most was how none of the graffiti had been covered up. It was like the city was made of it, this twinned transformation and discontent, and the storefronts that stood new and clean began to look unfinished, somehow, at least to me.

Though it wasn't all like that, especially as we approached

Mitte. The car took us by park after park, postage-stamp-sized in the middle of neighborhoods, and as we approached Greystone, we passed grand old beautiful museums, giant turnabouts, walls that gardens hid behind.

I pulled out my notebook to write it all down. Beside me, Holmes was looking out the window, too, but I didn't imagine she was taking any of it in. She'd been there before. And anyway, if I were her, I'd be deciding what I could possibly say to August Moriarty.

By the time we pulled up to Greystone, I had a full page of notes, and I hurried to finish them as the cab stopped.

"Come *on*, Watson." Holmes tossed a bill to the driver and dragged me out the door.

Greystone, it turned out, took up the top ten floors of a glass tower that loomed over the rest of the block, new and strange in its surroundings. Because it was private security—because it was Milo—we were put through a metal detector, a full-body scan, and two separate fingerprinting kiosks before we were sent up to him on the freight elevator. Floor after floor of office space. His penthouse was at the top.

"He knew that we were coming, right?" I asked Holmes for the tenth time.

"Obviously," she said as the elevator lurched. "Did you notice how hastily that retinal scan was set up? He's obviously watching his security feed with a bowl of popcorn. Jackass."

The elevator lurched again.

"Stop insulting him," I told her, "or we're going to plunge to our deaths."

Milo Holmes had always reminded me of an actor who'd wandered in from a movie set in another century. He had the same sonorous speech as an English professor, and I'd never seen him wear anything but a tailored suit. (One of those suits was folded up in my suitcase. I tried to feel bad about having filched it, and failed.) His offices were just like him—old-fashioned and stuffy, like the MI-5 of old spy novels. It was like he'd cherry-picked his favorite fictional references and rearranged them into a hodgepodge of mismatched places and times.

But I hadn't really expected the armed guards.

Two steps out of the elevator, and a pair of them stopped us, automatic weapons pointed at our chests. One started mumbling rapidly into her wrist, something about *unfriendlies* and *unauthorized access.*

"We were cleared. We should be fine," I said to the guards, my hands up. They didn't budge. "Uh. Should I be speaking German?"

The other soldier hoisted his gun to my face.

"I guess not." It came out sort of high-pitched.

Holmes, unbothered, was peering up into the light fixture. "Milo. I know you can hear me. Have you entirely forgotten your manners? You're making Watson squawk."

"Of course I haven't," her brother said, stepping out of a door that swung open from the wallpaper, as if invented on the spot. He nodded to his guards, and they shouldered their weapons, disappearing down the hall in the two-bit magic show that was Milo Holmes's bread and butter.

"Wasn't that fun?" he asked.

"No," I said. "Do you treat all your guests this way?"

"Only my little sister," he said, tucking his hands into his elegant pockets. "You know, you could have come up the visitors' elevator, and we would have had far less trouble."

"They *put* us on—"

Holmes lifted a hand to stop me. Her eyes were scanning the room. "You haven't updated your lobby. It still looks like an ugly antiques shop in here."

"It is, as you well know, not a lobby. This is my private residence," he said. "You've seen the actual lobby quite often. And now you've been x-rayed in it. Would you like to visit it again?"

"Yes, it is *so* good to see you spending your time on worthwhile causes like photographing my teeth when you could, in fact, be looking for our uncle. Or adding guards to the family estate."

"Who says I'm not?"

"I am. I'm watching you do nothing."

"You wouldn't know how to look."

She took a step toward him. "You monstrous pig, I knew how to read people before you knew your alphabet—"

"Oh? Because I've been holding my tongue about the fact that you and your 'colleague' there have obviously begun doing the nasty, and that—pity—it's not going very well—"

At that, Holmes lunged, and he dodged her, letting out a triumphant laugh.

"Guys. *Guys.* Where is he?"

"Who, Watson?" she asked.

"August Moriarty. The reason you two are fighting? I could be wrong about that. It's just an assumption." I looked Milo over, head to toe, the way I'd seen him do to me. "As is the assumption that no one's done the nasty to you in years. Three? Four?"

Milo adjusted his glasses. Then he pulled them off and began polishing them with a sleeve.

"Two, actually," a soft voice said behind me. "He never really did get over that comtesse, and I haven't seen any girls around here since."

Charlotte Holmes went completely still.

"Though it's been longer for me," the voice said. "So I shouldn't really be making fun. Speaking of, I hear I have you three to thank for breaking off my engagement. And I do mean that. Thank you."

Milo sighed. "August. It's good you're here. Lottie, I've given him access to my contacts. He'll show you around. I—well, frankly, I have more important things to do." He stopped at the end of the hall. "By the way, Lottie, Phillipa Moriarty called to confirm your lunch. I've left her number in your room."

With that bombshell, he left. I didn't have any time to process it. I'd been left with Holmes and Moriarty. And because I was—am—a coward, I waited until the last possible second to turn around.

August Moriarty was dressed like a starving artist. He had on ripped black jeans and a black T-shirt and steel-toe boots—black, of course—and his hair was cut into a blond fauxhawk. But while he was dressed like a poet, he had the polish of a rich kid, and his eyes were burning with an intensity that reminded me of—

Well, it reminded me of Charlotte Holmes. All of him did. In the picture of him I'd seen on his math department's website, he was smiling in a tweed blazer, and now he was standing here like her looking-glass twin. Before they'd even exchanged a word, it was clear that they had *done* something to each other, broken each other, maybe, or distilled each other like liquor, until all that was left was hard and strong and spare. They had a history that had nothing to do with me.

Maybe I was reading too much into it. Into him. Things between me and Holmes were tenuous enough already, though, and here was a gust of wind that could take the rest of it down.

A very polite gust of wind.

"Milo's said some nice things about you," he was saying as he shook my hand. He had a tattoo on his forearm, something dark and patterned. "Which is interesting, since Milo usually doesn't notice people that aren't holograms."

"I didn't know the two of you were close," I said. I had to say something. We were still shaking hands.

He had a strong grip. I pressed harder.

He laughed, a friendly sound. "We're both ghosts. Where else would you work if you legally don't exist? I'm fairly sure that Milo's scrubbed his digital footprint so clean that he wasn't even technically born. We have that much in common."

"That makes sense," I said, because he was still shaking my hand.

"I should probably also apologize for my brother. Do know that I never told him to kill you."

My fingers were starting to go numb. "I'm pretty sure I'm just the collateral damage there."

"Right, of course. Of course." A strange look passed over his face, and then vanished. "Sorry."

"So. Phillipa?" I asked. "Are you two . . . close? Do you know why she'd want to see us?"

"Not really," he said. "We haven't spoken since I died."

I risked looking over at Holmes. She hadn't moved, except for her hands, which were pressed against her sides. She didn't look nervous or scared. She didn't even seem like she was cataloguing him, the way I'd expected her to, taking in whatever changes the last two years had worked on him. What her betrayal had done. Whether he hated her for it.

She was just looking at him.

"I got your birthday card," she said quietly. "Thank you."

"I hope you didn't mind that it was in Latin. I didn't mean it to seem pretentious. I just wanted to—"

"I know. It reminded me of that summer." Her eyes brightened. "That's what you intended, right?"

August Moriarty was still shaking my hand. More accurately, he was holding it, because neither of us was moving anymore. He was staring at her like she was a penny at the bottom of a well, and I—well, I was staring at the space between them.

"I need this back," I said, and pulled my hand away.

August didn't appear to notice. "You must be exhausted from your trip. Both of you. You're here for the week, yes? I'll have Milo's body man show you to your room so you can settle in. You had lunch on the plane? Excellent. And tonight—well, there's a bar we should go to. Some things I'd like your opinion on, there."

"Aren't we going to talk about this Phillipa thing?" I put every bit of venom I was feeling into her name.

"Is the bar the Old Metropolitan?" she asked him.

"It's Saturday night, so it's where Leander would be."

"We'll go tonight. I can't imagine what he's— I can't wait any longer than that."

"The Old Metropolitan," August said, and there was a surprising thread of bitterness in his voice. "You just knew that, didn't you? How did you guess?"

"I never guess."

I cleared my throat. "We could have just asked my father. He's been getting daily updates from Leander since October. I'm sure he has a list of places for us to look. And can we talk about Phillipa? What does she want with you?"

Neither of them even glanced at me.

"Walk me through it. How you knew it was the Old Metropolitan," August said, drawing her over to a bench between the elevators. He sounded intrigued, and something else, something darker. "Step by step, and slowly. Charlotte, it had to be a guess."

"It's Saturday night," she repeated. "And I never—"

"No, you don't," I said, but I was saying it to no one.

I DECIDED TO FIND MY WAY TO MY ROOM ON MY OWN WITH-
out waiting for Milo's "body man," whatever that was. I couldn't
stand between Holmes and August for another second.

But it wasn't difficult to orient myself. Most of the doors
on the hall were keycode-locked—honestly, I didn't want to
know what was behind them—until I tried the one at the end
of the hall.

I opened it. I took a breath.

It was like being back at Sciences 442. Like being back in
Holmes's room in Sussex. It was like being back inside Charlotte Holmes's head.

The room was dark; unlike her lab at Sherringford, this
one had a window, but it was tinted so dark that no natural
light crept in. A series of lamps snaked down from the ceiling. Some half-finished chemical experiment was laid out on
a table, with a set of burners and white powder measured out
into piles. No shelves, but books everywhere, piled up beside
an overstuffed armchair, behind the sofa, on either side of a
white plaster fireplace, and inside its grate, too, like kindling. I
picked one up from the pile beside the door. It was in German,
with a bisected cross on its cover. I set it down.

In one corner, uncomfortably close to the chemistry set,
someone had brought in a twin bed. It was clearly a new
addition, much nicer than the shabby furniture surrounding

it. It was clearly meant for me.

I decided to camp out on Holmes's bed instead.

Milo (or his men) had built a loft for her, a bed bolted high up into the wall, as small and remote as the crow's nest of a ship. From up there, she could survey her tiny fiefdom. I wondered how old Holmes was when Milo gave her this room. Eleven? Twelve? He was six years older; he'd have been eighteen, at the beginning of building his empire, from the timeline Holmes had given me. And he'd given her a space of her own in that new life. As I climbed up the loft's ladder, I tried to imagine a miniature Holmes doing the same, a flashlight clenched in her teeth.

She must have felt like Milo's first mate, surrounded by his loyal men, in a ship's cabin of her own. Untouchable. Away from the world.

I knew what I was doing. By taking over her perch, I was gunning for a confrontation. Some sign that she still knew I existed. *Watson,* she'd say, lighting a cigarette. *Don't be a child. Get down here, I have a plan.*

August Moriarty wasn't a child. He was a man. That had been my first impression, and the one that ultimately mattered. I couldn't help seeing him as a standard by which I'd already failed. If he was the finished sketch, I was the unfinished space around it. Let me put it this way: I was five foot ten on a good day. I had on faded jeans and my father's jacket. I had twelve dollars in my bank account, and still, somehow, I was along for the ride, and the ride was in *Europe,* where my best friend paid for everything and spoke German to the driver and I tried not to feel like the cargo she'd strapped to the top of the car.

Time passed. Thirty minutes. An hour. I hated this line of thinking, but it was what I'd been left with.

To torture myself, I wondered what Phillipa Moriarty could possibly want with Holmes. Why she would agree to a lunch. I mean, I wasn't stupid. I had a few solid ideas— death, dismemberment—but going through Milo's mercenary company made me think she wasn't up to serving violence. A détente, maybe? Maybe she knew where Leander was being kept. Maybe she was going to tell us that she wasn't siding with Lucien in this ridiculous war.

Maybe she'd found out that her little brother August was alive.

As an act of desperation, I took out my phone to text my father. *What do you know about Phillipa Moriarty?*

The response was prompt. *Only what's been in the papers, and you've seen that, too. Why?*

What about a bar called the Old Metropolitan?

Leander went there on Saturdays to meet with a professor from the Kunstschule Sieben. One of the local art schools. A Nathaniel. Gretchen was another name that came up quite often.

The forgers Holmes had mentioned. *Any other places I should know about?*

I'll email you a list. I'm happy to hear that Milo's taking this so seriously.

I was pretty sure that Milo wasn't, and that he'd shoved us off on August because of it. I put my phone away.

After a minute, I pulled it back out.

When you were working with Leander, did you ever feel like you were his baggage? Like he'd insist on taking you along on a case, and then he'd run off and solve it without you?

Of course. But there's a way to stop feeling like that, you know.
How? I asked.

I don't know when my father became someone I trusted to go to for advice. It was an uncomfortable feeling.

My phone pinged. *I've put a hundred dollars in your bank account. Now run off and solve it without her.*

THE OLD METROPOLITAN WAS BUSIER THAN ANY BAR I'D been to in Britain. Not that I'd been to too many bars—but I'd seen enough. In Britain, you could have a beer with your dinner at sixteen if your parent bought it for you; at eighteen, you could order whatever you wanted for yourself. Germany's laws weren't all that different. One of the great ironies of my life is that I got shipped off to America for high school, a country that didn't let people drink until they'd nearly graduated college.

The Old Metropolitan was full of students. It was only a few streets away from the Kunstschule Sieben's campus, something I learned while wandering the neighborhood. When I'd left Greystone HQ, it was still late afternoon, so I decided to spend the time before nightfall cultivating a disguise. I'd watched Holmes remake herself in front of me, how putting a slight spin on her usual presentation turned her into an entirely different person. I'd asked her, once, what she thought of me going undercover. She'd laughed in my face.

Not this time. I bought a hat and a pair of shit-kickers at a thrift store. Then I found a barbershop and asked them for a haircut I kept seeing on the street, shaved on the sides and long on top. My hair was wavy, but whatever he styled it with made it lay slick and straight. When he finished, I put on my glasses and looked in the mirror.

I'd always had something that made grandmothers want to talk to me in waiting rooms. I looked friendly, I guess. I'd never been able to see it myself, but I saw its absence now. Grinning, I stuck the fedora on the back of my head, tipped the barber, and went out to find some dinner.

Simon, I thought. *I'm going to call myself Simon.*

I walked to Old Metropolitan with a gyro that I'd gotten from a sketchy-looking food truck up the street. Whenever I was in a new place by myself, I was always aware of how I was walking, what I was looking at, worried that I'd seem like a tourist and be slighted somehow for it. Tonight, I was wandering along like a local, licking the tzatziki sauce off my fingers, looking at the street art with disinterested eyes. Simon didn't care about the giant neon dragon painted over the Old Metropolitan's doorway, teeth bared like a warning. Simon had seen it a million times before. His uncle lived just down the block.

Simon was used to the crush of people inside, too, and so I kept my face bored as I pushed my way up to the bar. But I almost lost my composure when I looked over the crowd. Despite my new clothes and haircut, I was the least avant-garde person in sight. The girl next to me had pink hair that faded out to electric gold. She was gesturing with a giant glass of something, and it sloshed at me while she spoke to her friends in German. The only word I recognized was "Heidegger," who was a philosopher. Who I thought was a philosopher. Did I know that from *The Simpsons*? I tried to avoid eye contact.

Instead, I ended up staring down the bartender. "What'll it be?" he asked, clearly pegging me for English. I reminded myself that that was fine. Simon was English.

Jamie was panicking.

"A Pimm's cup," I said, with fancy posh-boy vowels, because I'd decided that Simon was rich, and because people drank Pimm's cups at the races I'd seen on television, and yes, it was becoming abundantly clear that Holmes was right, I was an awful spy, because if tonight was any indication, my entire knowledge of the world came from Thursday-night TV.

But the bartender didn't shrug, or raise an eyebrow. He just turned his back to make the drink. I made myself relax, one muscle at a time, and willed my brain to stop racing. I put my hat more firmly on the back of my head.

My plan had been to nurse my drink and eavesdrop until I heard the Kunstschule Sieben come up in conversation. Then I'd sidle over and introduce myself as a prospective student visiting my uncle over the holiday. *Maybe you'd know him— tall, slicked-back hair, English like me? Can I buy you a drink? Do you know a girl named Gretchen? I met her here last week—* et cetera, ad nauseam, until someone mentioned the last place they'd seen either of them, or Leander's mysterious professor, and I'd be off on a new lead before Holmes showed up on her blond Gaston's arm.

It had seemed fairly foolproof when I'd thought it up. Like all foolproof plans, it turned out to be ridiculous. First off, it was *loud* in the Old Metropolitan. I could barely make out what languages were being spoken around me, much less the actual words. Second, I hadn't counted on the intimidation factor. I'd never had problems in the past striking up a conversation with strangers, and I couldn't pin down why it was proving so difficult now.

Maybe because I'd spent the last three months talking exclusively to someone whose idea of small talk involved blood spatter.

She's ruined me, I thought, and sank down a little over my drink. The last bits of Simon scattered. What did I think I was playing at, anyway? I wasn't any good at this. I didn't even want to be here, in this bar, wincing against the Krautwerk turned up to eleven while the dude next to me played with his labret piercing. I leaned out to ask the bartender for my bill, but I couldn't get his attention.

When I sat back down, I noticed a girl across the bar drawing me.

She was being pretty obvious about it. Her sketchpad was braced against her knee, and she kept sneaking glances at me over the top. She had long glossy black curls and a cute upturned nose, the kind of girl I used to like, when I liked other girls. Before I knew what I was doing, I picked up my drink and headed her way.

Her eyes widened. Then she bit her lip. I was feeling pretty confident.

Well, Simon was feeling pretty confident.

"Hi," I heard him say. "Are you using charcoals?"

"I am. What do you use?"

"My dashing good looks." Where was this crap coming from? "What's your name?"

"Why?" She spoke with an American accent.

"Are you from the States?"

"No," she laughed. "But my English teacher was."

Simon sat down next to her. "I'm going to ask you a question, and I want you to tell me the truth, okay, love?" Jesus Christ. "Were you drawing me just then?"

She angled her sketchpad toward her body. "Maybe."

"Maybe yes or maybe no?" Simon lifted a finger to the bartender, who came right over. "One of whatever she's having—"

"A vodka soda—"

"A vodka soda." She hadn't instantly shot Simon down. He grinned at her. If there was a part of Jamie somewhere in that smile, both he and I decided not to notice. "Is it a maybe yes now?"

Her name was Marie-Helene. She was born in Lyon, in France, but the rest of her family lived in Kyoto. She loved visiting, she said, but really she wanted to live in Hong Kong someday. "It's like it's a present place that's in the future," she said. She was studying at the Kunstschule Sieben because, when she was a little girl, she'd gotten lost in the Louvre during a family trip to Paris and instead of getting scared, she'd found herself wandering entranced through the Impressionist wing. "I drew water lilies for years after that," she said. "I made my parents call me Claude, like Claude Monet."

Simon liked her. More than that, I liked her. She had an impish quality to her, like she was keeping a secret. But a small one, nothing Holmes-sized. She was nothing like Holmes, in fact, and it made me want to cry from relief.

"I *was* drawing you."

I snapped back to focus. "What?"

"That look you just had. You had it before, too. Like your grandmother died, but you're angry about it. It's—interesting. And a little disturbing." Marie-Helene turned her sketchbook around to show me. A boy in a stupid hat, staring down at his hands like he could find some answers there.

It was a good drawing. I hated that it was of me.

I forced myself back into my Simon-shaped cage. "I'm more handsome than that, aren't I?" he asked her.

"Yes." She toyed with her drink, looking up at me. "You are."

I didn't know what to do next, because usually, in this situation, I'd lean in to kiss her. Correction: what I *used* to do next was lean in, but that was at parties in people's basements, not bars—would that even work here? It was what Simon would probably do. I wanted to, I did, and still I didn't want to at all. Should I change the subject? Ask about Gretchen, the art forger Leander had made contact with? About her professors? Should I just kiss her and pretend it didn't make me nauseous?

The moment passed. She took a sip, then brightened. "Hey!" she said, waving a hand to someone over my head. "Over here!"

In an instant, we were surrounded by chattering girls. One was wearing a paint-splattered backpack, so I figured they were her friends from school. "Everyone," she said, "everyone, this is Simon, he's *British*," and in the flurry of introductions that followed, I thought I heard the name Gretchen. My pulse quickened.

"I was thinking about going to the Kunstschule Sieben next year," I yelled over the music. It was disco now, and louder. "I do video installations! Do any of you do video installations!"

"Yes!" the girl next to me yelled back.

"Can I ask you more about it!"

"Friday mornings!"

I wasn't sure if she'd heard my question, or if her English wasn't that good, but the crowd of girls was moving now, and Marie-Helene grabbed my hand in hers. An invitation to follow. I threw some money down on the bar, feeling thoroughly triumphant. We'd go to a party. There'd be other students there. Surely someone would know something about Leander, and I could go back to Holmes with *information*, something that she and August wouldn't have—

Or would. Because like a nightmare, she and August were standing between us and the door.

five

I HADN'T SEEN THEM COME IN. I'D SAY IT WAS A TESTAMENT to how good their disguises were, but they weren't dressed to fit in with this crowd. They'd taken the opposite tack from me. August was done up in full douchebag tourist mode, from his gelled hair down to his white sneakers and calf-high socks. Holmes stood beside him, fishing something out of her fanny pack. Her wig, mouse-brown, hung lankly around her face.

She glanced up. Her eyes traveled down to my hand, clasped with Marie-Helene's, and I thought I saw her blanch.

Either way, she recovered quickly.

"*There* you are," Holmes cried. I thought she was about to blow my cover when she turned to August and said, "I told you he couldn't ditch us for long."

Marie-Helene gave me a questioning look.

"They're my cousins, visiting from London," I told her, trying to reclaim the narrative. "And I didn't ditch them. They said they wanted a night to do touristy things by themselves."

"Well, tell them to come along." Her friends were already on the street. She disentangled her hand from mine and pushed the door open into the night air.

August and Holmes were on my heels. "What's your name?" she hissed.

"Simon. Yours?"

"Tabitha and Michael."

"Are you supposed to be siblings?" I asked August. The both of them were wearing brown color contacts.

"We are, but it's not believable. I'm much prettier than she is."

I grinned, then reminded myself that I hated him. "She drag you into this?"

"I am standing right here," Holmes said, stamping her feet a little in the cold. "Where are we headed, Watson? What have you found out?"

Nothing yet, but I didn't want to tell her that. I was still smarting about her and August ignoring me before. We were having lunch with Phillipa tomorrow? We weren't at all dealing with the fact that her mother had been poisoned? "I found out that French girls like Simon a lot," I said instead, and trotted to catch up with Marie-Helene and her friends.

The air had gotten colder since earlier this evening. I reclaimed Marie-Helene's hand under the pretense of warming it up. Was I aware that Holmes was behind me, watching? Obviously. Was I above doing things to make her jealous? Well . . . no.

It wasn't hard to like Marie-Helene and her friends, though. They chatted about the new Damien Hirst show going up the next week, and when, tired of maintaining my know-it-all pose, I confessed I didn't know who that was, they were kind about filling me in. Apparently he put cows in formaldehyde. This was art? Yes, they told me, it was. In a world where information was currency, I was usually bankrupt. It was nice, for once, not to be mocked for it.

"Where are we going, exactly?" I asked the girl with the paint-splattered backpack.

"Some of our friends rent from this super-rich art dealer. He has a house up ahead." With her chin, she pointed to a tall brick building on the corner. "The only catch to living there is that he can use it to throw parties on the weekends, when he's in town. You'll see why, it's a pretty cool space. We all usually go."

"But?" I asked, because her tone was darker than her words.

"But he's a creep," she said, shrugging. "He's like fifty, and his new girlfriend is always some baby Sieben student. A lot of these girls have dated him. It's like making a deal with the devil for a little while. You meet some people, you get bought some nice things, you sleep with a gross old man, and by the time he ditches you you've gained something from it. You'll be fine, though. He doesn't like boys."

My skin crawled. "You're Gretchen, right?" I asked, hoping she'd point toward who was.

"Gretchen?" She shook her head. "I'm Hanna. Marie-Helene was calling us her *mädchen*—her girls. Is that what you were thinking of?"

I was stumbling into some sleazy party based on something I didn't actually hear in a bar.

Marie-Helene pulled me up the steps to the brick building's door. "Our destination awaits," she said, ushering us in.

The main floor was surprisingly dark and quiet, but it wasn't our "destination." Without turning on a light, Hanna felt around to her right until she found a doorframe. "Down these stairs," she whispered. "Turn on your phone if you need light."

At the bottom of the stairs was a door, and beyond that door was a cavern.

Marie-Helene and her friends made a beeline for the bar in the corner. I was left standing with one hand on my hat, taking it all in.

The cavern didn't feel natural. The walls were lined with tile, and the ceiling had a perfect arch that meant it was manmade. A damp, sharp smell hung in the air. It took me a moment to place it as chlorine. I pushed past a knot of people and saw its source—a massive pool in the center of the room. One girl kicked her legs on an inflatable swan, holding her martini glass safely above her head. A pair of boys were dangling their feet in the water as they made out. Everywhere, a dim, fractured sort of light speckled people's faces, speckled the walls.

Without thinking, I turned to clock Holmes's reaction. It was what I always did in these down-the-rabbit-hole situations.

It took me a minute to find her, still standing up on the now-deserted staircase, and I caught the end of a transformation—a subtle one, this time. Somewhere along the way, she'd lost the fanny pack. One hand was hastily unbuttoning her cardigan, and the other was tapping some kind of lip gloss on her mouth. The whole process took less than a minute, and when she stepped down into the party, she was wearing a little black dress and a haughty expression. In this light, her mouse-brown hair looked soft and warm. She was recognizably the same girl as she was in the Old Metropolitan, and she wasn't at all.

On her tottering heels, she padded up between me and August. "Boys?" she asked, and on her cue, we took her elbows and led her into the party.

I leaned down to whisper in her ear. "Is this the part where we share information? Because I know how you came up with the Old Metropolitan. It's just something you've overheard back in Sussex. No magic there."

She glanced up at me. "It's all magic, Simon," she said, "if I'm to believe what you write about me."

"He's your biographer?" August asked. "Like Dr. Watson? Jesus, that's ador—"

"It is not *adorable.*" I pulled us to a stop at the pool's edge. Beside me, Holmes squinted across the room. The light from the water was freckling her cheeks, and I resisted the urge to touch her face, to see if I could make them scatter. "Of course I know it isn't magic. I'll prove it. Do you want me to tell you what you'll do next?"

She smiled, almost imperceptibly. "Go on, then."

I gave myself a second to look around the party. Hanna had been right. Here and there someone broke the mold, but really there were two kinds of people here: college-age girls and men who gleamed with that particular sheen of money. The girls were mostly in tiny dresses, but the men were all dressed differently, some in suits and some more like artists, some in rumpled black and some neatly pressed. Some had a dancer's build, or the anxious stare of a writer.

Next to us, a girl was flicking through what looked like slides of her work on her iPhone. "As you can see," she was saying, "I'm an excellent candidate for your opening."

Immediately, Holmes turned her head to listen.

Focus, I told myself, and looked around the room again. I was not going to make a fool out of myself, not with Blond Gaston over her other shoulder.

"There's a man in the corner," I said finally. "The one with the scarf and the round glasses. He's the best candidate for Leander's professor contact. What was his name? Nathaniel?"

Beside me, Holmes made a humming sound. She wasn't looking at him; her attention was fixed on the conversation behind us. "Explain your reasoning."

It suddenly seemed so important for me to be right. To get her to look at me, really *look* at me, the way I needed her to. Squinting, I considered the man in question, who was telling a story with his hands. "His body language. He seems much more relaxed than the other men here. He's not jockeying for status or trying to get laid; he looks like he's catching up with friends. And the people around him are at ease, too.

Look at the guy next to him—he's what, eighteen, and he just whacked Nathaniel on the arm while he was talking. Now he looks shocked, probably at his own gumption, and everyone's laughing. They're all comfortable with each other. He's their authority figure, but they like him."

With the calm electricity of a hunting dog in a field, Holmes stared down the man in the suit. The only problem was that it was a different man in a different suit.

"Plus he's handsome," I said desperately, trying to refocus her, "and people meet at the Old Metropolitan to walk down here on Saturday nights, and you said your uncle was involved with someone here, someone in this scene. Does Leander like redheads?"

Holmes grimaced at the mention of her uncle's sex life. "Yes, yes, fine, except we're not in a position to approach him, so it doesn't matter. None of us are done up like art dealers and you're a little too spot-on to play a prospective art student. You look like you just came from central casting. A disconnected undercut, Watson? Really?"

August smiled to himself.

"Marie-Helene buys it," I said, setting my jaw.

"That's because she thinks you're handsome."

"And you don't?"

Nathaniel was looking over at us now. I'd been staring. Quickly, Holmes turned to me, adjusting my collar. "You look ridiculous," she said. Her hands were warm. "I like you much better as yourself."

There was a trace of something in the air, sickly sweet and

familiar. Forever Ever Cotton Candy. The Japanese perfume that August had given her years ago.

"You look good, Simon," he was saying, reaching past her to clap me on the shoulder. "And really nice work, with the deductions." It came out unnatural, like he'd learned how to compliment people from an instruction manual.

"Anyway," Holmes said, pulling away from me. "We'll deal with him later. Big fish first."

"What big fish?"

There was a look on August's face, something strange and drawn, but when I glanced again it was gone. "Charlotte, we're going to go play pool," he said.

"We're playing pool? Don't you mean *in* the pool?" I paused. "Why the hell would we play in the pool?"

"Go off, then," she said, coiling a strand of hair around a limpid finger. She was already slipping back into character. "I imagine I'll work faster on my own, anyway."

Holmes and not-Holmes. Businesslike words in a porn star voice.

"I'm sure you will, Tabitha," August told her, annoyed, and steered me away. Past the bar, past a circle of overstuffed chairs, past a group of men in suits all smoking and checking their phones while a girl in a skirt served them drinks. I wondered if she was one of the art students who lived here, too. If that was part of the deal. I felt sick.

There was a pool table in the corner. Unlike the heavy, ancient ones in Holmes's house, this one was made of acrylic. You could see straight through its legs to the wall. Only the felt surface was an opaque white.

"This seems pointlessly complicated," I said.

"What does?"

"This party. This situation. This pool table." I kicked its leg. "Who got bored enough to make this thing?"

August was already racking the balls. "Are you any good at pool?"

I'd played some in the afternoons in a pub near my school. Which of course meant nothing, because I'd spent most of that time staring at Rose Milton, girl of my freshman daydreams. "Eh," I said.

"Well, it's all geometry and hand-eye coordination." He tossed me a cue stick and lined up his shot.

"Terrific. So the idea was to drag me into the corner and ritualistically beat me, and then explain why you and Holmes ditched me in Milo's Military Funhouse earlier?"

With a resounding crack, he broke the balls across the table. Two solids went in the far right pocket.

"Tell me," he said, leaning against the wall. "Do you ever get sick of playing the victim?"

It was so far removed from anything he'd said before that I thought I must've imagined it. "Excuse me?"

"Jamie, I've known you for less than a day, and you already flinch every time I talk to you."

"I'm not—"

"I haven't been anything but nice. What, exactly, is the problem?"

"You seem—either you're completely naïve, or you're a

fake. The way you talk to me is ridiculous. The way you look at her—" Deep breaths, I told myself. If I beat him into the floor, Holmes would kill me. "I guess I'm stripes."

"You are, but it's still my turn." His eyes were on the table. The solid-colored balls had all wandered into improbable corners. I was sure he was working out some mathematical solution. "Are you really that insecure? Or is it something else?"

"Do you know what you are to her?" I snapped. "Because I do."

"No, you don't. Not from what I can tell. And I wasn't asking you about Charlotte."

I glared at him. His ugly tattoo, his posh accent, his twenty-three-year-old bullshit confidence. "Then spell it out for me, genius."

"Maybe you need me to," he said, and with an elegant motion, he knocked another ball into a pocket. "Maybe I need to say to you, out loud, that I didn't diddle any children." Another shot. Another ball. "Or that I didn't feed her drugs. Or tell my brother to ruin her life and raze an American boarding school."

"Or almost have me killed," I said. "You didn't tell him to do that either. Is there some reason you're suddenly so mad at me?"

"I'm not."

"You are."

August's cue stilled in his hands. "I faked my death to escape my family. Jail time, too, but mostly them. My parents agreed to let me go; my siblings think I'm dead. I'm not the enemy. I'm not the bad guy. I thought I'd made that clear." His face was mercilessly blank, like he'd wiped off all emotion with a cloth. But his words sounded genuine.

"I—well. 'Enemy' is kind of a strong word."

"Jamie."

"Just—take your shot."

He looked back down at the table and, very deliberately, scratched.

I picked the cue ball off the floor. "You didn't do anything to me, so you don't need to feel bad. I don't need a pity win."

"No," he said. "I think you need a chance to play."

"That sounded like you'd been rehearsing it for a while."

He scowled. "I'm trying to be nice to you."

"Stop trying. You're not nice. Or if you are, you're out of practice." I paused. "I'm not very nice either. God knows Holmes isn't."

That pried a smile from him, a real one, if sad. "I am nice, Jamie. I just . . . I haven't talked to anyone in a while."

We traded shots after that. August began playing with an ease that he hadn't before, pointing out angles, lining up a shot for me when I couldn't figure out how to get my blue two into the side pocket.

"Are you in love with her?" I asked him as he sank another ball.

His face went blank again. Was it his tell? Is this what he looked like when he was upset? "Are you?"

"It's complicated." I watched him, but his expression didn't change. "If you aren't, then why did you look at her the way

105

you did? When we first arrived?"

August sighed. "I've been in Berlin for a few years now. I do data entry. Milo gives me a pile of spreadsheets—numbers, usually, about which air base has x number of metal gaskets—and I put it into a computer. They came from a computer in the first place, so it's totally unnecessary. It's fake-work. Make-work. There are actual things I could be doing for Greystone, but—"

"But you're a Moriarty." The waitress came by with her tray. I took a glass and offered it to August.

With a half smile, he accepted it. "Because of who my brother is, and who my aunt and uncle are, and so on, and so forth, I can't be trusted with sensitive information. Or an interesting job, apparently."

"Milo hates you that much?"

"Milo is a spymaster. God knows how that one worked out, for someone so determined to not leave their building. He doesn't hate anyone. He doesn't *like* anyone either. But he does love his sister, and she wanted me to have a place to go, so he did her a favor. I'm dead. Nobody out there can know I'm *not* dead. Nobody out in the world can recognize me. I had limited options. So I took it." He downed his wine in a determined gulp. "Do you want to know why?"

"Yes," I said, because I'd been wondering why for weeks.

"I took that job because there's a ridiculous war on between my family and theirs, and I wanted to wave the white flag. If I made friends with Milo, if I convinced my parents to extend an olive branch, if I was able to smooth things over . . . but I was younger, then, and stupider. My parents won't even talk to me anymore."

I whistled. August made an ironic little bow. "You know what they say about good intentions," he said.

"No kidding."

"So here I am. No friends. No family that aren't criminals or would-be ones. Just me, and a mathematics dissertation I can't finish researching, because dead men don't do postdocs, and I work on fractals. In Antarctica. There are no dead man ships headed that way anytime soon. I live in a sad little room in Milo's sad little palace. I can't leave the building because . . ." He shook his head angrily. "Look, when Charlotte walked in, I was . . . I don't know. It was like my past hadn't been erased after all. The good and the bad, all of it—it was like it still existed somewhere out there. I still existed. I didn't realize how lonely I'd been until I saw her."

"And it's as simple as that."

"She's my friend. Maybe it's self-destructive for me to like her, but I do." He shrugged. "I try not to blame her for what happened. Her parents—well, never mind. You can't keep her in a box, Jamie, and you can't let her do that to you, either. She and I were quite close, if you can believe it, and when it didn't play out between us the way she needed it to, she threw a grenade at me and ran away."

"August—"

"We were trained in the same way. We think the same way. We have the same self-destructive solutions to problems we face. . . ."

"So you're casual bros now? I don't buy it. You want me to believe you can just *hang* with the girl who ruined your life." The words came out more caustic than I'd planned.

August blinked rapidly, almost as if he was fighting off tears, and there it was, the real emotion I'd been waiting to see—and it was brutal.

"It's not like I have anything better to do," he said finally. "Dead, remember?"

I eyed him. Despite the clothes and the polish and the heaps of self-pity, he was hard to dislike. Later I would wonder if it was because he reminded me of a version of Charlotte Holmes who'd been raised by the enemy.

"Do you ever get sick of playing the victim?" I asked him, because I was good at taking those kinds of openings.

"No," he said, "it's actually quite fun," and he sank his last few balls one right after the other.

"Asshole."

"For reference, that's the only sensible way to answer that kind of question."

"Rack the balls, dickweed," I said, and for that night, at least, we were friends.

TWO GAMES LATER, MARIE-HELENE DRIFTED OVER IN time to catch me in the middle of a yawn.

"Long night?" She did that pretty-girl thing where she casually slid under my arm.

"No," I told her as August took his fifth shot in a row. "I'll win in the end."

I wasn't sure if I believed that. But Simon did. Simon liked how soft she was, too, and after a moment, I caught myself playing with the ends of her hair.

Honestly, it felt nice. Simple. When did I start thinking a good relationship had to be complicated?

Friendship I understood. There had to be an arc there, some kind of story that the two of you were telling just by being together. Something made up from what you wanted from the world and what you got instead. A story you reminded each other of when you needed to feel understood. *I saw you in the quad that day,* mine would go. *I'd always thought you would be blond. I always thought you'd be my twin sister. My other half. And then I met you, and someone killed the meathead down the hall, and you became something else to me.* Because other than our friendship, I felt like I had nothing to show for this year. Like I was a circuit board where all of the tangled cords ran straight to Charlotte Holmes.

And still it wasn't just a friendship. When I'd met her, I'd stopped looking at girls in the way I used to, and I used to look at girls all the time. More than look—I made out with them in my room to Radiohead turned all the way up. I texted them to say goodnight. I was a good boyfriend, while the relationship lasted—though it never lasted long. Still, they were never my friends, not the way that Holmes was, and I didn't know if what I was feeling was a kind of reversion to my former self. Was I re-becoming fifteen-year-old James Watson Jr., a pair of tickets to the Highcome School Spring Fling in my pocket? I was so much more now. I was past all the hopeless crushes, my inability to separate friendship and love.

Wasn't I?

I'd been thinking for so long that what I wanted from Holmes was—everything. Like this thing between us was a Wonderland rabbit hole, that we could fall endlessly and never hit the bottom. I wanted us to belong to each other, completely, in a way where no one else could come close. Maybe I felt this way because she was so strange and private and still, somehow, had invited me in. Me, out of everyone in the world. Maybe it came from how we met, the two of us together in a foxhole. Maybe I wanted her to be my girlfriend because I didn't see what could happen if I found myself wanting someone else. I wanted a stamp to put on our file: *All boxes checked. No one else needed.* She didn't want me to touch her, but she wanted to be near me all the time. *Closed circuit. Keep out.*

Son of a bitch, I thought, and it wasn't just because August had won this round, too.

"Too bad." Marie-Helene leaned against my chest. "If you're ready to give up, I can introduce you to someone. My drawing professor's here. He doesn't do video installation the way you do"—*Thank God,* I thought, *I couldn't BS a professor*—"but maybe he could talk to you about Sieben admissions for next year?"

August was silently racking the balls for another game.

"I'll be right back," I told him, because the person Marie-Helene was waving at was the man I'd deduced to be Nathaniel.

"Okay, Simon," August said, and I remembered how not-simple any of this was.

THAT WAS HOW I FOUND MYSELF STARING AT A SET OF charcoals in an industrial loft five blocks away.

"Think about *form*," Nathaniel was yelling. "Think about *style*."

"I'm thinking about killing him," I told Marie-Helene, who looked horrified. Holmes would have snickered, but Holmes wasn't there.

After an interminable hour listening to him gas on about *creating* from your *gut*, really *feeling* the *rawness* of the *world* in your *work*, I sympathized a bit more with Holmes and her aversion to expressed emotion. Talking about your feelings was a lot different from talking about "feeling" in the abstract. If this is what being an artist or a writer was like, maybe I wasn't one after all. Especially if it involved growing some neck-beard. Nathaniel's was as lush and overgrown as moss.

I decided that if this was the guy that Leander had been kissing, he was doing some serious slumming.

But Marie-Helene and the rest of his coterie hung on his every word. I understood why—he listened to his students' opinions, knew things about their lives. He teased Marie-Helene about her "new crush" within minutes of meeting me. I thought about Mr. Wheatley, my old creative writing teacher, and how good it felt when he'd taken an interest in my work last fall. (Even if he'd feigned that interest for his own messed-up, villainous reasons.)

So maybe Nathaniel was a blowhard. He seemed like a nice guy, underneath it, and I sort of felt bad knowing that I was the villain in this situation.

Unless he was a villain, too.

"You should come to Sieben next year," Nathaniel had said to me back at the party. "You're a nice kid. Smart. I can tell that you're smart. As usual, these miscreants are having a late night Draw 'n' Drink tonight and they've talked me into coming along. Why don't you show me what you've got? I can put in a good word for you with the admissions committee."

Hence, we'd gone a few blocks over to this industrial loft, which maybe belonged to Nathaniel—God only knew—and now I was holding a piece of charcoal the way I held a cigarette the one and only time I tried to smoke one. Which, for the record, isn't how you hold a cigarette *or* a charcoal.

"Is that what you call it? A charcoal?" I asked Marie-Helene, as the students around us shuffled around to look at each other's progress, beers in hand. Nathaniel was deeply engrossed in a girl's work on the far side of the room. I had no idea how to approach him again, and people were beginning to put on their coats. The night was almost over.

"No." Marie-Helene frowned at my sketchbook. "Simon, it's been an hour. Everyone else has drawn the still life. . . ." She didn't need to finish the thought. My page looked like it had developed chicken pox.

"It's experimental," I said, lifting my chin. "Very . . . Picasso-ian. My tutor always said my work was reminiscent of his Blue Period."

Marie-Helene made a face. I couldn't blame her, really. Simon was a pretty awful person.

SOS can you draw, I texted Holmes under the table. *I'm about to be exposed as a fraud. Are you busy? Can you come?*

The response was instantaneous. *Not busy,* she said. *Have experienced abject failure. Auctioneer steadfastly denies any idea of stolen work bought/sold, even when persuaded to speak.* (I didn't want to know what sort of persuasion she meant.) *Cannot draw but can fake it better than you. Address please.*

She was there ten minutes later, leaning over my shoulder. "Simon," she said, loud enough for everyone to hear, "are you still shy about drawing in front of people? He can be *so* self-conscious. Don't tell me he fed you some line about making 'experimental' art." With exaggerated slowness, Holmes shook her head at Marie-Helene. "Men. They're such self-saboteurs. Can you show me where the wine is? I just had the *worst* night...."

Nathaniel had been listening, because as Holmes led Marie-Helene away, he came over to me with a concerned expression. "Is that true, Simon? It's okay—I know it's a lot of pressure to work in front of more experienced artists. Do you want to talk about it?"

"Yes," I said, "very much," hating Holmes for fixing my whole FUBAR undercover op in about thirty seconds.

Nathaniel led me over to the corner kitchen. The loft was a giant, echoing space, brick walls and a concrete floor, but the kitchen only held a sink and a microwave. "Tea? I noticed you weren't drinking."

"I'm not much for it," I said, as Simon. "I'm already a bit nervous. A pint never does much to help that, for me."

113

"Odd. It's usually the opposite." He pulled a mug from an otherwise empty cabinet, filling it with water. "You're a nice kid."

"Am I?" I laughed. I sounded a bit insane.

"No, you are. But you seem a little sad. Is anything wrong?"

I shrugged. "Just feeling a little out of my element."

"I'm happy to introduce you around."

"Thanks," I said, hating that I wanted to say yes. "I think I need to take my time with that."

"Bad night, huh. Okay, I'll take the hint," he said. "So how'd you find out about the school here? We're not very well known outside of the city."

I decided to try for a direct approach. "My uncle lives here. I'm staying with him nearby. He couldn't come out tonight, but the Old Met is his Saturday night place, and he told me to check it out. Maybe you know him? Tall? Dark hair? He wears it slicked back—"

With a sharp crash, Nathaniel dropped the mug. "Oh— oh, God, I'm sorry, shaky hands, long night. You know. I can't believe—you're David's nephew? He never talked about his family."

Hook, line, sinker. So much for FUBAR. As long as David was, in fact, Leander's alias. "You know him?" I asked, as Nathaniel kicked the ceramic pieces into a pile.

"You could say that." He was avoiding my eyes. "And he's at home tonight? I didn't think—well."

"He is," I said blithely. "You know him. Cooking up a storm. Arguing with the crossword puzzle answers."

"That sounds like him," he said, which was good, as I had no idea what "David" would do on a Saturday night in. Or who exactly Nathaniel was to him. All I'd had was his name, that he was one of Leander's contacts. Maybe. Did that mean that he was under suspicion? Had he stolen paintings? Organized a forgery ring? Was he part of a drug cartel? Was he helping Leander out? Was he so surprised to hear about "David" because he knew he was being held somewhere or—awful thought—dead?

What the hell was I doing, and where was Holmes?

"I should get home, actually," I said, forcing a yawn. I needed to talk to my father. I needed to get him to give me the details. "He worries if I'm out too late. I'm sure he'll be glad to hear that I met you."

"Yes. Yes of course." Nathaniel squinted at me. I felt, suddenly, like an insect on a slide. "Tell him to meet me tomorrow night at East Side Gallery. Our usual corner, at the usual time."

That didn't sound sketchy or anything. "Yeah, okay."

"It's Simon, right?" His stare grew thornier.

"Right. See you!" Before he could ask for Simon's last name, I was out the door.

Holmes met me outside. Her arms were covered in goose bumps, and I gave her my jacket. She took it with a show of reluctance. "Is this our new status quo? You leave me to babysit your girlfriend while you muck up my investigation?"

"*Our* investigation. Hey, maybe I do. How come I ended up playing pool with your boyfriend while you threw yourself at some auctioneer?"

"Honestly, will you quit imagining that I'm some tarted-up Mata Hari? My espionage work is far more subtle than that."

"Really?"

"Really."

"Then how did you approach him?"

"I appealed to his sympathies."

"Holmes."

She paused. "I might have threatened to kill his shih tzu—"

"No. Never mind. Stop."

We looked at each other. After a second, she started to laugh. "Watson, do you even know exactly what Leander is doing here in Berlin?"

"No," I admitted. "Not exactly."

"I don't either," she said. "Shouldn't we get back to Greystone, then, and find out?"

SIX

Have you found him yet?

My father's text woke me at five the next morning. *Call me when you wake up. I need to know,* my screen read. I turned it around in an attempt to assuage my guilt.

We'd spent this past fall fending for ourselves because Holmes had been too proud to ask her family for help. *No more,* I told myself, and clambered down from her lofted bed. When we'd gotten in last night, she'd flopped facedown on the cot and gone instantly to sleep, as though her body recognized the rare opportunity to recharge.

I slept fitfully, and now that I was awake, I was anxious to get going. Ten more minutes, and I'd go wake up Milo. I'd get him to throw some real resources at the Leander situation.

Surely, with his help, we'd find Holmes's uncle within the day, and then we could get down to normal things. Museums. Curry shops. Christmas shopping, maybe, and for a moment, I wondered what I should get Holmes. Pipettes? A book on something bizarre, like anglerfish? August would get her something better than that. Something more inventive.

No, it was definitely better to focus on the task at hand.

Milo was waiting for me in the hall, as though he were a robot that had been left to recharge there all night. "Watson," he said impatiently. "Come along. Breakfast is in my kitchen."

As I trailed after him, I realized that his actual living quarters were on the other side of the floor. Holmes and I, it seemed, had been housed in the hallway just outside the rooms that held Milo's personal security team. He never said it out loud, but I got the sense that his sister was housed outside his penthouse for her protection and not because he thought she'd muck up his nice vintage carpet.

She was the first person I saw when we entered his rooms. She was framed by the floor-to-ceiling window, playing a song on her violin. I stopped in the doorway to listen. The sound was spectral, almost galactic in its runs and rivulets—it had an aching descant. A song for worrying. Except for her, the rooms were quiet. Milo had bustled back to the kitchen, busying himself with a coffee grinder. This morning he probably razed a small city. Now he was readying a French press.

His place had a musty sort of lived-in feel, all midcentury like the lobby but shabbier. On the plaid sofa, August sat with a mug between his hands, listening to Holmes's violin with closed eyes. I was surprised to see more feeling on his face now than I'd seen at all the night before.

"Jamie," August said as I dropped down beside him. "You've met Peterson, right? He's arranging a briefing for us on Leander. Holmes is waiting for coffee, but there's tea."

"Thanks."

He settled back into the cushions. "I love this one."

She'd changed styles. Now she was playing something straightforward and mathematical, which meant it was probably Bach. She was wearing a pair of my socks and her CHEMISTRY IS FOR LOVERS shirt and she was playing her ex-tutor's favorite song, and I wondered if this was as close as she came to feeling sentimental.

She paused, a note still fluttering in the air. "Peterson," she said to the doorway, her voice still thick with sleep. "So good to see you."

"Ma'am." He was wheeling in a kind of AV cart, but this one had twelve screens branching out from some kind of glowing processor.

Milo came in with a tray. He poured out the coffee carefully, in a way that suggested long practice.

"I would've thought you'd have someone to do this for you," I told him.

"I think you discount the importance of routine," he said. "My father always spoke about the importance of doing things for oneself, the same way every day. Frees the mind to focus on more important pursuits."

Jesus, I thought, imagining him going through this whole

ceramic-tray coffee ceremony alone, on this couch, as Peterson prepared his morning briefing. I'd surrounded myself with geniuses—the most miserably lonely geniuses I could find.

"Jamie." Peterson powered up the monitors. "Feeling better?"

"I am, thank you."

"We'll be speaking more generally than we normally do," he said in his affable way. "Mr. Holmes has requested that I bring you up to speed on the basics of art theft and law enforcement."

"Wouldn't the most expedient solution be to call the German government and ask them to tell you what Leander was up to?" Holmes asked, flopping down on the carpet.

"Mr. Holmes has in fact gathered that intel," Peterson said blandly. "But he believes you are all in need of an education on the subject."

With the air of long practice, Holmes waited until Milo raised his mug to his lips, and then reached up to whack his elbow. Coffee splattered down his front. She smiled her black-cat smile.

"When we're finished here, I'll fetch you a bleach pen and a new shirt," Peterson said to a sputtering Milo. "Now, as for your basic education on modern investigation into art crime . . ."

We learned that the art world is largely unregulated. There is no worldwide database that tracks the buying and selling of works of art, so it's incredibly easy for unethical dealers to sell stolen or forged pieces. Since most large governments only employ two to three full-time art theft investigators, those dealers can operate without any real fear of getting caught.

All of this is complicated, Peterson told us, by the staggering amount of art that the Nazis stole from artists and collectors—mostly Jews—as they fled Germany during World War II. Of course, not all escaped. When German Jews were put into concentration camps, their homes, too, were looted. Though the German government has made attempts to track down these pieces and return them to the families of their owners, many works of art have vanished altogether. In a field like this, it's easy for those pieces to reappear, magically—and for no one to ever realize that they're actually forgeries, despite the best efforts of authenticators.

"Essentially, it's lawless," Peterson told us, "and most law agencies have more pressing matters on their hands. Private investigators like Leander Holmes are often the last hope for those looking to track down forgers and forgery rings, networks of dealers selling art looted from Jewish refugees, or your token drug cartel using paintings as collateral. Since these are very small, exclusive circles, in order to investigate, he'd have to spend months establishing his cover before he could ever hope to gain access to any real information."

While he talked, the monitors behind him played an aquarium screensaver. I took notes on a pad that Milo lent me.

August raised his hand, like we were all in class. "How do my brothers fit into this? Lucien? Hadrian?"

Peterson hesitated. "Hadrian Moriarty is best known for paying off the leaders of corrupt countries to look the other way while he and his sister make off with their national treasures."

"Yes, of course," he said, turning to Milo, "but how do they fit into this particular situation?"

Milo made a hand motion, and the twelve screens switched over to a security feed. A number of different security feeds, and none of them black-and-white, as they were in the movies, but full, deep color. A beachfront cabana, complete with billowing curtains that framed a view of the ocean. A bedroom with a four-poster bed. Other scenes, other rooms—and the four monitors on the bottom, which all showed a different approach to the Holmeses' Sussex house. With a start, I recognized the woodpile where I'd last seen Leander.

Milo ticked them off on his fingers. "Your brother Lucien's latest hideout over here. And here, your brother Hadrian's pied-à-terre in Kreuzberg—really, August, do get yourself born into a better family next time—and his front entryway, and the view of his back windows, and one of his toilet, though for propriety's sake I've chosen not to show you that one. There's a rather large window in there, though, so I deemed it necessary." He flicked his wrist again, and the screens changed. "I have every angle of every room in our family home, including a camera on the septic tank, and two specialists who do nothing but watch these screens and synthesize their deductions."

"That doesn't answer my question," August said. Beside him, Holmes leaned forward to see the screens better, drumming her hands against her knees.

"If Lucien sneezes, I know about it. If he orders a different cocktail than what he usually has delivered to his sad little beachfront hideaway, it'll be one of my men bringing it to him. If he even *thinks* about getting into a car, it'll be missing three gaskets and the back right tire, and if anyone remotely connected with him takes a flight to Britain, it makes an emergency stop in Berlin, during which they are forcibly removed from the plane." Milo's voice was electric with hate. I shrank a little as he spoke. "I've stripped him of his resources and his connections. The last phone call he made was three weeks ago, to his sister Phillipa, and I had it terminated after one point three seconds.

"So to answer your question, if Lucien has something to do with Leander's disappearance, he is better than me at my own game, and I am the best. I told my sister she shouldn't worry, and so she won't. We'll sort this through."

Holmes looked up at her brother questioningly. He stared back down at her, his face still tight with anger, until she lifted the enameled coffee pot to refill his mug. Marginally, he relaxed.

She turned to look back at the screens. When Milo spoke, he was his usual dour self again. "As for Hadrian Moriarty, he's employing me."

I coughed. August lowered his face into his hands.

"Explain," Holmes said. She didn't sound surprised.

"Why, Lottie. I thought you'd be able to figure it out."

She took a breath. Thought about it. Then began ticking it off on her fingers. "The sort of services you'd provide to a man like that would be in the personal protection business. I can't imagine that he'd employ your mercenaries for anything else, unless it was the transportation of legally dubious artwork from one country to another, and as most self-respecting governments loathe you and your 'independent contractors' as it is, I doubt you'd get your hands that dirty for the sake of a Moriarty. Sorry, August."

From behind his hands, he groaned.

"So you're providing agents to serve as his . . . bodyguards. It would have to be bodyguards. But how did it come to pass? Hadrian would never approach you, not unless he'd gleaned that August was working for Greystone, and I imagine that if that were the case, we'd have seen some fallout already. Unless Leander's disappearance is the fallout—but no, he'd have gone for me directly. From what I've heard of Hadrian Moriarty and his six-thousand-dollar watch, he's not particularly subtle. No. You approached him."

Milo sipped his coffee.

"But why on earth would he agree? Even if he doesn't personally want me flayed and hanging on his wall, his older brother does, and I can't imagine Hadrian wanting to rock the boat without a good reason. What could you have offered him? You don't appeal to a Moriarty's better angels. Sorry, August"—August groaned again—"but you don't get traction that way, not really, and so you had to make him afraid." She read some invisible cue in her brother's face. "No. You didn't. You appealed to something he was already afraid of."

"Leander," I said, putting the pieces together. "He's afraid that Leander will expose his forgery ring."

"But he wasn't investigating Hadrian directly—*oh*. Leander was deep undercover. He might have kicked up some stray information that led back to Hadrian. And if no one in the government is paying any attention to art swindlers—"

"And then a Holmes comes along with a boatload of information, and takes it to the press—"

"—even if the government never goes after him, his international reputation is ruined," Holmes finished neatly. "No more lining his piggy bank with cash from plundered treasure."

August looked up. His eyes were miserable. "So you're feeding my brother information about Leander's investigation, you do his private security. And your men report back to you about what Hadrian is doing."

"Peterson," Milo called. "Please get these three some gold stars."

Maybe I was getting better at this. Maybe I was just the only one who was properly afraid. "Are you so morally bankrupt that you're willing to gamble with your uncle's life?" I demanded.

"The information runs both ways," Milo said. "I told Leander how to keep safely out of Hadrian's way. I told Leander how to avoid Hadrian. It was the only way to keep abreast of the situation. It's a lesson of my father's—it's always worth sacrificing safety for omnipotence."

"It isn't your safety you were sacrificing," I told him, and he set his jaw.

"So it can't be Hadrian who has Leander," August was saying, with palpable relief. "Or Phillipa, the two of them are inseparable. You're saying they're not involved?"

"Insofar as I can tell," Milo said, "no."

Holmes looked down at her hands. She wasn't angry. She wasn't upset. For a brief moment, she looked . . . crestfallen. As though she'd known, absolutely *known* the solution to Leander's disappearance, and had that surety taken away. I'd wondered why she hadn't been more outwardly worried about her uncle. Here was my answer. She thought that finding him would be as easy as tracking down August's brother.

She wasn't used to being wrong.

Scowling, she leaned forward to study Milo's security feeds again, as if the answer were there. Maybe it was.

I turned back to Milo. "Hadrian knows the details of Leander's investigation. And you don't think he's responsible for his disappearance."

Milo sniffed. "Leander wasn't anywhere near Hadrian's operation, not until very recently, when he ended up working a source—a dealer who also represented Moriarty interests. Hadrian heard about it, so I heard about it. And as soon as I did, I phoned my uncle up and told him to leave the country. To go stay with my father, who had connections that could shed new light on the investigation from a distance. It was enough time for the dealer to go to ground before Leander returned. Everyone happy. Everyone unharmed."

"Hadrian could have had agents in England," I said.

"He wouldn't dare. I have every inch of our house surveilled."

"And Phillipa—"

"Lottie has her own plans there. I imagine." He frowned.

"Either way, it's not as though you're in any danger. I'll send along a sniper or two."

"A sniper or two," August muttered. "You're all the same."

Beside him, Holmes moved her hands up and down in front of the screen. Nothing happened.

"Excuse me?" Milo said. "I'm juggling a number of flaming clubs here, one of which is *you*. I'm more than happy to find you a position in Siberia, August."

"Thank you. Really. I'm sure Leander appreciated this kind of meddling, too."

"Oh, yes," Milo said blandly. "He was thrilled."

"Hold on," I said. "If he wasn't hunting down Hadrian and Phillipa, what exactly was Leander investigating in the first place?"

With a small sound of triumph, Holmes jerked her wrist to the right. All twelve surveillance screens changed: a series of views of the Sussex home's front door. Her left hand made a sharp diagonal, and they all began to rapidly rewind.

Milo pursed his lips. "You're going too fast."

"I'm not," she said, and flipped both her hands upside down. The screens obediently stopped. "Those sensors are a ludicrous waste of resources, by the way. Whatever happened to a remote control?"

August coughed. "I designed the math for the sensors. It's based on a differential of—"

"Yes, yes, I know," she snapped. With an imperceptible motion, she set the screens going again. "Look here. The night

Leander disappeared. We have him and Jamie having what I'm sure was a very touching moment by the woodpile; here they go, one, two, back to the house. Through the window, we see the family assembled at dinner. Leander in his room." A flick, and the screen changed. "We're on a time lapse, inside. Milo only had still cameras within the guest rooms. They photograph every ten minutes."

"An oversight," he said, "that I've now rectified."

"Obviously. Here: Leander on his phone. Pacing, or at the very least moving about. Now Leander packing his bags. And here, in the front hall. He heads quickly down the stairs, holding his suitcases, and"—she flipped to the camera of the outside of the house, where a man in a black cap took off down the drive—"there he goes. Off screen, to a waiting car." She leveled a look at her brother. "Where did he go after that?"

With a sigh, Milo snapped his fingers. The screens went black. "We don't know where he is now. But we know where he was and what he was doing before. According to my contacts, the German government has hired him to infiltrate a forgery ring and compile enough evidence to prove their work as fake. These forgers have been knocking off the work of an artist from the 1930s, Hans Langenberg. The sheer number of paintings that have been 'recovered' has raised some alarm bells, so they're making this a special case."

A painting appeared on the screen. I blinked. It had that atmospheric quality I loved, all cobalts and grays with flashes of eggshell white. In the painting, a girl sat reading in the corner, bored in a red cotton dress. The man next to her turned a letter opener in his hands. Another looked out a darkened window. They were all clustered together in the painting's lone splash of light; the rest of the room was muted, unexplored.

"This is his most famous painting—*The Last of August*, it's called. He was German, from Munich. Unmarried, no family. Intensely secretive, and thought to be very prolific, though he only ever gave his agent three of his paintings to sell. In the last year, an actual trove of 'newly discovered work' popped up on the auction circuit." The screens were crowded, suddenly, with similar paintings, ones set in attic rooms and garrets, a back garden at night. Always a group of figures somewhere in the background, holding bright objects in their hands, both looking and not looking at each other. "They've stumped authenticators. It's impossible to tell whether these were Langenberg's work. And if this is revealed to the public, it could look like opportunistic forgers are benefitting off of genocide. Already there are murmurs that the money is lining neo-Nazi pockets. The German government wants this stopped as soon as possible."

The paintings were all appealing, forged or not, and I was disappointed when the screens shut off again.

August must've seen my face. "They're lovely," he said in that voice I hated, the one where he was pretending to be himself.

"Yes," Holmes said, to my surprise. "*The Last of August*. Funny, it's beautiful. They all are. And Leander was attempting to track down the supposed forger, examine their studio, find evidence that Langenberg's renaissance is a fake one?"

"That was his specific operation, yes." Milo nodded to Peterson, who began packing up the cart. "For his safety, I wasn't told more than that. But Lottie, this ring runs the length and breadth of Europe. Berlin is a fair place to start, of course, but I know for a fact that he was exploring connections in other cities. Budapest. Vienna. Prague. Krakow. This is a massive undertaking, and he could quite literally be anywhere. Yes, he stopped sending emails to Jamie's father, but he could be in deep enough that he doesn't want to risk exposure. Sending lengthy daily reports to your best friend, last name Watson, isn't exactly the height of subtlety."

"He called me Lottie," she said to him, a plea in her voice. "In his message. He never calls me Lottie. He didn't leave me a present when he left."

"Darling, everyone calls you Lottie." He stood. "Don't be a child. Leander could very well be in over his head. He could, in fact, be in danger. But he has been before, and he will be again. It's his job. I won't make it my business. Especially not when I'm in such a precarious position with Hadrian already. Do you think it was easy explaining to him that Leander had just suddenly decided on a sojourn outside the country of his own volition, and not because he was two seconds from stumbling on information that would uncover Hadrian Moriarty's dirty dealings? No. I have a line to walk here."

"This isn't that missing giraffe fiasco in Dallas, or that piracy case in Wales. This—it feels different. He disappeared from *our house*."

"And Father says he's fine," Milo said, as though that

was an irrefutable argument. "I know you're concerned, but I need to focus my extraprofessional efforts in a single direction. Honestly, Lucien is much more of a concern right now. If there's any chance he was involved in Mother's poisoning . . . and who knows? That threat could involve Leander as well. You can't argue that it would hurt for me to double down on Lucien Moriarty and on our family's security. Our mother is in danger, and while I know that she isn't Lottie's favorite person"—Holmes flinched—"I also know she doesn't want her dead. My men on the ground are examining the security breach. I'm getting weekly reports. I'm nearly done weeding through our staff. *My* concern is that Lucien is in Thailand, getting through to his men somehow, and I need to find out how."

"Which means?" August asked.

"Which means I'm headed to Thailand. Tonight. I need my own eyes on the situation." He smiled thinly. "I'll be back soon. I do have a war to run, you know."

I remembered Alistair saying that. *I was the architect of several wars.* Clearly the impulse to take on the world ran through the Holmes family. But his sister didn't have his same scope of his ambitions. Hers had a laser focus.

Milo was giving his sister a rundown of what agents she could turn to if she needed help, though I wasn't sure if she was listening. For his part, August was preoccupied, his eyes fixed on the cart as Peterson rolled it out the door.

"We have that lunch with Phillipa, which I'm sure will be totally fine and not at all awful and insane. And then Holmes and I are going to the East Side Gallery tonight," I told August, though she and I hadn't discussed it. "That professor, Nathaniel, had a standing appointment with Leander. It'll be interesting to see what happens when he doesn't show up. Especially because—is he that dealer that Leander approached? Before he left?"

But August was hardly listening. "He trusts me," he said. "He just . . . laid all of that information out, about my family, like it was nothing. He trusts me not to tell them what he knows or what he's doing."

I looked at him sharply. "Will you?"

"No," he said, barking a laugh. "I never would. I told you I came here to make peace, and I meant it. He's just never confided in me like that before. I don't know what changed."

Holmes was touching Milo's shoulder, leaning forward to say something in his ear. He shook his head, and kissed her briefly on the cheek. "I'll see you soon," he said, and with a nod to us, he left.

"Congratulations, August. You've been given codeword clearance to the file on your own family." She tugged at her CHEMISTRY IS FOR LOVERS shirt. "Can we please get on with our day? It's already seven a.m., and I want to have this wrapped up by midnight."

HOLMES ASKED AUGUST AND ME BACK TO THE ROOM TO "strategize" before our lunch with Phillipa, but August begged off, saying he needed to work.

"On what? You don't exactly do anything." Holmes raised

her eyebrow at the look I shot her. "What? He talks constantly about how he does nothing. I don't see how it's impolite for me to acknowledge that fact."

He put his hands firmly on her shoulders, like he was her tutor again. "Charlotte. I don't have any work to do. I'm—very politely—trying to ditch you so I can get an hour to myself. Unlike the two of you, I start to feel ragged after too much of all this togetherness."

"You could have just said so."

With a shake of his head and a smile, August took off toward the elevator.

I wondered where he was going.

"Don't tell me you're unfamiliar with the concept of the polite no," I said to Holmes as she opened the door to our room.

"I'm not. I simply expect more from my friends. Honesty is far more efficient than lying."

"Milo is just telling him that information to see what he's going to do with it."

"Of course. But I trust him. He chose to erase himself rather than turn me in. I doubt he's gone and changed his mind now." She thought about it for a moment. "And anyway, even if he is off trying to tell on us, he's overdue for a little selfishness."

"You're feeling that cavalier about it?"

Her smile was all teeth. "I said he could try. I'm fairly sure Milo still has a target on August's back. Hadrian can try getting information from a smoking pile of ash, but I don't think he'll succeed."

It was such an awful image that I had to laugh. "You're chipper this morning."

"I am," she said. "Gird your loins. I need to run through our strategy for our lunch with Phillipa."

"THE RAW BAR IS EXCELLENT," PHILLIPA WAS SAYING. SHE lifted a subtle finger, and like a bit of magic, a white-clad waiter appeared at her elbow. "Could I please have a split of champagne. Whatever your house champagne is, nothing fancy."

"Isn't champagne by definition fancy?" I asked.

"It's barely midday," Holmes said without looking up from her menu.

"Children." Phillipa smiled thinly. "Don't tell me you've never rinsed your oyster shell with champagne. What are they teaching you at that wretched school?"

I lifted an eyebrow. "How to frame children like us for murder."

This whole business was absurd. Phillipa had insisted on choosing the restaurant; Milo had been sent an address ten minutes before we left. He'd raised an eyebrow when he saw. "That restaurant opened in 1853," he'd said, loading us into a car, "and since 1853, it's been overpriced. Enjoy the Italian marble. I'll send some discreet security to sit nearby."

But we walked in to find that Phillipa Moriarty had booked the entire restaurant. She waited at a table in the back, under a glittering mosaic of a dragon. "Hello, all," she'd said pleasantly. "I hope this suits you?"

"Absolutely not. Unacceptable," Holmes said. "I want my

brother's men to see us through the windows. Up. Let's go."
And she led us to a table by the window, like we were children
she was taking to the principal's office.

That set the tone for the next wretched hour.

"Do you prefer New England oysters?" Phillipa was saying,
toying with her tiny fork. "I do, but it's so hard to ship them
across the ocean, and what's the point, really, when we have
such lovely Italian shellfish close at hand?"

"Where is Leander?" I asked, in the tone someone takes
with a small child. "I know you know."

"Fine," Phillipa said, ignoring her, "I'll choose them myself,"
and raised her finger again. She rattled off an order that might
as well have been in Italian, for all I understood it.

"Where," I said, "is Leander."

Grimacing, Phillipa adjusted her scarf. "They really could
turn up the heat in this place, couldn't they? Brrr."

"Where is. Leander."

This had been our plan, insomuch as we had one: I would
hammer away at Phillipa with the question she wouldn't
answer until she laid out her reasons for meeting us. *If she's
going through the trouble of arranging a lunch,* Holmes said,
*she'll want to pretend at civility. That gives us time to maneuver.
Hammer away at her. It'll give me time to learn her tells.*

"Where is Leander," I said. Then I ordered a soda from the
waiter. Holmes was still pretending to study her menu, but I was
sure she'd found a way to study Phillipa's face. The older woman
wouldn't stop fidgeting. It was subtle—she'd smooth a piece of
hair, or tug at a sleeve—but her hands were in constant motion.

135

Five minutes passed. Ten. Phillipa seemed to be waiting for something. I would've worried that our meeting was a diversion, but for what? It wasn't like Greystone HQ would be made vulnerable by our absence.

The oysters arrived on a shallow platter, on a bed of ice. Holmes's eyes narrowed, for a moment, in pleasure. She'd had them for the first time at my father's house in Connecticut when Abbie, my stepmom, had brought home a sack from the fish market, and Holmes had eaten nearly a whole tray. I knew her well enough to know she liked the ritual of it, the strange, beautiful meat, the tiny tools used to prize it out.

Almost reverently, Holmes lifted an oyster and studied it. "How are your orchids?" she asked Phillipa in a polite voice.

And just like that, Phillipa's mask slid off her like oil.

"I'll give you one chance to bargain with us," Phillipa said, placing her hands on the table. "It's more than you deserve, and you know it. Tell me where August is, and I'll negotiate on your behalf with Lucien. Hadrian isn't interested in treating with you, but I am. Surely that's why you called me here to this farce of a lunch."

"It's too bad that your gardener quit, and so suddenly," Holmes said, lifting the shell to her nose to study it. "That was just this morning, wasn't it? Milo did need someone to tend to his . . . carnations."

"There are other orchid gardeners," Phillipa said. "Here are my terms. I'll ask Lucien to give you two years. Two years' amnesty from the death sentence he's put on you—long enough for you to grow up, come of age, finish school. And then you'll disappear. Choose a new identity. A new name."

"Milo chose that gardener on my recommendation," Holmes said, turning the shell in her hands. "Oh, these just smell like the ocean, don't they? Makes me wish I was at home. In Sussex."

Phillipa paused. "In Sussex."

"Yes. With my very sick mother. And my missing uncle. Tell me," Holmes said, and reached across the table to pluck the tiny oyster fork from Phillipa's plate, "have you seen Leander Holmes recently? The last I saw him he was concerned about my . . . very sick mother."

"The better question would be where you're keeping my baby brother," Phillipa snapped. "Don't toy with me."

"Your brother," Holmes said.

"My brother."

"Which one? The child-murderer hiding out on a beach in Thailand? Or the antiquities thief with the receding hairline?"

"Did *nobody* teach you any respect?" Phillipa exploded. "No one! Did nobody tell you that being clever isn't enough? You need to be willing to *work* with people. I'm attempting to offer you an out."

"I will never work with you."

"I'm willing to call in men, right now, to take you to Lucien," she continued. "He might be done taking it slow. I'm sure he'd be willing to speed things up. Break your hands. Kill you. Let's see if I can get you out of the country and to Thailand before your bear of a brother can stop them."

"The waiter is texting someone," I told Holmes, not bothering to whisper. "He pulled out his phone the second she started yelling."

Holmes leaned forward. "August might be alive. And my uncle might be just taking a short jaunt across the Swiss Alps and forgot to tell us. Listen—there's no time, you've made sure of that. These are *my* terms. You order your brother Lucien out of hiding. You and Hadrian go to England. You *apologize* to my parents. And you tell me where my uncle is. And then perhaps I dig August up and see if he still wants anything to do with you."

"*Apologize* to them? For what—having the misfortune of producing you?"

"For poisoning my mother," she said quietly. "For trying to kill me. For taking what was a mistake and blowing it up into a horrible international war."

I'd been half-turned, watching the front window, and there they were—cars pulling up against the curb, like dark beads on a white string. "We have to go," I said. "Now."

"Those terms are unacceptable." Phillipa sat back in her chair. "No, Charlotte. Remember that you fired the first shot. August will come to us in time."

"Holmes," I said, keeping my voice even, "they have guns."

With a fingernail, Holmes dug the meat out of her oyster and dropped it onto her plate. She poured a draft of champagne into the empty shell. Tossed it back.

"There'll be a time when you regret not taking my offer," Holmes told Phillipa, and then she and I ran like hell.

Through the maze of tables, through the strangely bustling kitchen, and then instead of out the back door—"There'll be men there, too," she hissed—she dodged a surprised line cook and yanked me into the walk-in freezer, slamming the heavy door shut behind her.

"Your brother better be two seconds away," I told her, coughing, "because that thing locks from the outside."

"By key code," she said, pulling out her phone. "Didn't you see? This is a very fancy seafood restaurant, can't be letting people see you freeze your Dover sole— Hello, Milo, could you please hack the walk-in freezer at Piquant? Watson's stubble is starting to freeze. Change the code and then send someone to fetch us."

She hung up. We looked at each other.

"Milo just told us this morning that there wasn't any way that Hadrian or Phillipa had your uncle captive," I told her. "So what was that all about?"

"Milo can be myopic. Thinking you know everything is dangerous," she said. "I know the Moriartys are involved. I'm sure of it." She said it so fiercely that I took a step back.

"Orchids?" I said, an attempt to defuse her. "That was your master plan? To poach away her orchid gardener?"

Her eyebrows were beginning to bead with snow. "She's won several international awards for her flowers," Holmes said. "I thought Milo could use some pointers. Grow a tree or two in his penthouse."

"You are *awful*."

"I know," she said, and grinned.

"So all that, back there. It was just a pissing contest."

"It was me giving her a final chance." She sighed. "Sometimes I'm far nicer than I should be."

"I'd hate to see you when you're mean," I said. "God, it's cold. I think I can feel all my teeth. How long until your brother's men get here?"

"I think they were on the roof. Just another minute or two. I don't hear gunfire, that's good." She stomped her feet a little against the cement floor. "Watson?"

"Holmes?"

For a long second, she studied the ground.

"I left my coat back at the table," she said, and when she looked up, I saw that her eyes had gone glassy and sad.

I took a step forward. "Hey," I said softly. "What's wrong?"

"Did you know that when my uncle goes away, he always leaves me a present? He didn't this time. He didn't . . . the last time he went, he left me a pair of gloves. They were black cashmere. Fingerless. Perfect for picking locks." She looked down again, shoving her hands in her pockets. "I wish I had them now."

Five minutes later, they opened the door. There was ice in my mouth and snow on my shoes, and Holmes had stopped crying. Though really, I guess she'd never started.

BACK AT GREYSTONE, WE BYPASSED THE SECURITY CHECKS by the simple expedient of telling them to fuck off, and rode the elevator back to our room. Holmes had that sort of deliberate silence around her that meant that she was brooding. Ten more minutes of this, and she'd start chain-smoking under an avalanche of blankets.

"I didn't get to eat any lunch." It was the sort of deliberately stupid comment I'd make to draw her out of herself. It also happened to be true. "I sort of wanted an oyster."

"We'll go," she promised. "You can always get a sandwich from Milo's penthouse. He keeps a spread in there, usually."

"No one will snipe me when I get in there?"

"No one will snipe you," she said. "Where's your phone?"

"I left it here. Why?"

"We went to meet a Moriarty and you left your phone at home? What if we were separated?"

"We weren't separated," I said irritably. I really was hungry. "I still don't have anything to tell my father, and he keeps texting me."

"Check it now," she said, sitting straight down onto the floor. After a quick once-over, she hauled a book out of one of the stacks beside her.

There it was, that familiar mix of dread and anticipation I always felt when she told me to do something like this. I climbed up to my loft and dug my phone out of the tangled sheets. I had a text from a number programmed in as FRENCH LOVE INTEREST. *Simon*, it read. *Do you still want to get coffee this afternoon? I'd love to talk more about my paintings.*

I swore. Down below me, Holmes smiled to herself, balancing her book on her knees. She must've dug my phone out in the night, but how, I couldn't imagine—when I'd left that morning, she was starfished out in the same position she'd been in when she fell asleep. Still, she'd managed to send Marie-Helene the world's most awful text:

Hi luv, hope u don't mind. Tabitha gave me ur number. Ace wingwoman she is. Fancy a cuppa tomorrow?

"Holmes. This is wretched. This is like British by numbers."

"Can't help it. It's what you sound like when you're playing posh." She bit her lip. "Isn't that right, *mate*."

Aren't you the sly one, Marie-Helene had written back. Jesus Christ. *Sending your cousin to do your dirty work! Yes, of course I'd love to see you.*

Luv to see ur paintings and talk more about them. Sorry was a bit shit last nite at ur teacher's. Got nervous.

"Simon wouldn't have used an apostrophe if he's too lazy to type out a full word."

She looked innocently up at me from the top of her book. "Bloody hell, I made a bleedin' mistake."

Why nervous? Marie-Helene had asked, and added a line of angel emojis.

Isn't it obvious? Ur beautiful. U kno it 2.

Blush emoji.

"No," I groaned. "No. Absolutely not. This is like a L.A.D. song. This is like my sister's L.A.D. fan fiction."

"I learned quite a bit from your sister," Holmes said with some satisfaction. "I learned that when you were a toddler, you once insisted on wearing your underwear *outside* your trousers for an entire week. I saw the photos."

"*No.*" I was going to murder Shelby, and creatively.

"I also learned every word to every song on L.A.D's debut

album." To my surprise, she started warbling, *"Girl / yeah girl you're beautiful / you know you're effin' beautiful—"*

I threw a pillow at her. She dodged it nimbly. "How can someone with a private music teacher have such bad pitch?"

"We all have our own personal skill set, Watson. Not all of us are professional heartbreakers."

"Is there a real reason why I'm meeting Marie-Helene for coffee this afternoon? Or are you just feeling punchy?"

She lofted the book up in the air. *Gifte*, the title read, on a marbled textbook cover.

"Are you asking what I want for Christmas?" I asked. "Or should I suddenly be able to speak German?"

"Poisons, Watson. The word means poison. There are some things you can't tell from surveillance footage and from frisking the housekeeping staff, as much as Milo would deny it. If I can't do anything about Leander . . . I'm going to run some things I know about my mother's medical history. Try to narrow down what she's been exposed to, and from there, determine how it's gotten into the house. Milo's gone, you know, and now I have access to his *labs*. To his techs! It's going to be an excellent afternoon."

"I thought we'd have this case solved by midnight," I said.

"We will."

"*This* case. Not the one with your parents."

"Obviously, they're connected. Occam's razor, Watson. How often are your family members kidnapped and poisoned inside the same week?" Her words were flip, but her voice wasn't. "The simplest explanation is the truest. Always. So I'm

143

boning up, as it were. While you're using this girl as an in. Pump her for information. Turn on that skeezy laddish charm."

"Any more gross puns?"

"I'm just not up for it—"

"Stop." What did it say about us, that the best we'd gotten along in days was when we were planning my date with another girl? "Fine, I'll get a look inside Marie-Helene's studio, ask her friends some leading questions, try to get a read on Nathaniel before we stake out East Side Gallery tonight. But I'm getting a sandwich first."

"Yes, good." Like she was donning a cape, Holmes threw her ratty robe over her clothes and tucked her book under her arm. "And Watson," she said, "wear your fedora," and she snickered to herself all the way down the hall.

MARIE-HELENE LIKED MY HAT. SHE LIKED MY BOOTS, TOO, and the band shirt I wore with my ripped jeans, which wasn't exactly a good thing, since I'd never listened to them.

"And anyway," she was saying, holding her latte in her gloved hands, "Faulkner's always been my favorite, but I like Murakami a lot, too. They're so different, it's hard to choose between them."

"Oh," I said. "Sure." We were standing outside the café where she'd wanted to meet, a half block from her studio. She'd pointed it out to me earlier—the steepled roof, the brick walls—and I was waiting for an excuse to ask to see it.

"And graphic novels. I think they're what got me drawing in the first place." She sipped at her drink. The fuzzy ball on the top of her hat bobbled back and forth. "Are you okay? You look distracted again."

I forced a smile. "Just a bit lost in my thoughts, love," I said, and I was. I wanted to move things along. I wanted to be back at Greystone with new evidence. I wanted to know when talking to a French girl about our favorite authors on a snowy street in Berlin stopped being my idea of a perfect Sunday. All I really wanted to do was get to her studio so I could rifle through her things while she was in the bathroom.

Sometimes I wondered if hanging out with Charlotte Holmes had made me into a monster. At times like this, I knew it for sure. "So how did you get into art?"

"Well, once I got lost in the Louvre—wait," she said, frowning. "I thought I told you that already, at the Old Met."

She had. I backtracked. "No, of course. Ha. But that was when you decided you *liked* art. I meant, like, when you wanted to, uh, *make* it."

Marie-Helene raised an eyebrow, but she gamely launched into a story about seashells, and her grandmother's spoon collection, and a pencil she stole from her postman. It was a well-told story, funny and smart. I stopped listening almost immediately. Instead, I took her hand in mine and set off toward her studio in a wandering sort of way.

"Do you have any of that old work up there?" I asked when we reached the door.

"I don't," she said. "Are you trying to get me alone, Simon Harrington?"

The last name Holmes had given me. "I might be."

I watched her think about it. The tip of her nose was pink in the cold, and she was wearing some bright lipstick that made her look like she'd wandered in out of a fairy tale. And I didn't want to kiss her. How did I not want to kiss her? I'd been completely ruined.

"Okay," she said shyly. "I'll show you my paintings."

"Is anyone else around?" I asked as she fiddled with the keys.

"It's only a few days till Christmas. I'm going home tomorrow, but I think that I might be the last one here."

"Good," I said, too eagerly. There'd be fewer witnesses, fewer occupied studios, and I wanted to dig around. If I could, I wanted to rule out Nathaniel's students as suspects. I liked Marie-Helene. In another life, I could've liked her a lot, and I wanted to stop wondering how I could use her as a tool in our case.

The studios were dark, except for the pale winter afternoon streaming in through the windows, and Marie-Helene didn't bother to flick on any lights as we went along. Not until we got to her space at the end of the row, and she hoisted herself up onto her worktable, kicking her legs.

"Hi," she said, biting her lip.

Crap, I thought. Because of course. Of course I'd be expected to make a move here. Touch her neck. Kiss her; hell, maybe sing her an L.A.D song—do something to live up to the ridiculous texts Holmes had been sending.

They *were* ridiculous texts, and in more ways than one. There had to have been a way to arrange this meeting without all that over-the-top flirting. If they'd gotten friendly last night, why hadn't Holmes gone and met Marie-Helene herself? She was the better detective. We both knew it.

Okay, I'd been kind of petty that night before, keeping my arm around Marie-Helene, bragging to Holmes that the French girl liked me, *Ha-ha, I don't care that August is hanging around, I have someone, too,* and yeah, it was kind of a dick move, but I thought she'd brushed it off, and *Oh my God,* I thought, *she's totally setting me up. Either she knows I'm going to totally cock this up, or—*

Or she knew I was going to cock this up, *and* she wanted me to go after Marie-Helene and leave her, Holmes, the hell alone. I could see it now, her laughing to August about it—*You know what Watson's like,* she'd say. *It's never been about me. He likes every pretty girl.*

Well, there's a pretty girl right now, I thought, *that wants me,* and I let Simon come crawling out of his cave. I slipped my arms around Marie-Helene's waist and kissed her like a man coming home from war.

Here was another point under the "monster" column: it was a good kiss. She leaned into me, she put her hands in my hair, she pulled me down into her like she wanted me, like I wasn't the terrible person Holmes thought I was, like I was somehow good enough for a girl like her.

Like Marie-Helene, I mean. Of course that was what I meant.

With a small noise, she drew me in closer, pulling out the tails of my shirt so she could touch my stomach. Her hands were warm, but they were still in her gloves. We realized it at the same time, and laughing, she pulled them off, one, two, with her teeth. Something pulled hard in my chest, something open and raw. I wanted to get my hands under her jacket. Unbutton her blouse.

A bigger part of me wanted to be back in Sciences 442, knee-to-knee with Charlotte Holmes, while she talked to me about her vulture skeletons.

"Hey," I said to Marie-Helene, out of breath, "hey, you're leaving tomorrow. Isn't this a little fast?"

"I don't think so." She traced a finger up my arm.

"I think—I think it is for me, actually."

With a show of surprise, she sat back. "Simon, you're a gentleman," she said, teasing, but I could tell that she was hurt underneath it.

"Not like that." I ran a hand through her hair. "I mean that I actually wanted to see your art." True, but not in the way it sounded. "And I want to see you, too, again, after Christmas." True, sort of. "When are you coming back?"

"This wasn't—" She sighed. "I broke up with my boyfriend last week. I don't want . . . I don't want to see you after Christmas, okay? I wanted to hook up with you because I thought you were leaving, and I . . . when I go back to Lyon, I'll probably see him. I didn't want him to be the last person I'd been with."

"Oh."

"Sorry. Too honest?"

It wasn't. Both of us were in too deep; it just wasn't with

each other. "I'm fine," I said, and it was completely true.

Marie-Helene smiled a bit sadly. "You're cute, you know. I just . . . my heart's somewhere else."

"That's fair." I offered her a hand, and she hopped down from her worktable. We looked at each other, and I laughed a little at it all. The cup of paintbrushes. The straightforward way she'd shot me—Simon—down. That I was in Germany at all, with a strange girl in her art studio, and that Charlotte Holmes had set it all up to see what I would do.

"While I'm up here," I said, "would you show me some of what you're working on, art-wise? Or is that a bit weird?"

She giggled. "A bit weird," she said, wandering over to a stack of paintings by the wall, "but sort of nice. Yeah, okay. How about this one? It's a riff of one of the Turkish baths in Budapest. I really loved the tile—look, I wanted to represent the mosaic I saw there in abstract. I used these brushes. . . ."

Even though the canvases she showed me were all clearly originals, studies of places she'd seen, landscapes that had stayed with her, I found myself interested and asking questions. Real ones. At first, I was trying to distract myself from how I was still uncomfortably turned on—a case of my body acting without my brain's permission—but she spoke with such authority about the work she made, rifling through canvases in her little fur-collared coat. I was coming to realize that I always found that compelling, that kind of mastery and passion, that she could be talking about her rock collection this way and I'd still want to know more.

We'd come to the back of her finished work. "These last

few are exercises for class," she said. I caught a glimpse of a piece that looked familiar.

"Wait," I said. "That looks like—well, Picasso, actually."

"That's because it is."

I raised my eyebrows at her. "It is."

"Simon," she said, ruffling my hair, "you're really sort of adorable." While she pulled out the painting for me to get a better look, I decided that I needed to do something about my haircut.

"It's a take on the really famous one, *The Old Guitarist*. For Nathaniel's forms and figures class. All first-year students have to take it. He's really into imitation as a teaching practice."

"What does that mean?" I asked, peering at the painting. It was obvious what it meant, but I wanted to hear her say it. Especially because this didn't seem like an outright copy. I didn't know much about Picasso, but I was pretty sure that the guitarist in his painting was a man. This was an elderly woman, wrapped around an instrument that wasn't a guitar.

"It's a *kokyū*," she said in response to my unasked question. "My father has one in the house. It belonged to my great-aunt. They're beautiful, aren't they?"

"Yeah." I reached out to skim my fingers across the canvas. "Why doesn't he have you come up with your own ideas?"

"Because, when you're searching for your own style, it can be useful to try on those of successful artists. Nathaniel says we should see what we can steal from them. So, like, if I imitate Picasso, really try to do the same thing with my brushstrokes that he did with his, I'll probably fail, but I'll understand something about his process and so," and she put on a Nathaniel voice, "'I'll learn something about my own! About my soul!'"

"He really loves his souls," I said.

"Yeah." Her smile faded. "He got kind of angry at me for changing out some of Picasso's elements here. Said I was straying too far from the assignment. During critique, he said the nicest things about the paintings that looked like exact copies. It seemed kind of stupid, honestly. I was still working with Picasso's style."

I was pretty sure I knew the answer to my next question. "Does he just have a thing for Picasso?"

"No," she said. "He works in conjunction with the art history teacher. Hands out a list of painters that she teaches in her first-month overview. It's like this whole project—we study the painter we choose, their life, their history, really get a feel for their work. It counts for both classes."

"Who else do people imitate?" She gave me a funny look—I was asking too many questions. I stuck my hands in my pockets and looked down. "I'm just . . . it'd be good to have a jump on this assignment if I ended up coming here."

Marie-Helene laughed. "I'll do you one better," she said. "Go get me another coffee from the café, and we can try a little breaking and entering." At my shocked look, she amended, "Into my friends' studios. What did you think I meant?"

At that moment, she sounded so much like Holmes that my stomach turned. Was that why I wanted to immediately run off and do what she told me to? *Stupid, so stupid,* I thought, *what is it with these girls? Why do I always end up trailing after them?* But this one studied under Nathaniel, and she had a group of friends who were forging paintings, whether or not they knew that was what they were doing, and no, I didn't want to be with her, but she had this immaculate spray of freckles across her nose, and so of course I told her yes, what kind of latte did she want this time?

"YOU KNOW, THIS MIGHT BE THE BEST NOT-DATE I'VE EVER had," Marie-Helene said, pushing open the door to her friend Naomi's studio. It wasn't real breaking and entering, of course; there wasn't even any lockpicking involved. People had their personal supplies stored in strongboxes under their tables, but the spaces appeared to be communally used.

"Naomi did her project on Joan Miró. A lot of people did. Professor Ziegler was pretty funny about it, actually," she said, and now I had Nathaniel's last name. "He had an unofficial prize for the best one and hooked them up with some kiosk outside the Centre Pompidou—the museum—that sells imitation paintings to tourists. Supposedly you make pretty good money doing it."

Naomi had imitated Joan Miró. Rolf, in the studio next door, had chosen Da Vinci. The next was Twombly, all painted squiggles and sparks, and then a black-and-white Ernst collage, where a girl in an old-fashioned gown held an iPhone to her ear ("Nathaniel really hated that one," she said), and then an *American Gothic*, a really terrible imitation of *Starry Night* (actually, I thought, maybe Simon *could* go to this school), and finally, as I caught Marie-Helene not-so-subtly checking the time, we wound up in her friend Hanna's studio. The girl with the paint-splattered backpack, the one who warned me about the men at the pool party.

"She's from Munich," Marie-Helene explained. "She really loves all the twentieth-century German painters. A lot of us don't like taking art history—we'd rather make our own—but Hanna really works hard at it. She's a great artist, and she's really smart."

Langenberg. I kept my face neutral. "As smart as you?" I asked.

"You tell me," Marie-Helene said with a shrug, and began to pull the paintings back one at a time for me to see.

They were all surrealist landscapes. Every last one of them done in clashing neon colors, horrible to look at. No hushed scenes in sitting rooms. No dark colors. No people, even. And maybe my taste in art was just underdeveloped, or maybe I was just frustrated to again have hit a brick wall. But when we got to the last of them, I knew I was done.

It was a relief.

"Maybe I just drank too much last night," I told her, taking off my hat to rub at my temples. "I think I just need a nap. Sorry to be so lame."

"Not lame," she said, and took the hat from me to prop on her own head. She grinned. "I actually had a lot of fun today."

I had, too. Almost a normal kind of fun, when I used to go hang out at the pub on long afternoons, having the kinds of conversations where I didn't feel like I needed an encyclopedia, a dictionary, and a scorekeeper. Where my friends liked me and I liked them, and that was the whole of it. When I could go home and bicker with my sister and read a book in bed and not worry that everything I cared about was retreating slowly out of my grip.

The kind of fun where nobody's shooting at you, I thought, and when I took my hat back from Marie-Helene, I kissed her on the cheek. Before I could pull away, she snaked a finger through my belt loop. "I could see you when I come back," she said quietly. "I think I might like that."

"I'll be in London," I told her. "But if you ever come out that way—" *Don't call me,* I wanted to say, *because you're lovely and deserve better than an imaginary posh asshole who doesn't like you as much as he should.*

"If I do." She kissed me on the corner of my mouth, a slow kiss, an unexpected one. It wasn't chaste, and it wasn't romantic—it was a suggestion, an ellipsis. I closed my eyes against it.

"See you later, Simon," she said, and I dragged my heels back to Greystone, not sure what I'd say to Holmes when I got there.

I WAS SO LOST IN MY HEAD THAT I DIDN'T NOTICE THE CAR trailing along behind me. At first I thought I was imagining it. But the sky was bleak and whispery with snow, the roads nearly empty, and the black car crept down the street like a moving tumor.

I slowed at a crosswalk. The car slowed, too. When I ducked through an alley and out onto a different road, the car was there moments later. Finally, I stopped at a corner, my hat in my hands, and I waited.

It pulled up to the curb. The back window rolled down.

"Mr. Watson," the voice said. "Do you need a ride?"

The click of a gun cocking. It wasn't a suggestion. I got in.

seven

THE BLACK CAR DIDN'T TAKE ME TO A CELL, OR A WARE-house, or a secluded field with a pre-dug grave. I wouldn't have known to be afraid if it had, because I couldn't see where we were going. When I climbed into the car, I was immediately grabbed and blindfolded, my hands tied with what felt like a zip tie. All I'd seen before I was bound was a man in a suit with a black bag over his head.

What the hell was going on?

"James," the voice said, inflectionless. The slip of the bag-mask being pulled off. "Before we begin, I'd like you to know. This is not my voice. I've employed this man to speak to you on my behalf. He's being fed his lines."

I strained my ears, and I could hear the light tap of fingers on a screen across from me. There must be a seat facing mine. Someone else sitting there, writing his words on a tablet. I kicked my foot out and connected with someone's knee.

A gasp of pain. A shuffle. The safety being switched off on a gun. Maybe he wasn't typing on a tablet, after all. But I wasn't given time to consider it—I was thrown against the door, and after a scuffle, they bound my legs.

"I have no intention of hurting you, idiot child," the voice said. "Stop flailing about."

There was a pause while everyone settled back down. The car took a slow turn to the right. If I were Holmes, I would've tracked our route by the number of turns we'd made and deduced where we were going. Three? Four? I wished I had a map of the city committed to memory, the way she did.

But I didn't. I had to get over it. I focused instead on the car's interior—how many people were in here with me? Two, I knew for certain. When the voice spoke again, I listened for the dead places in the car, where his voice hit resistance. Three, maybe?

"This is not your fight. This was never your fight. You're putting Charlotte Holmes in danger."

The voice was English. That was a useless deduction, because I was surrounded by bloody English people, and it wasn't his real voice, anyway.

"Actually," I said, hoping to keep them talking, "I'm pretty sure you're the one putting her in danger, Hadrian."

I was pretty sure it wasn't Hadrian in the car with me, but it was worth a shot. Who else would have a fleet of black cars and bother kidnapping me to make their point?

(That said, I'd noticed that the Holmeses had at least one of these black cars, and a driver who took them around town. So did Milo. I wondered if a black car appeared in your garage the morning after you came into some money, like some kid's movie. Frog chauffeurs instead of coachmen. A bloodthirsty art dealer instead of your fairy godmother.)

The voice paused. "According to my instructions, I'm supposed to laugh at you now."

"Go ahead?"

The voice managed a kind of embarrassed chuckle.

More soft tapping sounds, but the voice spoke again before they finished.

"I won't give you my identity. It's not important. Know that I am an interested party, and I want you to begin booking your travel back home. You have no particular skills. You know this. You're a fairly standard teenage boy. You have no use but to be used."

"I know it's fun to be cryptic, but that last thing made zero sense." I wanted the voice to keep talking, because as I wiggled my hands, I realized the zip tie wasn't as tight as it needed to be.

"Think of yourself as a package. It's Christmas, so picture a nicely wrapped present. Charlotte carries it around. It's heavy in her arms, but it's pleasing to look at it. Maybe the package talks. It's witty. It's flattering. It makes her feel special, and she likes that feeling. And one day Charlotte leaves it somewhere in public, and poof, it is taken from her. Charlotte is sad. Then furious. Charlotte will do anything to get her present back. Horrible things. Things that will end in her death, or imprisonment. We don't want Charlotte to do these things."

"So in this weird children's story you're telling me, I'm a talking package." I'd put my wrists between my knees, and slowly, slowly, I worked one curled hand out of its binding. "That's a pretty stupid extended metaphor. Did you fail English class? You were more of a math person, weren't you?"

A pause. "Go home, James. You know that you can't offer her anything."

My hand was almost free. With my elbow, I felt as unobtrusively as I could for the location of the door handle. "I do make a pretty mean pasta carbonara."

The car slowed. Were we coming to a stoplight?

"Go home," the voice said sadly, "or we'll call your father."

I laughed. I couldn't help it. "Please," I said, "I haven't talked to him in a few hours, he'll want an update," and when I jerked my hand out of the tie, I pulled the door open and tumbled out of the car.

Wheels skidding on concrete. My fingers yanking off my blindfold. Honking, someone shouting, and a mess of cars pulling around me, but I'd learned at least one thing in the last few months. Before I crawled the two feet to the curb, I committed the black car's plate number to memory.

I TOLD THE CRYING BYSTANDER THAT I HADN'T BEEN KID- napped. I told the other one that she didn't need to call the cops. She did anyway, so I told the police my friends and I were doing a German fire drill. No, I didn't know the name of the driver, or the person the car was registered to. I'd just met them today. No, I didn't want to make a statement. Yes, I'd pick my friends better in the future. No, I was fine walking down the block to Greystone, because that's where we were, within sight of Milo's headquarters, and I wanted to be spared the indignity of being driven the final five feet.

I limped the rest of the way there. I'd sort of wrenched my shoulder in my roll out of the car. Scratched up my hands. They were still battered from a run-in I'd had this fall with a two-way mirror, and it didn't take much for them to start bleeding again. The guards at the Greystone front door took pity on me. This time, I was only subjected to a retinal scan.

I needed to find Holmes, though I wasn't looking forward to it. Breaking news: I got into a strange car where someone told me I was useless. How was your afternoon?

No one in our shared room. No one in Milo's penthouse, at least the areas I was allowed into—I definitely wasn't going to ask the guard in the hall to let me search his bedroom. I asked her if she'd seen Holmes or August, and she shrugged, like it was beneath her to answer.

"Well, is there a lab here? One that's usually off-limits to Holmes?"

"If you're referring to Charlotte, then yes. Ninety-four percent of this building is 'off-limits' to Mr. Holmes's sister."

"I've had a very bad day," I told her, "and I'm one hundred percent sure you know where she is. Will you just take me there?"

Down three floors and around the corner, and the weary guard led me to a keypad-locked door. She punched in the code and nosed the door open with her rifle. "Our audio-visual laboratory."

The lab was the kind of bright-white clean I associated with the dentist. Computer terminals were set up in a cluster in the center of the room, and big buglike speakers and screens mounted on the walls. Holmes sat below a cluster of those screens. She'd taken one apart with a screwdriver—at least I assumed that's what she'd done, because she had a toolbox beside her—and now she was plucking at a series of black wires with a pair of pliers. She was whistling something tuneless and gleeful, so I assumed it was going well.

August Moriarty had scooted up a swivel chair behind her. He leaned over her shoulder, saying something into her ear.

"I have a Watson for you, Miss Holmes," the guard announced.

Neither of them moved.

I cleared my throat. "A bleeding Watson, who's been kidnapped."

August stood up. Holmes wrenched her head around.

"Thanks," I said. "If I want to get your attention next time, should I be an actual bomb?"

For the record, I was in a really bad mood.

"Your hands," Holmes said, and she crossed the room to me. "What happened to your hands this time?"

I held them up, letting the blood drip on the floor. "Black car, plate 653 764. Lavender air freshener. Two people in the car, maybe three. I'm not sure. I was blindfolded, I didn't get the particulars, but I think they drove around in a circle. It took about five minutes—"

"Watson, I don't need a report just now—"

"They told me I was useless. That I should leave you here and go home."

She looked at me steadily. She didn't say a word.

"And when I rolled out of the car, I think I dislocated my shoulder. August, could you? I need it put back into place."

He went pale. "Isn't there a doctor on the Greystone staff?"

"Oh, for crying out loud," Holmes said, "what on earth did they teach you at Oxford," and after mapping my shoulder with her palms, she made me lie on the floor. Then she stuck one foot on my stomach and jerked my arm back into place.

I shouted. Louder than I needed to, maybe. I took a breath. Straightened. I tried my shoulder. The pain wasn't any worse— it had lessened slightly.

"It would probably be a bad idea for me to ask you for painkillers," I said to her as she helped me to my feet.

"Probably," she said. "Though I might have something in my shoe, if you want me to look."

I looked sharply at her, which set off another spasm of pain, and she put up her hands. "Watson, please, I'm joking. The plate number you gave me is one of Milo's cars. The cars in his personal fleet all start with 653. I'm sure he's just worried about your safety. This isn't exactly your mission."

I wasn't looking for reassurance from her, but I also wasn't looking for her to join in to that particular chorus. "Right, then," I said. "Your brother wouldn't, I don't know, call me and ask me to leave?"

"I'm sure he appreciated the theatrics of it all. Lavender air freshener? That sounds wretched enough to be him." She took one of my arms by the wrist and peered at my palm. "These are fairly minor abrasions. I'll call down for some bandages, and we can get back to it."

"Back to what, exactly? How have you spent your afternoon?"

"Picking apart that screen."

"I didn't realize you'd started up an AV club in my absence."

She frowned at me. "That was the security feed we were running. It stopped working. I'm fixing it."

"Don't talk to me like I'm a child."

"Stop acting like one, then. How was Marie-Helene?"

"How do you think she was?"

"Stupid enough to find your little act charming."

"She isn't stupid."

"Really," she said. "I consider myself to be fairly intelligent, and right now I find both you *and* Simon obnoxious. How do you square that?"

I kept my voice cold. "I made out with her until she showed me a floor's worth of forged paintings. They were done as assignments for a Sieben class taught by Nathaniel Ziegler. I didn't see any of Langenberg's work, but I didn't get through the whole building. It doesn't matter. We have enough to know this is the connection Leander was exploring. I know this isn't exactly *my mission* or anything, but if I were to guess, I'd say that Leander was just trying to track down the intermediaries. Figure out how the money was changing hands. You always follow the money, right? It's like hot potato. Whoever's left with the cash in the end is the guiltiest one."

I'm not stupid. I've never been stupid. I got good grades. I paid attention when someone was teaching me something, and I made it a point to learn it fast. Fine, I didn't have Holmes's training or her aptitude, but just because I wasn't a genius didn't mean that I wasn't smart.

And no, this wasn't my mission. It was *our* mission. Her uncle was missing, but he was my father's best friend, and I had as much of a right to be there as she did. I was done taking a constant backseat. Taking bullshit from strangers who hauled me off the street at gunpoint to dress me down. I was done with the way August was looking at me, even now, with the kind of indulgence you showed to a well-behaved Chihuahua.

"You want this solved by midnight?" I said, rubbing my shoulder. "Then I'll get my father to give up the IP addresses on Leander's emails if he won't give us the emails themselves. Your uncle had to live somewhere while he was conducting his investigation. Let's *go* there. Shake it down. Someone run Nathaniel Ziegler through Milo's criminal databases. Can we get some known associates? It was smarter to send me on a date with an art student while you played mechanic here at home?"

Holmes stared at me. I couldn't tell what she was thinking.

"Your uncle is *missing*, Holmes."

"Jamie," August said, a warning.

"Whatever. I don't care. August, you've been here all afternoon? Haven't hijacked any black cars today?"

"No," he said, inflectionless.

"Then *what have you been doing?*" It was hard to keep from shouting. I needed to see some answering anger flare up in her face. Any reaction at all.

August stepped forward to put a hand on her shoulder. They looked at each other. He shrugged; she nodded. It was the kind of wordless back and forth I was used to having with her.

"My mother," Holmes said at length, "is now in a coma."

"A *coma?*" I stared at her. "I thought the poisoning was an isolated event. I thought—"

"We thought wrong."

"Shouldn't this be our priority?" I asked, starting to pace. "Shouldn't we put the rest of this on hold? Go back to England? Your mother's life is on the line here."

She regarded me evenly. "No."

"You're sounding kind of heartless right now. Just so you know."

"These things are *connected*, Watson. My mother? Leander? If I solve one, I'll solve the other, and I'm so sorry if it offends your delicate sensibilities if I happen to love my uncle more." Visibly, she swallowed. "I love her, too, you know. But—I need to prioritize. My mother can take care of herself."

"From her coma."

Behind Holmes, August glared at me.

Her expression was a mirror of his. "I've only heard about

this from my brother's intel. My father hasn't told me anything at all." Annoyed, she gestured to the screen. "Milo is beaming me footage from Thailand so I can review it for myself, but no one, and nothing, has entered the house that wasn't there yesterday. Milo just fired the whole staff, as a precaution. The only people—" With a sigh, she raked back her hair. "My father and the doctor are tending to my mother. That's all I can tell."

"And Lucien?" I asked.

"Moriarty hasn't made any kind of move. Not that Milo can tell. Nothing that he can stop."

"I'm sorry."

She slipped out from August's hand and crossed to me. His eyes tracked her across the room. "I'm tired, Watson," she said. "I'm working two cases at once, and they both concern my family. It's not like anything I've taken on before. Milo's stupid surety isn't helping. I'm positive he's missed something. I know who the culprits are. I just don't know how they've done what they've done."

"Don't you usually reason *from* the facts?" I asked her. "Instead of assigning blame and working from there?"

Holmes shrugged, but I could tell I'd hurt her. "I'm not Sherlock Holmes. This isn't a case study. My uncle is missing, and the only possible answer is that it's the Moriartys behind it. One way or another, they've done this. Sorry, August."

August grimaced.

"Is there any value in having Milo . . . remove Lucien?" I asked.

"And Hadrian?" she asked. "And Phillipa? And their

bodyguards? Why do you think they haven't taken us out directly? Why do you think they haven't sent us Leander's body via parcel mail? Put a bullet in my mother's head?"

Rubbing my shoulder, I thought about it. What was the only worse thing than the confirmation of your greatest fear? "Because the uncertainty is worse."

She spread her hands as if to say, *There you have it.* "Are you done berating me?"

"What about my ideas?"

"They have value," she admitted. "Of course they do. Of course *you* do. What do you take me for? Some kind of machine? If I wanted a yes-man, don't you think I'd find one that wanted to 'yes' me more often?"

I bit back a smile. "That's fair."

"Don't you think," she said, drawing closer, "that there's some irony in someone taking the trouble to anonymously kidnap you? If everyone keeps insisting you're unimportant, you have to ask yourself why."

"I'm sorry about your mother," I told her quietly.

"I am, too." She considered me for a moment, eyes bright. "Should we divide up the work, then? You'll call your father? I'm sure August wouldn't mind doing some data mining in Milo's systems, he was hired to do that sort of thing"—August shrugged—"and if you don't mind, I'd like to spend more time with Milo's security feeds. When I was younger, I was made to find my way through my own house, blindfolded. I know every room. This feed is missing some."

"Was Milo trained that same way?" I asked, wondering

why he'd skip surveillance, wondering why we were all apparently wandering around with our eyes covered.

"No," she said absently. Her attention had drifted back to the broken screen. "He was always away in our father's study. He speaks five languages, but I doubt he's ever seen our basement. Shall we regroup in an hour?"

But when I reached the door, she cleared her throat. "Watson?"

"What?"

"You only—you kissed her?"

Her back was to me. "Yeah," I said, wishing I could see her face.

"Will you see her again?"

"I don't think so."

Holmes bent her dark head over the tangle of wires on the desk. "That's all," she said finally, and when I left, August was at my heels.

"I'm going to call my dad," I told him. "Can you give me a minute?"

"Do you two fight like that often?"

"No. Well . . . yes. Lately, I guess we fight like that a lot." I shrugged. "I'm sorry you had to see it."

"I don't know how you two are still friends."

"That's kind of bizarre, coming from the aberrant Moriarty who can't get mad at the girl who ruined his life."

His eyes wandered over to the closed lab door. "Isn't getting past it better than the alternative?"

"It depends what the alternative is."

"Is there one? A sane one, I mean." He sighed. "I don't hate her. I'm not a terrible person."

I watched him, the sad mask of his face, the dark clothes edged bright against the fluorescent-lit hallway. "You could be a decent person," I told him, "and still not like her."

"Then what am I left with?" His mouth twisted into a smile. "I'm her friend. And because I'm her friend, I'm going to go do some data mining for her. For free."

"You're hunting down art forgers," I called after him as he set off down the hall. "You can be excited about it. I give you permission not to be a sad sack."

"Sorry about your shoulder," he said. "Just so you know." And he was out of sight.

I wasn't sure if he was just being very English, or if August had actually orchestrated that whole blindfolded joyride. Access to Milo's cars? His team? Resources? *I should be mad about this,* I thought. *He had a gun pointed at me by proxy. He told me to leave all this and go home for Christmas. He . . . well, he threatened to call my father.*

No. I was crazy. He wouldn't go that far just to prove a point. Just to get me to get safely home. Would he?

Breathe, I told myself. *Friends don't kidnap friends.* If we were friends. I took a deep breath. I needed another opinion.

When I called him, my father picked up on the second ring. "Jamie," he said, too eagerly. "News! Tell me!"

There was a commotion in the background—the crackle of a party, a child crying. "What time is it there?"

"I'm at your stepmother's family's Christmas brunch."

"Oh, I don't want to bother you," I said. "Can I call back—"

"Yes! That's such an interesting, complicated problem! Oh, no, Abbie, I need to go take this outside—it'll only be a minute—no, go ahead and play without me, ha! I'm so sorry to miss another round of charades—"

"Having fun?" I asked him. For some reason, I'd never stopped to think that my father had a whole new set of in-laws. I wondered how they stacked up against my mother's family, the Baylors. On her side, I had one cousin. He was a fifty-five-year-old accountant.

"I'm on the porch." I heard him slide the door shut behind him. "There are so many of them, Jamie, and when they're not burning down the kitchen, they're giving Robbie fireworks to set off in the backyard. It's been a hazardous holiday."

My half brother Robbie was six. "They sound a little like you."

"If I watched professional wrestling instead of solving crimes," my father huffed. "Well, what have you discovered? Or are you calling to apologize for ignoring my texts?"

"I haven't discovered anything. Milo's doing all the work."

"You and I both know that Milo is doing none of the work, or else Leander would have been delivered home this morning. Tell me what you've found."

I filled him in on the day's findings, including my brief kidnapping and my theory as to the perpetrator.

"Well, it certainly sounds like a ham-handed attempt at altruism," he said. "You're not badly hurt? Then no harm done,

170

really. August does seem like a nice young man, from what you've said."

Maybe I was mad at him, after all. August *and* my father. "Thanks for your support."

He ignored that. "It's good to hear that you're coming up with some strategy of your own. It sounds like your poor Charlotte is distracted, and with good reason. It's terrible to hear about her mother. Emma might be a bit of a witch, but no one deserves that."

"You've met them? Holmes's parents?"

"A few times. They were quite fun when we were younger. Emma's a brilliant chemist, you know. Works for one of the big pharmaceutical companies. Mostly I saw her flex her skills when she made us cocktails. Molecular mixology . . . anyway, she and Alistair came to visit us in Edinburgh, when Leander and I were flatmates. Alistair would tell us wild tales about his exploits in Russia. I always thought of him being a bit like Bond. I'm sure that was the image he wanted me to have of him, anyway."

"What happened?" They sounded nothing like the people I'd met.

"They got married. Had Milo, and then—and please don't tell your friends this—they went through a bad patch and had Charlotte, I think, as a fix-it. People do that with children sometimes. It's a terrible idea for everyone involved. But Alistair had gotten sacked by the M.O.D.—"

"I thought the Kremlin tried to have him assassinated," I

said, "and that the government made him retire for his own safety."

"Is that what Charlotte told you?" He sighed. "I don't know for certain what happened. I got the impression, from Leander, that he'd gotten caught feeding classified information to the Russians. It's not important. Either way, he lost his job. They were having money problems—you've seen that house, it's absurd to imagine the upkeep—and they were fighting about it, and so they had a child. That child was Charlotte. And while I love your friend, Jamie, I don't think she's ever made anything easier for anyone."

I bristled. "That's an awful thing to say."

"The state of her parents' marriage isn't her fault," he said. "But she put extra weight on an unsteady foundation. They're not happy people, Alistair and Emma Holmes. Not the way Leander is. Not the way I imagine myself to be."

"I know." My father could be called a lot of things, but miserable wasn't one of them.

"Try to keep that in mind as you're going through all this with Charlotte. It can be so easy to get bogged down in it. The darkness. The heartlessness. Not in Holmes, of course. Well, sometimes . . ." I didn't know what Holmes he was talking about, there. I don't know if he did. "Besides, you're young, much younger than I was when I got mixed up with this lot. I don't want it to ruin you."

"Why won't you let me read Leander's emails?" I asked. He'd mentioned his friend's name so many times, always with such . . . longing. It didn't sound romantic. It didn't sound unromantic, either. It sounded like he was mourning the loss of a limb.

He was silent for a moment. "Well, he says a few things about his niece that aren't very nice."

"Really? They seem really close."

"They are," he said. "But she's a teenage girl, and makes mistakes, and—oh, dammit, those emails are *private*, Jamie. They weren't meant for you. I'm sorry to put it so plainly, but I need to make you understand. I'm so far away from all of it, and thank God for that, because the last case I took with him? It almost killed us both. I have small children. I live in America. I need that distance, but . . ."

"But you can't cut him off completely."

"Yes. Well. Listen, I'll send you the IP addresses from his last few emails. Maybe Milo's grunts can make something happen on that front. Hold on—" He covered the receiver with a hand. There was some muffled conversation, and when he got back on, his voice was ridiculously jolly. "Well, son, I've been told that I need to go sing about figgy pudding! Happy I could help with your girl problems! We'll talk more soon. I'll send what I promised. Love you, Jamie."

"Bye, Dad," I said. "You too."

"So. Nathaniel Ziegler," Holmes was saying an hour later, spinning back and forth in her rolling chair. "Was arrested for possession three years ago. Want to know the address?"

"Let me guess." August paused for dramatic effect. He was sprawled on Milo's couch. We'd taken over his penthouse, despite the complaints of his staff. There was more space here than in our room. "221B Baker Street."

"Yes, you're a rare wit, August. Have a cookie. The address, in fact, is one we visited last night." She gave us a street name ending in *strasse*. "Would the underground pool ring a bell?"

"The place was raided?" August sat up. "During a party?"

"According to the report, he lived there."

I remembered what Hanna said, about the art school girls who hung on older men's arms for money and connections. "I wonder if that was how he met Hadrian."

"It certainly fits." Holmes frowned. "And Leander's supposed to be meeting him tonight, Watson?"

I thought back to my conversation with Nathaniel at his loft. "Yeah, if he shows up. The way he reacted when I told him that Leander was hanging out, back at home, it was like . . . it was like he knew that wasn't possible."

"You mean to say, he reacted like he knew Leander was dead."

I shifted in my chair.

"Leander isn't dead," she said. "I know it for sure."

"For a fact?" August asked. "Or for sure?"

Holmes lifted her chin. "He can't be dead," she said, and there was only the slightest quaver in her voice.

I had a lot of experience fighting Holmes over her outlandish assertions, but I didn't have the heart to insist that, yes, in fact, her favorite uncle could be lying in a ditch somewhere. "We can. So?"

"So. It's seven o'clock already. I doubt Leander's 'usual

time' for meeting Nathaniel was any earlier than eight. He's been at this for a while; he wouldn't want to meet even at twilight. He'd want the cover of darkness. Still, I have access to the cameras covering the corners in case he shows early." She swiveled her chair to look out the window. "East Side Gallery is a big place. It's a tourist destination. We need a plan to make this meeting work for us."

"You do have an entire company of trained men at your disposal," August said.

"Do I?" she asked. "Even if they'd follow my lead, using other people's men leaves a rather large margin for error."

"You really think your brother would hire subpar help."

Holmes snorted. "You've met my brother, haven't you? No, we do this alone."

"You could kidnap Nathaniel," I said, only half-joking. "Hey, maybe August could do it."

He started. "Better not," he said.

Was that an admission of guilt? I was going to murder him.

"And what? Torture him back at home until he tells us that he thinks Leander's dead?" She got to her feet. "*Think*, would you."

The ceiling fan whirred. The clock in the kitchen chimed the hour. Holmes paced in front of the window, talking to herself.

For my part . . . well, I had no part. What could I possibly suggest? "What do we even want from Nathaniel?" I said aloud. "His ties to Hadrian Moriarty? We have August, there.

He's a better link than Nathaniel could ever be, if we need to flush Hadrian or Phillipa out. She's already asked us for access to August. Look—do we want Leander back, or do we want to solve the crime he was investigating?"

Holmes and August looked at each other.

"What? Is that a stupid question?"

I thought about it while we suited up. It only took a few moments to put myself into my Simon guise—a hat, a vest, the steel-toed boots. I was playing him again in case Nathaniel managed to catch sight of me, since I didn't look dissimilar enough from Simon to convincingly claim I was anyone else. But as I parted my hair in the mirror, I realized that it was weirdly comforting to be him again. Simon. I knew how he walked, talked. How he thought. What he'd say. I didn't always know those things about myself.

To my surprise, Holmes didn't have her wig cap on. She didn't have on a costume, either. She'd changed into a new pair of black jeans, a black button-down shirt done up to the collar. With her usual intensity, she was rooting through a makeup case.

"How are you doing yourself up?" August asked her, adjusting his fake nose. "Tourist? Nanny? Sorority girl?"

"Myself," she said, looking in her hand mirror, "in the other universe where I'm an art student desperate for lodgings." With a small brush, she began doing her eyes up in silvers and blacks.

"Won't that be a hazard?" August asked. "You could always go redhead—"

"If you want to help, you can fetch me a curling iron," she told him. "And after that, you can decide how badly you want Hadrian to continue thinking you're dead."

"That sounded like a threat," he said mildly.

She took the iron from him and plugged it into the wall. "Either you're in or you're out. For the record, I'm fine with you staying here. I'm sure Milo has some data entry you can do."

He stared at her for a moment, his face drawn. "I'll go," he said, with a barely concealed edge. "I suppose I already have my nose on."

EAST SIDE GALLERY WASN'T ONE. OR IT WAS, BUT ITS NAME made it sound like it was tucked away in some snooty building, where people drank champagne and bought paintings for millions. I don't know why I'd expected that here, a city where art was everywhere, transforming everything, a public act of reclamation.

Because East Side Gallery was the Berlin Wall. The wall that had divided the east part of the city from the west, a result of World War II and later, the Cold War, a symbol of a divided, unequal Berlin. One run by outside forces, separated by a wall that was barbed and booby-trapped and separating the poor, Communist-controlled eastern side from the richer, capitalist west. After demolition finally began on the wall in 1990, artists began painting murals on a mile-long section. Long, uncanny, evocative murals, of men wandering against a dark screen like ghosts, of doves and prisons and melting figures in the desert.

We approached it on foot, and I lagged a few steps behind

Holmes and August, reading a short history of it all on my phone. The last few weeks felt like a history lesson I'd only caught the tail of, one on Berlin but on London, too, on love and inheritance and responsibility. It was like I was trying to read the cheater notes on the last century right before a midterm.

All of this made me feel really young, something I wasn't used to, not when I was next to Holmes. She operated with such absolute confidence, even when the playing field was thick with adults. But now, walking this strange, lovely city after dark, the hint of snow on the wind made me pull my jacket a little tighter around myself, wishing I was home with Shelby and my mother, watching TV under a blanket on the couch.

We weren't the only ones out after dark. Tourists clustered in front of a mural made of handprints, fitting their own palms against the wall. A street artist was selling painted tiles on the corner, playing quiet Europop from a battery-operated stereo. A pair of girls took turns taking pictures in front of a mural that depicted long twirling locks of hair. The blond girl laughed, tipping her head forward so that her curls spilled over her face, and as the other girl snapped photos, she said, *Yes, you are my queen.* Holmes brushed past them, August at her heels, and the brunette girl said, *Forget it, I want* her *hair,* looking after the two of them with longing.

They made a striking pair, Charlotte Holmes and August Moriarty. He looked, as usual, effortlessly cool—this rankled, especially when I knew my own came with a good bit of trying.

He'd dyed his fauxhawk a temporary dark brown, and his false nose turned up at the end, but he was wearing his typical ripped jeans and bomber jacket. And Holmes strode beside him, looking now like a weapon made real. Her eyes were rimmed in a thick black that made her irises seem translucent. Her hair was a tumble of slept-in curls. She had a dark portfolio bag under her arm, and she walked like she had somewhere to be.

We were still ten minutes from eight o'clock, the earliest she thought he'd show. But the East Side Gallery was a mile long, and though Holmes was checking her phone to see if Milo's grunts had caught sight of Nathaniel on their security feeds, we hadn't spotted him yet. I was beginning to feel like we were too out in the open. There weren't any cafés around for us to hole up in if we were spotted. The road beside us was busy and broad, and there was no cover for us to duck behind. So we kept walking.

Until, half a block ahead of us, I saw Nathaniel blowing on his hands on a street corner.

My phone buzzed. Holmes had noticed him at the same time I did. *Approach him,* her text read, *and tell him your uncle's sick.*

This hadn't been the plan. At all. *Uh I barely escaped the last time,* I typed back.

He's early. He's going to see us. Better we make it intentional— at least you're here at the right time. See if he'll take you back to his flat. We'll follow.

And what would he do to me there? If he was working with Hadrian Moriarty, if, despite Milo's intelligence, he *knew* that Leander was dead, the only thing he could be doing here tonight was baiting a trap he'd set for us. We'd hardly made it out of our lunch with Phillipa unscathed.

I had to ask myself again—what were we even doing here?

Ahead, August was saying something in Holmes's ear. She shook her head violently, but he ignored her. Half-turned to me, and nodded.

Then he took off at a jog to meet Nathaniel Ziegler.

Holmes stopped short. I was still a few steps behind. And August had a hand on the art teacher's back, steering him away from us, saying something to him I couldn't quite hear.

"He's asking Nathaniel to take him to Hadrian," she said, turning to me. She looked ready to spit nails. "He's buying us time."

"For us to do what?"

"To go raid Nathaniel's horrible house for evidence," she said. "Come on."

IT STARTED TO SNOW.

The trip across town took an agonizing twenty minutes in traffic. Holmes kept scrubbing fog from the window and glaring out into the road, like she could will the other cars to disappear. We didn't know how much time we'd have. We didn't even know if Nathaniel still lived there, in that house above the cavernous pool, the place he'd been arrested for possession.

"Did it say what kind of drugs he'd had on him?" I asked her, at length.

"Pot, I think. I don't know how actively prosecuted it is. Someone might have had to rat him out to get the police's attention. I'm sure his being a teacher didn't help." The car slowed to a halt. "Finally," she said, and shoved a bill at the driver, pushing me out the door with her other hand.

I pulled on my gloves. The façade of the house loomed above us, a warning. "Is there a reason we aren't taking a Greystone car?"

"My brother's men. My brother's cars. My brother having bugged my left shoe this morning, and the right one yesterday. My brother who thinks that he and my father are infallible and that the rest of us are imbeciles." She barked a laugh. Her breath came out in a cloud. "Do you know that, in the footage he has, 'Leander' has to look down to find the doorknob to our front door? The house he grew up in. He doesn't reach for it automatically—he looks for it. It's not *him*, Jamie. Who knows how he was really dragged out of there. They could have dressed someone up like him for the cameras. Milo says I'm imagining things. He thinks he can't make mistakes. And I play into it. I haven't done anything for myself since I've been here, I've just relied on him, and I—"

She pivoted on her foot and made for the front door, but I caught her elbow and steered her back.

"Take a breath. Don't look at me like that—*breathe*. You can't go in there like this. Breathe."

She glared at me. "You are not my meditation tape."

"And you're mad about something that isn't Milo."

We stared at each other, inches apart. Her pupils were

blown wide. I wondered, for an awful moment, if she'd taken something or if she was just upset, and I hated myself for not knowing how to read the distinction.

"August is going to throw himself back in with them," she said, a rush of words. She was standing too close to me. I could feel the heat of her breath. "He's going to get himself taken down, too. I can't—they're *monsters*, Jamie, and I swear to God I'm going to prove it." She grabbed my hand. "There's no time, we have to go in. Look. You're my stepbrother. I'm starting at Sieben after Christmas. We're looking for a place to stay until then, because my mom just threw us out—"

"Stop," I said, and brushed the snow out of my hair. For the barest second, she leaned into my hand. "I have a better idea."

The girl who answered the door had a pierced nose and a scowl. She said something to me in German.

"English?" I asked her, and she nodded curtly. "Sorry. My friend left her camera at a party here last night. She said this guy was asking her about it—brown hair, fortyish, really loud. She thinks he teaches at the art school. Do you know who he is?"

"You think Professor Ziegler could have stolen her camera?" the girl scoffed. "No." She started to swing the door shut.

I stuck my foot between it and the doorframe. "Sorry," I said again. "I'm not saying he stole it, I'm just wondering if he found it. She thinks she left it by the pool."

Holmes nodded beside her. Her body language mirrored the girl's—hand on cocked hip, a snarl. Strangely, it seemed like it made the girl more at ease.

182

"I already said his name was Professor Ziegler," she said. "His email is on the school website. I have to go."

I smiled at her, but I didn't move my foot. "Did he ever live here?"

"Who are you?" she asked, crossing her arms. "Why do you care?"

"My camera," Holmes said, in a low, accented voice, "cost me three months serving drinks to assholes."

The girl sighed. "Ziegler used to live here. The only man who *ever* lived here until the school found out and made him move. They didn't like that he lived with all college girls."

"Not his students?" Holmes asked her, disgusted.

"College girls. Not Sieben girls. But Ziegler's friend owned the building, and so he got cheap rent. Whatever. Not important. Ziegler doesn't have your camera. He's not a thief, just a creep." After a moment's pause, the girl shifted her weight and said, "I'll look for it. Your camera. Come back tomorrow, ask again."

"Who's his friend?" I asked. "Ziegler's friend?"

"For the love of God," the girl said. "His name was Moriarty," and she slammed the door against my foot, once, twice, three times, until I pulled it away and limped triumphantly down the steps.

"That was rather straightforward," Holmes said.

I could feel my pulse in my crushed big toe. "Well, I guess I'm not very subtle."

"It's been thirty minutes." Holmes checked her phone. "Feel like doing one more?"

Three long blocks and an alley, then four flights of stairs. Holmes moved like a dog on the scent. We were surprisingly close to our next destination.

It only took us a few minutes to ransack Nathaniel's loft, the place we'd been to last night, where the Draw 'n' Drink had been. Holmes had me pull up the public records on the building while she rifled through the sketches that the Sieben students had left behind.

"This place is owned by the school," I said, peering at my phone in the dark. "On the school webpage, it looks like it's listed under faculty housing. I think. The translate function is saying it's 'house for grown bears.'"

She took the flashlight out of her teeth. "Clearly, he doesn't live here full time. Check the bedroom."

"What bedroom?" I craned my neck to look up into the loft. "The only thing up there is an easel."

"Exactly," she said, taking the sheaf of sketches and slipping it into her portfolio bag. "There has to be a third residence. Some place where he actually lives. Hold on, I'm going to give it the loft once-over. Look for loose boards. Footprints. That kind of thing."

Holmes usually didn't explain her methods to me. "Need any help?"

"No," she said, with a bit more sharpness than necessary.

I raised an eyebrow at her.

"We don't have enough time," she amended. "And anyway, you haven't gone through that closet yet," and she hoisted her bag over her shoulder and zipped up the stairs.

The closet had a sad-looking jacket in it and a man's left snow boot. The kitchen cabinets had some mismatched wineglasses; under the sink, there was an old, disgusting plunger. Other than the chairs and tables I'd seen here the other night, the loft was empty of anything interesting. And God knew I couldn't read clues into dust trails or windows cracked a half inch open. I looked around the loft with some disappointment. Surely, somewhere here, there was a clue to where Leander was being kept. There had to be—

"I found something," Holmes said, pounding down the stairs. "Look."

Forms. A thick stack of them. The top one said INVOICE, and below it, an address for Hadrian and Phillipa Moriarty. This painting for this amount of dollars. This painting for more. It was an inventory of all the work that Nathaniel had sold to Hadrian, his counterfeit middleman.

Langenberg, one of the pieces said, followed by an item number. I ran my finger down the list. *Langenberg, Langenberg, Langenberg . . .*

"Where did you find that?" I asked.

"Under the floorboards. With this underneath. Look."

It was a business card, dog-eared and scuffed. DAVID LANGENBERG, it read. CONSULTANT.

"That's descriptive," I said. "This was all in the floorboards?" Almost like she'd just materialized them.

"*Langenberg*," Holmes said impatiently.

"I can read," I reminded her. "I thought that Hans Langenberg didn't have any children."

"He didn't. But he might have nephews. Great-nephews. Leander was posing as 'David,' right? David Langenberg. Simple." She tucked the card and the papers into her portfolio. "Did your father text you those IP addresses?"

"Earlier, while we were at East Side Gallery." I showed her the list on my phone. "I haven't had a chance to look through them yet."

"Send them on to Milo's grunts." She smiled at me, sleek and satisfied.

"I thought you were just complaining about Milo's grunts doing all the work for you."

"Let them." She closed the space between us, put her fingers on my chest. I almost recoiled—was I being played?—but then she scuttled back, like she'd only then realized what she'd done. "I'm starving. Don't you want to get dinner?"

Charlotte Holmes was never satisfied. Charlotte Holmes was never hungry. Charlotte Holmes was never the girl who convinced you to get a naan pizza and root beer floats from a sketchy little place in the tourist district, but that's exactly what she wanted to do.

In the shop, we sat in the window, watching the snow fall. She picked the pepperoni off the pizza a piece at a time while I made notes on the IP addresses in my journal.

"This one, they pinpointed to Kunstschule Sieben," I said. "So at least one of the emails Leander sent was from there. Maybe he followed Nathaniel to school. Or maybe it's the same IP address as that faculty housing."

Holmes nodded, making a giant stack of pepperoni with her fingers. I wasn't sure how much she was paying attention.

"There are a number from cafés. Milo's team sent along some names. It looks like Leander visited a Starbucks . . . do you think it's down the street from where he was staying? The last one is from this address, here." I pointed to it with my pencil. "It's in a part of the city we haven't explored."

"Okay," she said.

"Are you listening?"

"Uh-huh." After considering it for a second, she popped the giant stack of pepperoni into her mouth. "Oh my God," she said, her mouth completely full. "I didn't think I could pull that off. My calculations were right!"

I'd never seen her act like this before. "What are you *on*?" I blurted.

Holmes gave me an affronted look, the brunt of which was undercut by her chipmunk cheeks. She chewed for a minute and swallowed. "We found proof. Definitive proof. Haul Nathaniel in, question him, and you'll have your link to Hadrian Moriarty. I'm sure August has him en route to Greystone right now. We'll find my uncle before the day is out, I'm sure of it."

Holmes's instincts hadn't been wrong this fall, when she'd refused to consider August Moriarty as a suspect in Lee Dobson's murder. But this felt different. It wasn't sentiment, or nostalgia. It wasn't wishful thinking, either. It felt . . .

"Too easy," I said to her. "Isn't this too easy? All the information you need is under the floorboards?"

Holmes rolled her eyes. "Occam's razor, Watson. I've texted August and told him to bring Nathaniel back to Greystone tonight. But he said he won't be home until late. We have some time to kill."

She was trying to distract me, I knew she was, but the glee in her voice was contagious. "Well, what do you want to do?"

"A date," she said.

"A date." I blinked. "What kind of date? Are we talking, like, dancing? A movie? A soda shop?"

"Better." Shy, suddenly, she dropped my gaze and looked out the window. "Something . . . well, something I love. Something we can only do here."

"A German something."

"Well, when in Rome," she said, and that was how we ended up at the Christmas market at Charlottenburg Palace, three days before the holiday itself.

At first glance, it looked like a sea of candles bobbing in a dark pool. Tents, white tents, rows and rows of them lit from within like clouds of daylight in a line, all topped with light-up stars and wound with garlands. People were crowded around them in earmuffs and gloves, drinking from mugs and eating giant frosted cookies. It was silly, and charming, and a little bit weird, and honestly, I loved Christmas. I always had. I was missing my family something fierce, tonight, thinking of wrapping presents around the fireplace back at home.

And then there was Holmes, who was acting like she'd had a near-death experience and come back to tell me all about the light. She was relieved, I realized. Bone-crushingly relieved.

When, in our last case, she'd realized August wasn't to blame, she'd acted the same way. Talked nonstop. Ate everything.

Ate . . . everything.

"Have you had stollen?" she asked me, pulling me over to a booth staffed by a jolly old man right out of a Hallmark special. *"Was kostet das?"* she asked, pointing to the both of us. The man answered, and she pulled a handful of euro coins out of her pocket.

"What am I eating?" I asked her as she handed me a slice of jewel-dotted bread.

"Stollen," she repeated impatiently. "Sort of like fruitcake, only it isn't wretched. Milo usually ships it home for the holidays. That, and a fir candle to light up next to the artificial tree."

Gingerly, I tried it. It wasn't bad at all.

Cookies next, then mulled wine that smelled like cinnamon and cloves. We wandered through the stalls, eating from brown paper bags, getting our gloves covered in crumbs. We'd stopped on the way so that Holmes could retrieve her jacket from Piquant, the restaurant we'd eaten at with Phillipa, and now she flipped the collar up to keep the snow off the back of her neck. Then, with a self-conscious laugh, she reached over to do the same to mine.

"Otherwise it'll go down the back of your shirt," she said, her fingers brushing against my hair. "Don't want that."

I shivered.

This side of the market was playing Handel over its speakers, but as we wound over to the giant, light-up Ferris wheel, the music changed to American Top 40. The tail end of a song about sneakers, and then—

"Oh my God," I said to her. "They're playing L.A.D."

"I think I just heard the twelve-year-old girl behind me say the same thing."

"Shut up," I said, "or I won't take you on the Ferris wheel."

"You're assuming that I want to go."

"Of course you do." I paused. "Do you?"

She smiled crookedly at me, her mug of mulled wine clasped between her hands. A little bit of powdered sugar was on the tip of her nose.

"Yes," she said. "I want to."

We stomped our feet next to each other in the line; she was doing this thing where she'd lean against my arm for a second, but if I looked down at her, she'd pull herself away like a housecat caught on its back.

"I want car number three," she said, when we neared the front.

"Why?" I asked.

"Haven't you been paying attention? It's the one that's the swingiest."

"Swingiest isn't a word."

She smiled at me, that one particular smile I hardly ever saw, the one that could open padlocks, Yale locks, bank vaults, the one that was a trapdoor down into everything. I reached out and touched the tip of her nose. My finger came away white with sugar.

"It is now," she said quietly.

The ride operator was appropriately toothless, and the boys above us kept throwing popcorn down at our heads, and when our car stopped, it didn't stop at the top to give us a view of the city—instead, we jerked down to the stop before we disembarked, the perfect place to stare up at everyone else's feet.

"It only goes for two minutes? For five euros *each*?" She dug through her brown paper bag. "I wish I had something to throw myself."

"You've never been to a carnival before?"

"I rode the London Eye with my Aunt Araminta. She believed in taking my brother and me on 'excursions.'" Holmes made a face. "She gave us clothes for Christmas, a size too large, 'to grow into.' She's the sort of person air quotes were invented for."

"Leander said that the Moriartys killed her cats," I told her, and then blanched. I hadn't meant to bring that up. Not just when we were on the other side of this case (*But* are *we on the other side of this case?* a voice in my head asked), but when we were getting along so well.

But Holmes just nodded. "Totally did her in. She sells honey, now, from her apiary, and doesn't talk much to anyone. I haven't seen her in two or three years." Our spangled metal car tipped forward, then back. "Are they ever going to let us off this thing?"

"I thought you liked the swinginess."

"It's making me nauseous."

"Just close your eyes and enjoy the L.A.D. It's 'Girl I See U Dancin.'"

"You knew the name."

"*Girl I see u dancin / something something ransom*—oh, come on. You love it."

"*I* love it? I think that's your job."

I wrinkled my nose at her. "I know your deepest, darkest secrets, Charlotte Holmes. Don't you give me that."

The smile on her face went frozen and forced, all at once, like a gust of cold wind from the north, and as I opened my mouth to ask why, the ride lurched forward again.

eight

WE MADE IT BACK TO HOLMES'S ROOM AROUND MIDNIGHT
to find August Moriarty waiting at the door, hat literally in
hand.

"Where's Nathaniel?" she asked him, an edge already in
her voice.

"I let him go," he said.

She started, like she was keeping herself from lunging at
him. "You ask for my trust, for all of our trust, and then you go
and drag away the man I want to question and you *announce*
yourself and everything you know to Hadrian Moriarty and—"

"We didn't see Hadrian. My brother's gone to ground,
Holmes," August said. "I don't know where he is. Nathaniel
doesn't know where he is. And neither does Milo, though his

193

being on a red-eye flight does limit his resources somewhat."

"So why did that compel you to let Nathaniel go?" I asked him. "We have a stack of invoices here, for forgeries Nathaniel's students made that he sold to your older brother. We have a business card for David Langenberg, Leander's alias that we found in Nathaniel's apartment. And you let him rabbit? Just like that?"

"Because he doesn't know where Leander is," August said, "and this has never been about the Langenberg paintings. I don't care what you found."

"You're sure he doesn't know." Holmes took a step toward him. "You're sure."

August shook his head, as if trying to clear out noise. "I'm sure."

"How?" I asked. "How are you being so cavalier about this?"

"I pulled up pictures of Nathaniel's elderly parents. They're in a home, north of the city. I had its name within seconds. Its address. I threatened to kill them, tonight, if I even *imagined* he was lying." His voice broke. "Do you remember what my last name is? Or do you need an explanation for why he believed me?"

"There's a link," I said to Holmes. Anything, anything to defuse this situation. "We have the link. We know your uncle was posing as a Langenberg—"

"We don't know that," she said. "We don't know *anything*."

"But—"

"Go to bed, August," Holmes said, opening her door. She

shut it behind us so emphatically it was like she was sealing off a tomb.

"That was loud," I said.

"There isn't anything left for us to do tonight. We have to wait until tomorrow."

"Are you sure?" To my embarrassment, I stifled a yawn.

To my surprise, she turned to look at me. Really *look* at me, like she was straining to see some faraway sign.

"Watson, you look like hell. Haven't you been sleeping?"

"Not since October." I leaned against the wall. It felt good to put my weight against a solid surface. "Is this you saying you're worried about me, or are you really feeling the hard truths thing tonight?"

Holmes started to snap back a reply, then stopped herself. Very deliberately, she reached up to put her fingers against my face. "I'm worried about you," she admitted. It didn't sound practiced, that admission, as it did when August was trying to be nice. Really, I didn't think either he or Charlotte Holmes were nice, at their core. At their best, they were kind. It was that kindness that prompted Holmes to lead me over to the ladder to her lofted bed. "It's more comfortable than the cot. But you know that, you've been sleeping there."

"What are you going to do?" I climbed up and got under the covers.

"I don't know," she said. "Plan B. Whatever plan B is."

"Don't stay up too late."

"I won't." She stared up at me, one hand on the ladder. She'd undone the top three buttons of her shirt, and I could see the white line of her collarbone. "I might be—tired later."

"Okay," I told her, as cautiously as I could. "I might still be here."

Did I want her to climb into bed with me? Did she want to? Would knowing the answer to either question change what we were going to do?

Across the room, she rummaged through her suitcase for her pajamas, then called out that she was changing. I turned my back, trying not to listen to the rustle and slip of fabric, trying to remind myself how tired I was. I *was* tired, I realized with some wonder. I'd been exhausted and unable to sleep for so long.

Honestly, I'd never forgotten what Lucien had said to us in Bryony Downs's apartment. *It's good to know what matters to you,* he'd told Holmes. *So very little does. My brother didn't. Your own family doesn't. But this boy* . . . Meaning me. The pressure point. The weak point. A thought I tortured myself with on the nights that I stuffed my head under the pillow and tried not to feel the dot of a sniper's rifle on my back.

The door open and shut softly. Holmes had slipped out, and my eyes were already closing. Before I passed out, I took out my phone. *We're closing in,* I texted my father, though I didn't think it was true. *Will you please reconsider sending Leander's emails? I won't read them. I'll have Milo skim them for what we need.*

Pretense, all of it. He knew I'd read every word, just as Milo knew that Lucien was targeting his parents, and I knew, for a certainty, that neither Holmes or I knew what we wanted at all.

When I woke, it was hours later; I could tell even in that windowless room. My stomach was growling, and someone was speaking. A male voice. I sat up, too quickly.

"Lottie, I'm fine. I'll see you soon." The voice again, tinnier this time, and then broken into pieces. "Lottie, I'm fine. Lottie, I— Lottie, I'm fine."

Holmes sat in a small oasis of light. She was cross-legged on the camp bed with a laptop, a lamp beside her, and her hair hung in her face as she hammered on the keys. "Dammit," I heard her say. "Goddammit."

"How's it going?" I asked, and she jumped.

"Watson," she said. "One of the techs showed me how to peel apart a recording into layers, to isolate background noise. I've been working with Leander's phone message. What time is it?"

"I have no idea." I checked my phone; it was ten in the morning. "Did you find anything?"

"There's something. An echo . . . the kind that—" She went to play it again, and then, without warning, she slammed her laptop shut. "Shit," she gasped, exhaling through a hand. "Shit."

"Come up here." I didn't know if the thought would be at all comforting, clambering up into bed with me. From the look she leveled me with, she was skeptical, too. "Not like that. Just—come here."

She climbed up the ladder and sat next to me, our backs against the wall, surveying her little kingdom.

"Lena's been texting me," she said.

"Any news?"

"Why are we in Germany, Germany is lame," she said, in her quoting voice, "and also Tom has started wearing that Nuclear Winter body spray, which has Lena simultaneously turned on and disgusted."

"Sounds about right," I said. She smiled. We both knew that she adored her roommate, and that we would never mention that fact out loud.

"Every room you settle into looks like this," I said instead. "The clutter. The weird textbooks. Where do you even get those textbooks? And the lab table. Always with the lab table and the blowing things up. It's like all of it stays in some little box inside you that . . . bursts open when you take a moment to settle down."

"That's precious, Watson."

I grinned. "It's true. You know it is. You're like a turtle with your world on your back."

"There's not a lot you can control, you know. Where you're born. Who your family is. What people want from you, and what you are, underneath it all. When you have so little say in it all, I think it's important to exercise a measure of control when given the opportunity." She smiled, ducking her head. "So I blow things up."

"Did you hear that? You almost said something profound. You came *so close.*"

She pushed her sock feet against the edge of the bed. "Leander liked to talk about the importance of control. No one would ever guess it. He's famously lazy, you know, he lives like an absolute sloth. Goes from one house he owns to another, violin in tow, picking up the odd crime when it suits him. Living off his trust fund, eating out in restaurants. Going to *parties*." She said the word with such disdain that I choked on a laugh.

"Parties! You know what they say—first, the parties. And before you know it, they're on to the murdering."

She rolled her eyes. "Watson. Some people don't like to read. Or they don't like sport. They don't like the routine of it, or the slow pace, or the fast pace, or the noise. Whether it seems too intellectual or too base. But I'm an anomaly if I don't like parties or restaurants? It's wrong if I don't like the idea that there are a demanded set of responses and that I'll be judged on how well I can provide them?" Putting on a little-girl voice, she said, "'Yes, please, I'd like the salmon, it looks lovely! Could I bother you for another soda? Ta!' I hate the idea of performing a role when I haven't written the script myself. I need more of a purpose than I want to get a chocolate pudding without the waitress calling the police on me."

I made a mental note to dig up the rest of that story later.

"Leander *excels* at that kind of thing," she said, "because he has some genetic aberration that makes him good with people. They like him. They trust him almost immediately, and because he can pass as a normal sort of man, he can be invisible. Left alone. He says the right things, and people approve of him and move on." She looked at me. "I've always wanted to be invisible, and because I want to be, it's impossible."

"What kind of life do you want for yourself?" I asked her.

"After all this? After school, after Lucien?"

She thought about it for a long minute. I had no idea what she'd say. Holmes had always had such a tenuous connection to her surroundings, like she was more real than anything around her. At school, she walked around with a backpack full of books, but they were like props in a stage play. I knew, of course, that she had to go shopping for shoes and shampoo, but I couldn't imagine a world where she did so, and last week I'd watched her trimming her hair in the sink and wondered if she'd taught herself to do it from a YouTube video, because I couldn't imagine either of her parents showing her how. But I couldn't imagine her looking at YouTube, either.

Maybe it was just me. Maybe she was so endlessly fascinating because the world hadn't ever scratched up against me the way it did her, leaving her raw and unhappy and wanting to disappear. She used grocery-store-brand shampoo, I knew, because I'd used her shower back in Sussex, and I'd stood there smelling it, the water beating down on my face, because it was impossible that a girl like that shopped at the same stores I did, because, despite my best efforts not to, I'd romanticized her beyond all sense, because even if I wasn't in love with her, I couldn't see myself loving anyone else.

"I want an agency," she was saying. "A detective agency, a small one. In London, because it's the only proper place to live. We'll take back over Baker Street. It's a museum, now—none of my family wants to live there, it's too gauche for them—but it would make you happy, I think, and anyway it has all the original furnishings, so we wouldn't have to shop for them.

Furniture stores are horrid, aren't they? And we'll take cases. You can deal with the clients, comfort them, take notes. We'll solve them together, and I'll handle the finances, since you're so terrible at maths." She paused. "It sounds childish, when I put it that way. I imagine in practice it'll feel rather adult."

"Is that it, then?" I asked her. It came out quiet, though my thoughts were loud and cluttered. I'd never imagined that she'd daydreamed like this, not the way I had. "Is that what you want? I'm in those plans, when you imagine them?"

"If we both make it that long." She tipped her head back against the wall to look at me. "You're determined to take on all this responsibility for mistakes that I've made. I'm beginning to think you *like* having a target on your back. So if you insist on staying, I might as well make a place for you. I—"

I kissed her then.

I kissed her slowly. Patiently. It was always too desperate between us, the clock nearing zero, the last secret about to slip out, or too cautious, or too clinical, an experiment gone wild and wrong. It was a huge, impossible thing, kissing your best friend, and each time we'd tried, we'd managed to fuck it up so badly that the next felt even more impossible.

I wanted to give her an out. I always did, especially after Dobson. But God, it was hard. When she leaned into me, her fingers tracing the hollow of my throat, I had to clench my hands not to touch her back. Then she slipped a hand underneath my shirt, and I forced myself to pull away.

Her breathing was coming fast. "What if we weren't doing this? If we were just friends? You'd still come along. You'd be there, with me, in London. Say you would."

"I don't—we've never been just friends, though, have we?"

She smoothed out the sheet between us, avoiding my eyes. "You wouldn't want me either way, then. You wouldn't want me as just your friend."

"You're asking me for everything—"

"'Everything' doesn't have to mean *this*," she said, her voice breaking, and when I reached out to touch her, she flinched away. "'Everything' is a minefield, Jamie. I don't know when I'm going to make a misstep. Maybe it'll come two years from now, and what then? If you've already shackled yourself to me, will you resent me if I stop wanting to be touched? If one day, I wake up and it's there, my own private hell is back and everywhere around me, and I won't let you ever kiss me again? You wouldn't be able to leave me, at that point. You're an *honorable man*. But I know it. No one could sustain that. Bit by bit, you'd just—you'd go." She laughed. "God, I just want to burn it all down now, so I can know the worst thing that could happen. So I can control it."

I stared at her. "You'd what? Tell me to leave?"

"Or I could sleep with you." The look in her eyes was cold. "That would have the same ultimate effect. Making you leave. Ruining it all."

She was pushing me away. She had veered too close, and now she was overcorrecting, and she was overcorrecting with *knives*. I couldn't do it, I couldn't sit there another second and listen to her say these things, and horrifyingly, I was still turned on. I needed her as far from me as possible. "Get out."

"This is my room. You're in my bed. Where do you want me to go?"

"Anywhere else. I can't—get *out*, Charlotte."

An awful moment passed, then another, and when she climbed down the ladder, she walked straight out the door.

All the time we'd been talking, my phone had been buzzing with texts. They were from my father, apparently; it was six a.m. in the States. I seized on it now as a distraction. Anything to keep my mind occupied.

Why are you asking me again? I've told you already why I won't send them.

Dad, I wrote. *I don't see any other way. Milo's in Thailand. Holmes just ran out on me. I can't make bricks without clay.*

No response.

Unless you can come out here and look for him, I don't know how else we're going to get Leander back.

I'll send them.

I stared at his text for a long minute. *Are you sure?*

Yes. You should know that you'll be staying at my house for every school break until you're fifty.

Noted, I said, channeling Holmes without thinking much about it. When I realized I had, I turned the ringer off and stuffed my phone in my pocket. I lay back down, and forced myself to try to get some sleep. Forced myself to stop listening for her. She'd come back in, or she wouldn't, and either way, I couldn't face the world yet. What would I do? Go console August Moriarty for threatening someone who might have kidnapped Leander?

I finally accomplished it, sleep, though it was the middle of the day. My dreams galloped away from me. They were soft and threatening all at once, incomprehensible in their noise. When I woke, I felt around for my phone. It was dinnertime. The day had slipped away. I needed to wash my face. Get my head on straight.

I ran into August in the corridor, sending a series of rapid-fire texts of his own. He looked exhausted. "Rough day?" he asked.

"I could ask you the same thing. Where's Holmes?"

He waved the question off. "I saw her a few hours ago. She looked like she was off to draw blood. What did she learn while I was out? She wouldn't say."

I made a noncommittal noise.

"Anyway, I had some information for her," he said. "A friend of mine came through with an address. There's a party spot some of the art dealers go to. Turns into a semi-respectable kind of gallery during the day. It's Monday, so it very well might be dead, but I thought it might be worth a look. It's a place my brother Hadrian might pop up. Lots of artists. Lots of coke. That sort of thing."

I didn't think I'd heard him right. "You told Holmes that."

"Yeah," he said, still looking at his phone. "I thought we'd maybe check it out tonight."

"Where is she now?"

August shrugged. "Getting dinner?"

"Back up. You just effectively told a clearly upset Charlotte Holmes where to find coke in a strange city."

August gave me a hard look. "Coddling her is a terrible idea, you know. Charlotte always knows how to find coke. She's a recovering *drug addict*. How do you think that works? I trust her to know her limits. You can't really do much else."

"You can't." I got up in his face. "You knew her for how many months, when she was fourteen? What kind of limits do you think she has?"

"My brother," he growled, "is an addict, so yes, I *do* know something about it, and unless you just completely shattered her world in half, I can't imagine this being a situation that . . ." He trailed off. All at once, the blood went out of his face. "Oh my God, Jamie. What have you done?"

nine

ALL I COULD THINK IN THE BACK OF THE TAXI WAS, THERE *needs to be a German compound word for feeling both guilty and enraged.* Holmes had said just hours ago that I was always willing to take on the responsibility for her mistakes. Here I was, proving her right. What rankled me the most was that August had immediately asked what *I* had done, as though I'd been callous enough to reach in with my two hands and break her heart. She'd done that herself. Hadn't she? She'd said I'd leave her if she was hurting. She said I'd sleep with her and run.

God, I was going to throw up. I fumbled for the controls to try to crack the window and let in some air. The cabbie started ranting at me in German until August intervened, leaning between the seats to reason with him. Their voices grew louder and louder, and I thought I'd puke right there on the floor.

I focused my breathing, the way I did during rugby drills, until my stomach stopped roiling. "Distract me. Where exactly are we going? Who gave you this information?"

August settled into his seat, glaring at the back of the driver's head. "It's at an art squat. Used to be an old department store, and then it was a Nazi prison. Now it's almost like a city unto itself. There's a café, a cinema, ateliers—it's a shared space, and sometimes they'll do an open studio night. You walk through with a glass of wine, look at what the artists are working on. If you're a dealer, it's a good chance to see what's out there, though it's best if you keep those intentions to yourself. They don't love businessmen."

"You sound like you've done this before."

He smiled grimly. "Dead men hobbies. My name around here is Felix, by the way."

"Felix? Really?"

"Shut up, Simon," he said in such an uncanny impression of Holmes that I couldn't stop myself from laughing.

August had the cabbie drop us half a block away, so we approached the building from the rear. It sat on a low, grassy hill, a huge Frankensteined building against the darkening sky. I could hear music playing as we approached, though I couldn't pinpoint from where. The doors were a panicked red, covered in glitter and nails and little paintings of eyes. I hesitated, my hand on the knob.

"Wait—" With an expert hand, August pushed my hair back from my face. "Button your shirt up to the collar. Tuck it in. Cuff your pant legs. No, further. And ditch your socks, you wear your trainers without them. You don't speak much, but not because you're scared, all right? You're bored. Get a drink in one hand and scroll on your phone with the other."

"Did you learn this from Holmes, or the other way around?" I asked him as I looked for a place to stash my socks.

"We had remarkably similar childhoods," August said, his eyes as hard and blank as stones. "Let's go."

The building was strangely lit, with staircases that crawled up along the walls. I didn't have any trouble imagining it as an old-time department store—the walls had a tall, molded look to them, and the staircases were wide enough to hold a steady stream of shoppers. But the paint had all chipped away. Chunks of the walls were missing, like an angry hand had scooped them out. Now everything was painted electric blues and yellows, the walls and the windows and the stretching ceilings, and while most of the murals were abstractly beautiful, here and there I caught a glimpse of a drawn-on face hidden inside the paint, its eyes watching me.

"August." The hair on my arms was standing up.

"I know," he said, and held a hand up while he listened. "The music's coming from up above—the third floor, maybe? We'll try up there."

We climbed the stairs slowly. August assured me the

building was structurally sound, but there was something so precarious about a place that had been repurposed so many times, like its essence had been stripped bare in the process. On the second landing, we stepped to the side as a crowd of tattooed girls pushed past us, laughing. One of them shot the kind of smile at August that girls at Sherringford sometimes aimed at me.

False walls had been built throughout the third floor, breaking up the giant space into smaller rooms. Studios, I thought. August had called them ateliers. None of the walls reached the ceiling, so you could see the cluster of lights each artist had set up to illuminate their space. A table was set up near the stairs, and August filled two plastic cups with vodka and soda and handed one to me, his eyebrow lifted slightly. *Don't talk*, the look said. *And don't drink this either.*

He shambled along slowly, sticking his head into studios, greeting people in German. *"Ja,"* he'd say, *yes*, and jerk his head at me with an apologetic-sounding murmur. Then we'd stand for a minute while he chattered at some shaved-head boy about his giant metal sculpture of a pickle. I kept scrolling down my phone. I had a text from Lena: *where are u guys what happened to London so bored.* I ignored it, and instead, pulled up the collection of Leander's emails, but I couldn't pay any attention to those either.

I was listening for the edges of Holmes's voice. I noticed that August always kept himself turned toward the atelier's open door so he could see if she walked by. Slowly, we made our pilgrimage. A set of televisions, all playing black-and-white newsreels from the 1940s while disco music blared. A set of toes made from ceramic and gold, arranged on a pink platter to look like snack food. Tiny paintings of naked girls presented by a smug-faced man I wanted to punch in the throat. Instead, I scrolled through Leander's emails, not really reading them. All this to get them, and now I was too sick to focus. *Dear James*, each one began, *Dear James, Dear James.*

Then I came across one that began *Dear Jamie*, dated early this December, and for a minute I let myself stop listening for Charlotte.

> Dear Jamie, I don't know why I had the urge to write to you by that name. No one's called you that since I have! I've been spending all my time hanging around these art school teachers and their little student flocks. They all have so much overwhelming affection for each other, these students, like they're all drowning and simultaneously holding each other's lifelines. Honestly, I don't see how they don't all end up at the bottom of the lake that way, but here they are, welding and sculpting and drawing under their teacher's benevolent eye. Nathaniel even goes to their parties. I think he fancies himself a little in love with me, which is good for my purposes, but of course, terrible for his. It's always a bad idea to fall in love with your dealer. . . .

I hoped he was referring to dealing art and not to drugs. Though, watching the eyes of the artists around me, the lines between those worlds seemed blurred. Some were sharp as tacks, tour-guiding their work, teasing August in German about something that made him blush. And some sat in the corner, smiling, smiling, smiling, their hands clasped in their laps like it was the only thing that could keep them from flying apart.

Another studio. It felt like an hour had passed, but since I was staring at my phone, I knew it'd only been ten minutes. It was taking everything in me not to chuck it at this painter's head and start scaling the walls, calling Holmes's name. *There's a really good chance that she's fine,* I told myself. *She's almost always fine.* But the painter was monologuing at August, using his hands to explain something, and so I settled into a plastic chair to read the rest of Leander's email.

I hear Hadrian's name everywhere. I can't stress to you how much of a fortune he's made, and while I don't think he's involved in this particular Langenberg fiasco, I do know he has connections I could use to push the case along at a more reasonable clip. Milo's been keeping me informed, but only so I can keep myself out of Hadrian's way. Honestly, I wish my niece could time her meltdowns more appropriately. We've had a détente with the Moriartys for almost a century. Of course you manage to talk me into an art crime case just after we've burned the white flag. I always thought the whole thing would be worth it if Charlotte and August had really gone whole hog on the Montague-Capulet romance. Imagine that story! Still, he wound up dead and my poor girl wound up banished, so I suppose it has shades of Romeo & Juliet after all.

If I sound flip, it's because I feel flip. I don't know how

much longer I can live as David Langenberg; he has horrible taste in ties, and his studio flat is freezing. Not to mention that my sister-in-law is once again ill (fibromyalgia, wretched disease) and without her income—honestly, I'm a bit concerned that Alistair won't be able to hold on to the family home, not with the way he's been spending. I'm due for a visit anyway, so I'll see what I can do. He's always been a good help in my cases. And I'd like to finally meet your son!

I just wish we were smoking those ridiculous French cigarettes in our Edinburgh garret again, setting off the smoke alarm. And your cooking was awful, but God knows I can't do it for myself. I miss you, James. Take care of yourself.

I'd been expecting something much more clinical. The kind of step-by-step analytical exercise that Sherlock Holmes was always telling Dr. Watson he should write instead of his "stories." But these—they weren't case updates so much as letters, the kind you wrote to someone you knew so well you could imagine them beside you, even when they were across an ocean, living out another life.

My father had cut out his own replies. I tried to imagine them. Of course he'd been worried when Leander had stopped writing to him—it sounded like he was Leander's only lifeline in a difficult, months-long case. He'd been living as David Langenberg. As someone related to the artist? Someone with a financial stake in what happened to Langenberg's new work? That email had been near the bottom of the set. There were only two more after that.

Dear James, I had an interesting encounter this evening. On the way out of my flat, when I had hardly put on my Langenberg persona, I was almost run down by our Professor Ziegler. We'd plans to meet for dinner, so it wasn't a surprise to see him there.

I know I haven't really spoken to you about the particulars of my relationship with Nathaniel. "My" relationship. David's, more like, and you'll forgive me my modesty. His modesty? Suffice it to say that a certain amount of romantic promise had to be made to ensure his continued interest in our little project. But we've never been in a position where I ran my hands through his hair.

Nathaniel is a handsome fellow. He kissed me on my front step. He'd surprised me with flowers, and I decided to play it up. I put my arms around his neck. I—

I can't write to you about this. You know my feelings on this, and every, subject, Jamie.

I still dream about you sometimes, you know. But I suppose I can't write to you about that, either.

(I pulled a hand over my eyes, and then I kept reading.)

He was wearing a wig. I hid my surprise, but while I'm too good at this game to show it on my face, I think he could feel the shift in mood. But we went out for currywurst down the road, as we've done a few times before, and discussed the fortune we were making, from his students, from his own work. Do you know I've come to love Langenberg's paintings, even when they're done by Nathaniel's hands? There's an ache in them, a loneliness. An isolation. Is it pathetic to say that I have art in the blood? I do. I am an artist. My medium is unseen, but I am one all the same.

I want to see him paint a "Langenberg." Not just because I don't think he's the one who's been painting them, this blue-eyed Nathaniel, with his twice-broken nose. I don't think Nathaniel is Nathaniel at all. He looks like a blurred version of his photo on the school website. Him, and not him.

I've spent the night watching these odious interviews online. Did you know that Hadrian Moriarty has that same nose? And yet they look nothing alike. I've felt that face. I've had my hands in his hair.

I think I might just be going mad.

Maybe it's all this isolation, making me paranoid. I'm not sure. But I can't face the indignity of asking my nephew for his assistance. I'm going to the family home tomorrow. I need to see my brother.

August was trying to get my attention, but I shook my head tightly. There was one more email to read. It was dated two days later.

Dear James. I'm sorry I didn't write you yesterday. I'm at the family home, remembering how to be myself, trying to shed the last of this monkish grifter.

It's good to see your son. He takes after you in almost

every way, and like you, he's in over his head. Charlotte is . . . different. Wary. Untrusting. She'd never been very forthright, but this sort of animal fear is new, I think. It doesn't have anything to do with your Jamie, and still it does, somehow.

I caught Charlotte alone this afternoon. We had a long talk about her father. Certain changes are going to be made in that house, and she needed to be aware. That girl. Strong chin. Strong voice. She understood immediately.

Would it mark me as weak if I told you that sometimes, in my cups, I pretend that she's my daughter, and not Alistair's?

There's more to sort out here—finances, Charlotte's schooling. Emma's in . . . a situation, and they've called in a doctor. There's more to it than that, but that's all I should say. Privacy, you know. I'll be back to Berlin as soon as I'm able.

Happy Christmas. Roast some chestnuts for me.

That was it. The last one.

It was so hard to wrench myself back to the present. I made an effort to remember, to put words to the cold twist of panic in my stomach. *Holmes is here. We're looking for her. You have no idea how you're going to find her.*

And Hadrian Moriarty—was he Nathaniel Ziegler? I'd thought myself a genius when I'd picked him out of the crowd. When he invited me back to his loft. Nathaniel feigned panic when I mentioned Leander's name, and I thought, *Yes, a sign that I've found the man I've been looking for,* and had no idea how right I was. Was Hadrian masquerading as Nathaniel? All the time, or only for these meetings? Was he teaching college classes, or was he just meeting Leander in that empty, echoing faculty housing at night?

It was a half-formed hunch, in Leander's email. He didn't think he was right.

But God, what if he was. *Reason through it, Watson.* Because August Moriarty had seen Nathaniel last night and *let him go.* What if he had been conspiring with his family all along? What if he and Nathaniel hadn't gone to see Hadrian because Nathaniel *was* Hadrian?

What if all of this was a ploy to get us where Lucien Moriarty wanted us?

Frantically, I scrolled up through the previous emails. Looked through them faster now, all pretense gone. We were still standing in that same damn atelier, and when I glanced up at August, his attention was fixed raptly on the artist's face as he spoke. His own voice had grown quieter.

I took a look around me. This artist was interested in painting more traditionally than the others we'd seen—at least, his canvases weren't flashing neon lights or cut up into tiny strips. They were portraits. Each had a dark head, looking to the side, the expression obscured. All charcoals and grays, with flashes of eggshell white. What the paintings depicted was different from the false Langenbergs we'd seen, but they all had a definite similarity to *The Last of August.*

The artist didn't look like Nathaniel Ziegler. He didn't look like Hadrian Moriarty, either, and maybe they were one and the same. This guy was all of eighteen.

When he saw my expression, August held a finger up to the artist. "More vodka?" he asked. "Then we'll come back."

I had to keep a lid on my suspicions for now. We had to find Holmes.

August Moriarty kidnapped you, a voice in my head whispered, *and you still thought he was on your side. How could you be so stupid?*

"*August,*" I hissed outside the studio's entrance, but he shook his head tightly. *Later,* he mouthed. As we wound our way back to the table of drinks, I wondered if Holmes was even here. Maybe she'd stolen herself away to a coffee shop somewhere to think. Maybe she was still in Greystone HQ, playing scales on her violin, having shaken off our fight right after it happened. Maybe she'd done the sane thing, for once, and called someone to talk it over—though who, I didn't know.

No. I needed to focus on the now. I felt like she was here somewhere, and from the look on his face, he felt it, too. "Bathroom," he said, and pointed to a door far across the cut-up room. "Since you asked."

I nodded. We'd split up, then. *Trust him for now,* I reminded myself. *You'll have to deal with this later.* I crept slowly toward the restroom, looking up from my phone to throw quick glances down the aisles. There were voices, everywhere voices, but I didn't hear Holmes's. Which could mean nothing. I remembered the time she'd dragged herself under my father's porch and taken the rest of her stash all at once, sitting in the cold dirt like a blank-faced doll. It'd been like pulling teeth to get her to talk, until she opened herself up to spill out everything.

One long black flood of confession.

The ateliers were fewer here, and the suspended walls held dark little dens instead. Couches, and a television playing Netflix. A more elaborate bar, with rack after rack of liquor bottles reaching up to the false ceiling, the wall behind it chalkboard-painted and covered in strange little sunbursts. A few that were empty of everything but people laughing, people dressed like artists and people wearing suits, and I wondered about those strange little open spaces, who "owned" them, if anyone, who decided who came in or went out.

And still I didn't see her anywhere, until I did.

She was the golden-haired girl in a sea of men. My gaze had skipped right over her, and then I'd seen those eyes of hers, colorless and cold and strange.

Quickly, I backtracked and grabbed another cup, sloshing cranberry juice into it with shaking hands. *She seemed fine,* I told myself, *she's talking, she's happy, it's fine,* and I tried to summon up the confidence I'd need to wander into a room full of strangers and pull her out. Where was August? I couldn't see him. I didn't know what her cover was, or what she was doing—or God, even if she would come with me if she saw me.

I approached again, slowly. I didn't want to scare her off. At the edge of the crowd, I dodged the waving arms of a bearded guy ranting about Banksy, and put myself into Holmes's line of sight.

She didn't seem to see me. As I watched, she plucked an offered cigarette from its pack. "Anyone got a light?" she asked in her low, hoarse voice. These artists spoke English, then, or at least recognized the gesture, because three different men fumbled out their lighters. Holmes leaned forward into someone's gold-plated Zippo, and for the barest second, she locked eyes with me. Mouthed *not yet*, jerked her head.

August must have read the signals, too. "I didn't think this was your kind of scene," he said loudly, emerging from behind me to take the cup from my hand. "Thanks for getting me a drink."

"I lost you in the crowd." One of the men ran a finger over Holmes's bare shoulder, and she giggled. "Is this your kind of scene?"

"No," he said, low in his throat, and it wasn't in response to my question. "I know that man. Michael!" August called with a wave.

The closest man to Holmes, the one with the most muscles and the least gray hair, saw August and gave him a cursory wave back. He clearly wasn't interested in anything August had to say; instead, he bent to whisper in Holmes's ear. She beamed up at him. "Ooh, where?" I heard her ask.

"That's Hadrian's bodyguard," August murmured. "His personal bodyguard. He doesn't work for Milo. I didn't know he'd be here tonight."

"Is that how you know this place? You've been here with your brother? Hadrian?"

August nodded, the barest movement.

"Is your brother here?"

A hesitation, and August shook his head no.

He *had* been. He had been talking to his criminal cretin

of an older brother all this time, under our noses, and I could feel my hands seizing at my sides, wanting to strangle him. If we weren't in public—

"Michael," he said to me, loud enough to broadcast, "come on, let's go get a drink."

The giant man held up his cup in response as he walked away. Holmes was already tripping after him, her fingers tangled with his.

"Call your brother, you jackass," I told August. "Tell him to get his bodyguard home. I'll follow her."

I felt torn in a way I couldn't remember feeling before. In the past, I'd always respected her boundaries, especially when she was in disguise, trawling for information. Either I followed her lead or stayed out of it entirely. My stakes in this situation were lower; my stakes were always lower. My father may have asked us to ask after Leander, but he wasn't my uncle. I might have been in Holmes's house when it happened, but it wasn't my mother that Lucien was poisoning.

I had tried to convince myself that it was *our* mission. I was wrong.

But it was my best friend who was raped, my best friend who did coke and oxy and anything else that wasn't bolted down. She was also the one who could always take care of herself, but here she was, following the giant German bodyguard into what looked like a small square room repurposed into coat closet (*In an graffiti-covered art squat?* a tiny part of my brain asked, *A coat closet—is it art?*), and *dammit, dammit—*

Because it was December, or because it was an art

installation (who knew?), this closet was filled with coats. I hid myself behind a floor-length fur, and though I couldn't see anything, I heard the two of them talking just fine.

"I've watched you since you come in," he was rumbling. "You bright up the room."

"It's hard to miss you, too, you know. God, you must work out—look at your arms! You're so much stronger than *my* bodyguard. And better looking." She giggled. "Do you want a job?"

I couldn't make a diagnosis. I'd never seen Holmes on coke; I didn't know what it did to her. What it did to anyone, actually. What happened, in the movies? Didn't it make you talk quickly, feel more confident? Was that heroin?

"I have many years' contract with my employer. He is . . . angry man."

"Oh, I'm just teasing! He isn't here, is he? I don't want you to get in trouble."

Sometimes it made my head spin, thinking how much of Holmes's spywork had to do with telling stupid men what they wanted to hear.

"Tonight, no. He send me to check on a man who paints for him, but he is not here either. He is stupid. Does not return his calls, and he owes him work. This will get the man into trouble. I will go to East Side Gallery after, since sometimes he is there." A rustling sound, like he was backing her into a rack of coats. "You come with? After, we party."

"This is a party. We could party now," she murmured. My head washed with static. *She can handle this,* I told myself. *She always handles it.*

A wet sound, like kissing. The rustling grew louder.

"Wait—" And she sounded so unsure, so scared, that I had to shove my fists into my pockets. "My old boyfriend is here sometimes. I don't want him to hurt you."

"Hurt *me*?" This was apparently a new concept.

"No—not that he could, but I don't want there to be a scene." A sly note in her voice. "I broke his heart. Have you seen him? He's really tall, and handsome. Older. He has slicked-back black hair." Leander.

"Him? You date *him*?"

"It was a mistake," she babbled, a girl backtracking. "I'm sorry, a mistake, I'm just worried about you—"

"No. You don't worry about him. My employer has taken care of it, yes? Now—"

That wet sound again. No, a different wet sound, and a man's tortured wheeze, a whimper, and before I fully knew what I was doing, I had shoved myself out from my hiding place, fists up.

In time to watch Holmes slam her elbow into his throat a second time. He slid down to the floor, dragging an avalanche of coats down with him.

"He tried to reach up my dress." With a shaky hand, she straightened her wig. "Let's go. Now."

We made a break for the stairs. Even now, even with her mouth tight and trembling, she was playing the part she'd assigned herself—what looked like some blond version of Marie-Helene, down to the clothing. Was that how she crafted a persona? Ran her scanner eyes over some girl she'd just met and then re-created her, hours later, with a wig and a set of painted-on freckles?

Behind us, a buzz kicked up. When I turned to look, I saw a man come tearing out of the coat closet only to be grabbed and hauled away by—August?

"Faster," Holmes said, and we pounded down the brightly painted stairs, past the burned-out chandelier and the door with its painted eyes. In moments, we were outside and tearing down the hill. But I hadn't paid attention when we'd first arrived, and there was nothing around us—just the lumbering shapes of factories and trucks stretching out to the skyline.

"Where are we?" I asked her, but she grabbed me by the elbow and hauled me along. At the end of the block she skidded to a stop and pulled me around the corner of a warehouse. I searched my pockets for my phone. "I have something to tell you about August." No response. "He's in touch with his brother. He's been talking to Hadrian, I think all this time." Nothing, still. "Holmes?"

She'd knelt on the curb, her hands braced against the concrete. Once, twice, she threw up into the street. I got down beside her to hold back her hair, the long strands of the wig cold and stiff in my fingers. A cold wind snapped down the street. She didn't shiver, but any minute now, it was going to snow.

"Are you okay?"

"Fine." She coughed, then pulled off her wig and threw it to the ground. The wig cap. The false eyelashes. Without them, she was almost herself again, a girl in cast-off black clothes with desperate eyes. "Can you call a car?"

"I don't have any reception," I told her. "Yours?"

"I'll ask Milo."

"Isn't he in Thailand?"

But she didn't say anything else for a long minute. Instead, she looked out across the road stretching out and up to the art squat. The wind kicked up again, scattering her hair across her face.

Wheels on gravel. As we both watched, a black town car came around the corner. It didn't have plates.

"I wonder who he bugged this time," I muttered, opening the door, "you or me."

The driver was another of Milo's silent, dark-dressed men. After we settled in the backseat, Holmes waved at him. "Home."

We were quiet for a long minute. Absently, she asked the driver for a plastic bag; he handed her one as though he had a supply on hand. I wasn't sure what to say after the way we'd left things back at Greystone. I turned it over in my head—an apology? An interrogation? How to tell her about what I'd learned from Leander's letters? She met with him, the last one said. They talked about how things would change at her house. Should I start there?

At first it seemed like we wouldn't talk about it at all. She took out her phone and began tapping away—to who, I didn't know—and only when she'd finished did she speak, in a hoarse, cruel voice that I'd only heard once before.

"You want to talk about this."

I sighed. "I need to tell you something about August."

She drew a breath. "Watson. If you're telling me you're

concerned about his loyalties, I'm uninterested. He might be in touch with his family. He might be unwilling to babysit me. I don't care what reason you've dug up, but at the moment, I'd rather rely on him than you. This brings us to my second point. One moment."

Very neatly, she threw up again into the plastic bag.

"Two," she said. "When you told me to get out, I did. This is me getting myself out. I want *out*. I don't want this horrifying iteration of you that no longer has any faith in my ability to keep a handle on myself because I am having *boy problems*." She said those last words with a snarl. "Am I made of glass now? You come to find me, and you don't tell me straight off that you've gotten new information about my uncle?"

"How did you know that?"

Holmes stared at me like I was a moron. "You're honestly asking me that question."

"*Holmes.* August is talking to his brother again, and I don't care if he thinks he's doing us—me—a favor, it's incredibly stupid. What did he do, wander into his consulting rooms dressed like a bookseller? Surprise, I'm not dead, and oh look! We're re-creating history—"

"Shut up, Watson. Just get out. Look, we're at a red light—I'm sure you could find your way home. Do you have reception to call a cab?" She glanced again into the rearview mirror. The driver didn't look back. "Do you need me to come with and hold your hand?"

I set my jaw. She was coming at me like a bulldog, in the back of a town car that smelled like puke and was taking us to

God knows where, but there was no way I'd let her get a rise out of me.

Holmes glanced again out the back, then at the driver.

"Why do you keep looking out the window?"

"We're passing the Berlin Wall. Are you completely help-less with geography, or do you really not know where we are?"

"I—"

"Look it up. We're not far from Greystone HQ."

She was flustered now. Scattered. The car was going faster. I waited a second before I asked, "Are you feeling all right? Do you need—"

"I am clearly not physically ill over something that you have done to me. You might be dense, but right now you're being extraordinarily stupid."

I knew her well enough to know when she was pissing me off on purpose, but this had a different feel than usual. Usually, when she went after me with teeth and nails, it was because something else had frustrated her and I happened to be in the same room. She liked to have something concrete to fight with. It wasn't my favorite thing about her, but it wasn't the worst, either, and she normally ran through her rages in a minute or two.

And yes, we'd had a heart-wrenching fight earlier, and yes, it might've been something we couldn't come back from, but when Holmes was truly angry with me, she didn't throw out petty insults or tell me to look up the Berlin Wall on my phone.

The last time she went after me with this kind of vicious-ness, it was to chase me out of her lab before we were both killed by an explosion.

It couldn't be true. I turned to stare out the back window of the car. It was dark, and I didn't know the city, but I also didn't think I remembered the giant industrial buildings we were passing now. We were going deeper into whatever neighborhood we'd been in. We definitely weren't on our way back to Greystone.

Holmes was staring at me. *Look at your phone,* she'd said. So I did.

It was back in service. She'd been texting me this whole time.
THIS ISN'T A GREYSTONE CAR
GET OUT
I SENT AN SOS TO AUGUST AND MILO THEY'LL COME FOR ME
GO
GO NOW

Before I could begin to form a plan, or say, *No, I'm not leaving you, we'll get ourselves out of this,* the car came to a crashing halt. Even though I was buckled in, I slammed forward into the divider.

"Get out," Holmes said hoarsely, not bothering to whisper. "They're not interested in you."

What is happening? I wanted to ask, and *Why is this happening now?* The driver climbed out and slowly rounded the back of the car.

I reached out for her hand.

"Jesus, Watson," she said, and her face was clear and shining. "This is going to get ugly."

"I know," I told her. "I'm not going anywhere," and the

black-clad driver yanked me out of the car with his massive fists and shoved me up against the windshield.

I put up a good fight. That was my job, wasn't it, to be the brawler? I was playing my role. He had a normal face, the face of a dry cleaner or a dog walker or an old friend of my mother's, but he was some stranger, someone I'd never seen before, and he was punching me in the face. It was stupid to be so surprised at it. All we did was lurk around the edges of this kind of danger, so why was it such a shock to be hauled into the center of it by my shirt and then have my nose broken?

"*Run,*" I yelled. Where was Holmes? I couldn't see her anywhere. I was trying to buy her time. This man had a hundred pounds of muscle on me, and I wasn't a skinny kid. When he hit me in the jaw, I heard something splinter. It didn't matter. I couldn't hear, couldn't see, and it wasn't because of the blood streaming down my face. It was because I was furious.

I hooked my leg around his and took him down. *Thank God for rugby,* I thought with some bitter, distant irony, because I had him on his back now. He was scrabbling against me, ready to fling me off, and I knew nothing about street fighting, when it came down to it, but I did know to jam my fingers into his eyes. With his forearms, he flung me backward and lumbered back up to his feet.

Through the blood in my eyes I saw Holmes behind him. What had she been doing? Why hadn't she run, gotten help? But she was here, wrenching the driver's arm behind his back. With her cool, calm efficiency, she kicked out his knees with her sharp-heeled boots, but she was calling for help all the while.

He turned and gave her a shove that sent her sprawling on the ground.

I shouted her name. I shouted it again. Was this the warehouse district? I listened for cars, sirens, any sign of human life, and then I stopped listening, because all I could hear was the driver's grunts as he slammed his fist into my stomach. I tried to heave him off me, but I couldn't. It was like I was being beaten up underwater: time was moving that slowly. It was so impersonal. I'd never known that fighting for your life was so invasive and so cold. Had it been five minutes? An hour? On the pavement behind him, Holmes groaned and sat up, her face scratched red with gravel, and I couldn't look anymore because he was punching me in the mouth.

I told her to run, or tried to—I ended up spitting out a thick stream of blood, and just as the driver pulled back for another blow, I saw Holmes struggle up to her feet.

"Don't kill him," a voice said, but it wasn't hers. Where was I? "My brother won't be happy."

I think the driver nodded. I couldn't see, not out of both eyes, and my head was beginning to loll on my neck. "Sorry, kid," he whispered, two words so surprising that I almost choked, and when he hit me again, it kicked me off the ladder of consciousness and sent me falling down, down, down.

ten

FIRST AND FOREMOST, I SHOULD SAY THAT I AM PROVIDING this account under great duress, and only with the reassurance that Watson will not read it for a period of eighteen to twenty-four months after the events in question. Contrary to what he believes, I don't take any joy in upsetting him. He asked me to fill in some particulars about the period of time in which he was incapacitated, and to tell it in a way that appeals to the reader. *No info-dumping, Holmes,* he'd said.

If I'm to do this, I'll do it on my own terms. Here are the facts: we were locked in Hadrian and Phillipa Moriarty's basement. It had a very plush red carpet on which Watson was currently sprawled. They had tied me up, but I'd made short work of my bindings. All of this was August's fault.

I'm not sure if you remember this particular detail from his last account of our adventures, but it takes Watson an absurd amount of time to wake up after he's been knocked unconscious. You might make the argument that I shouldn't know this. That a good partner would in fact actively and successfully prevent such occurrences.

Your assumptions would be correct. But I do *try* to prevent such things. Why else would I have left him in Milo's sad little hotel? (Before we'd arrived, I'd asked my brother to stock our room with paperback classics and murder mysteries—Jamie Watson's poison, if you'll excuse the expression—and I hoped that he'd be engrossed enough in *Slaughterhouse 5* to not notice that, from time to time, I would slip out to do some work on my own. The fact that Milo ordered those books in German is an unfunny joke and hardly my fault.)

Yes, I was upset with Watson. I was quite upset, in point of fact, but it was nothing in comparison to the anger I felt when I saw his worried-sick face over the shoulder of my mark. Of the two of us, I am the only one who has successfully solved a crime. I am, in fact, the far more competent partner, not to mention equipped with far better foresight. These aren't boasts. These are quantifiable facts.

Here is something I can't say to Jamie Watson: I can't be your girlfriend because I'm terrified you'll try to wrap me in cotton and hide me away. "Try" being the operative word. He needs saving far more often than I do.

But there, at least, I'd failed. Watson laid out on that plush carpet was disturbing for a number of reasons. Every few minutes I made sure that he was breathing, and in the time between, I sat on my heels beside him, considering our situation.

The basement had no visible doors or windows. Our phones had been confiscated and the back of my head was bleeding. I would give myself, and Watson, ten minutes of rest before I began ripping apart the wooden furniture to fashion myself a weapon.

My father trained me to prioritize in situations like this. *Make a concrete list,* he'd said. *Be unsparing.*

A list, then. What were my priorities?

1. Keeping Myself Alive. Note that it may appear mercenary to put this first, but anyone who doesn't have this at the top of their list is a parent or a liar, and I am neither. Not to mention that failure to keep myself alive renders the rest of this enterprise moot.

2. Keeping Jamie Watson Alive, as his reckless disregard for his own safety works against him. Neither of us believes that we personally need caretaking; the other disagrees. He and I find ourselves at an impasse. As very recent events have proved, Watson will throw himself into a physical altercation he knows he will lose in an attempt to buy me time to run away. Clearly he needs caretaking, if not a thorough head examination.

3. Recovering My Uncle. Because Leander never goes without leaving me some small present—a book on vivisection, a pheasant quill—and nothing can rouse him in the

middle of the night. There is quite literally no situation I can imagine that would lead my uncle to willingly leave his bed between the hours of ten and four. Most importantly: he has never, *ever* called me Lottie, not since I told him I hated the name when I was seven. That said, he can and does take care of himself; for that reason, one would argue I should move him further down the list.

4. My Parents . . . how to put this? Ideally they would remain living. That said, I cannot imagine them as anything other than alive, anyway, as they are capable, ruthless, and wealthy enough to make the best of those two other attributes. (Jamie would call them "vampires." This term also has appealing qualities.) I am aware of their disappointment in me, which I once found motivating, and now find tedious; I have a somewhat vague desire to rescue them just to prove them wrong. That said, I don't wish them to be poisoned, though I can understand Lucien's desire to give it a shot.

That is one of those things Watson wouldn't want me to say out loud. *You're awful,* he'd say. *They're your* parents. At times, Watson is far too sentimental. I've yet to see him with a puppy, but I imagine it would be too much for me to handle.

Nota bene: my brother does not appear on this list because he has approximately seventy-two thousand armed guards and an ego the size of a small blimp.

All of the above items have been carefully ranked. They all must come before #5, the hardest of all, which is to Keep

Watson Happy. (One might argue that I rank this the lowest on my priority list because it proves to be the most difficult, and I dislike failure.) What does Watson want? To have us at our happiest and also to be in romantic love. In our case, because I am a "bit of a broken robot," to use his words, these two things are mutually exclusive. He is a boy and he is in love with me, but only because the world bores him. His world is boring because it loves him, you see. Of course it does. And so it all comes so easy to him, and his world grows wretched and long, and he begins casting around for something of interest in all that dark. If I am broken, at least my hazard lights are appealing to a boy like him.

Personally, I've often thought that Watson and I had all the trappings of a standard romantic relationship—absolute exclusivity, obsessive intensity, constant arguments, crime-solving—and have been confused as to what more he wants. Sex, of course, but that's a small thing. An unwieldy, impossible, giant small thing.

(My last romantic relationship wasn't categorically romantic, per se, but it certainly also involved crime. Carload of cocaine, local constabulary, etc.)

Watson still hadn't stirred. By my count, I had three more minutes before I should begin dismembering an armchair.

Looking down at him, at his closed eyes and battered face, I began to think. I thought perhaps Watson had a brain injury. Perhaps there was a chance that he wouldn't wake up, perhaps I would be left in this basement, alone, and then killed, or even worse, rescued by my omnipotent asshole of an older brother and then left to contend with August Moriarty, Human Conscience, alone, and if so I wouldn't ever see Watson again do the thing where he almost trips over a curb when crossing the street and overcompensates by windmilling his arms, and if that was the case I would certainly never again be able to say his name, *Watson*, in the way I say it to him, with affection and also a certain kind of despair, and then I forbade myself from thinking any more about Watson at all.

The best way to help him was to disregard him for the time being. I've often found this to be the case.

The basement was sparsely furnished, and I took the likeliest-looking chair and broke off its legs by bashing it against the floor. Taking the sharpest-looking piece of wood, I tested it for length and weight and then knelt again next to Watson on the floor. I checked him over. He was still breathing, his eyelashes beginning to flutter, but he didn't respond to either my touch or my voice. With luck, in another two minutes, he would be ready to go.

I reviewed what I'd gathered about our situation.

This wasn't Hadrian and Phillipa's primary residence; no self-respecting *bon vivants* would live in the warehouse district, and the walls were cinder block under their paint. We'd been taken to some secondary property.

From the mix of preserving chemicals in the air, I assumed that we were in a facility where they falsely aged the art they produced.

Even if I broke us out through the window well, I'd still have an incapacitated Watson and an empty road in the middle of nowhere. Milo was in Thailand, and while I know he kept a tail on me most times, I wasn't sure how or how quickly he'd respond to my texts. (Before they'd taken my phone, I had sent a contingency message to an old friend, asking for aid and transportation. I would wait on that.)

Any bug Milo had placed on me had been hacked by the Moriartys, most likely after Hadrian's bodyguard regained consciousness and called his boss. That car had come at my request. (I took the next twenty-seven seconds to locate that bug—he'd had it sewn into the sleeve of my jacket—and then crushed it with my boot.)

Really, this was August's fault as much as anyone else's. If my read on him last night was correct (one untied shoe, his keys nearly falling out of his back pocket), August had immediately ditched Nathaniel and gone to Hadrian for help in finding Leander. August, like me, was never that untidy. August, even when driven to his absolute limits, would never threaten to kill a man's parents. August would assess the situation and go to his brother to attempt to broker a deal.

Milo had called it exactly. *He'll go to Hadrian,* he'd said in my ear, right before he left, *and when the dust settles, we'll know exactly how he's involved. Just bide your time.* Who, indeed, needed money and resources when one had a Moriarty with a heart three sizes too big?

I couldn't blame him, really. Families were complicated animals.

Through the thick walls, I could hear a banging sound upstairs. It had the hollow ring of someone battering a wooden door. August, most likely, in full martyr mode. I hadn't quite forgiven him either for bringing Watson to that party. *Boy problems*, I thought to myself, and when I tapped Watson's shoulder again this time, I did it rather harder than I needed to.

His eyes flew open. "Holmes," he said. It was a horrible croaking sound. His mouth was swollen; his jaw, too. And his eyes. And his nose was broken.

Looking at him, I began deciding which of Hadrian's fingers I would stomp on first.

"Don't talk," I told Watson, because I didn't want him to strain. "Listen to me. I'm about to scream. I'm telling you so that you don't physically react. There will be a body. I'll remove it. We'll haul you up the stairs, and one or the other of them up there will give us an address, and then my contact will help us arrange transportation to Prague."

This was more information than I usually gave, so I was unsurprised by Watson's apparent confusion.

"Ready?" I asked.

He blinked, which I took for assent.

I made my preparations. With my fingers, I streaked the blood on my forehead down my face. I coated my hands in it. I hefted my makeshift club, feeling something like a warrior god, and positioned myself behind the locked door.

Then I began to cry. Softly at first. I turned up the volume slowly, as one would a dial, letting the tears call up a corresponding thickness in my throat. When I began to keen, I wanted the sound to be genuine.

"Jamie," I whispered. He turned his head to look at me. I

could tell it hurt. *Not you,* I mouthed, and said his name again. "Jamie—oh *God,* Jamie. Please don't. Please—please breathe." (This part was necessary; I didn't know if anyone was standing on the other side of the door.) "You can't be dead," I said, and took my voice louder, higher in pitch. I hunched my shoulders and brought my hands up over my face. "You can't be. You *promised.* You promised me London, you— God, could you just breathe? Please, start breathing again. I'll do anything, I don't care what I am to you, I'll be anything, do anything, please, please—"

By then I was taken over by it, the grief, the fury, and I let myself dig in deeper, deeper, as far down as I could go. I'd lost him. He'd gone, not in the way I'd imagined, him slamming his way out the door in the middle of the night (we'd be in uni, or he would, as I belonged in uni as much as I belonged anywhere else, which was to say not at all, but we'd have a little flat, maybe in Baker Street, that would have a kitchen and a good library and at least one room in which no one was allowed to speak to me under any circumstances barring fire, and it would be good between us, until one night we'd be in bed and the old horror would rise up in me again, where he'd touch me and I'd well up with it, that feeling of *wrongness,* how I'd been suckered into letting anyone touch me like this again, how had I *allowed* it, who was this person and why was he *touching* me and it was a con, I'd been conned by him or myself or both of us, and I'd either break down entirely or throw him out, and in the end, in how it played out in my head, it was always me throwing him out, and I'd want him to

238

leave as much as I never wanted him to go) but we wouldn't have that, would we? We wouldn't even get to that point. He'd be taken away from me by something else, something before that, some peripheral affair I'd dragged him into, something like this—a missing uncle, a man with a taste for my blood, and he wouldn't leave on his own two feet—no, instead, we'd have a gun or a virus or a knife to the throat or this, him yelling for me to run while I stood like some dumb animal, watching a Moriarty bullyboy take him apart piece by piece, and I was useless, and then we got into shelter only for me to watch him die on the ground, and *Watson*, I heard myself say it now, aloud, *Watson, please, please,* and I broke down into some approximation of hysterical sobs.

If you're going to take on a persona, my father used to tell me, *it can't be a persona. You have to believe it.*

I was very good at what I did. I believed all of it, everything. Always.

I was so caught up in it, in fact, this private recitation of my worst fears, that when the door did swing open, I nearly forgot what to do.

But I was in position, hidden behind the door and out of view. I hefted my table leg.

"Where's the boy?" the thug said gruffly, taking two steps into the room, and it was mere luck that he didn't see me and more that he had no one behind him.

"Here," I said, and knocked him on the head. He went down with the usual speed. I took the ring of keys from his hand and rolled him into the corner. Luckily he was not the man who'd roughed up Watson, or I would've struck him again.

"Mmph," Watson was saying, and when I returned to his side it was clear that he was only semiconscious. It took some coaxing, but I managed to get him to his feet, propping him up against my shoulder. He's largely muscle, which makes him quite heavy, and while this was something I had of course noticed (and yes, appreciated, I am in fact a heterosexual human girl), I didn't like having to haul him out the door. He supported some of his own weight, but not nearly enough.

The hallway was empty, as I knew it would be, and there was a set of stairs on either end. I stood there listening, aware that Watson was bleeding on me while I in turn bled onto the carpet. While I calculated the odds of either staircase being the more direct route to our destination, I thought also about the state of my boots, which Lena had coaxed me into buying on something called a flash sale site, an experience I found traumatic enough to never want to do it again. A timer ticked down, telling me how long I had to keep these hypothetical boots while I typed in my bank information, and it made me think of all the false scarcity we had in our lives, *one shoe left! act now!, one more day for this sale!*, and the way the boy leaning on my shoulder was coughing now, low in the throat, was ringing an awful bell somewhere in my head, scarcity and plenty, boom and bust, this being the only time in my life that I'd ever have this and then it would be over, done, never—

But that was the undercurrent to my thinking. The rest of me, as always, knew what to do. The west hallway. We would take the stairs one at a time.

I had been waiting since last night for the Moriartys to make their move. Here we were.

Review your facts, my father said, *before you build deductions on top of them.*

The facts were obvious. This is what I had deduced:

We were being kept in the basement because we were children and therefore supposedly collateral. Milo had gone away—I'm sure that last night, Hadrian had managed to weasel that fact out of his guileless little brother—and Hadrian saw his opportunity. He would make a point to his older brother Lucien that he was capable of doing what, to Hadrian's mind, Lucien could not do—that is to say, punishing me for what I'd done to baby brother August. After all, I was still alive.

This is all idiocy, of course. Lucien was doing a lovely job. My mother poisoned? My father somehow still in fine fettle? A multitude of cameras in the family home, a live-in physician, and no evidence to be found? Was I or was I not puzzling through this at least once every seven minutes? Yes, of course I was. If Lucien was interested in killing me, I would be dead, Milo or no. No, toying with me was Lucien's hobby, and one's hobby stops being a hobby once it's buried beneath an angel statue in an excruciatingly posh cemetery.

I had never worried about Lucien murdering me; I worried about Lucien murdering Watson. Think of the endless mental trauma—it would be exquisite, a masterpiece of revenge. Think of the iterations! Exhibit one, in which I am framed for Watson's murder. Exhibit two, in which I do in fact kill Watson: for example, am put into an impossible situation where

I must slit his throat or see a city explode. Exhibit three, in which I do and Lucien explodes the city anyway. Exhibits four through twenty-nine, the last of them so wretched I couldn't even consider it.

Watson leaned more heavily against my shoulder; he'd stopped moving his own legs, but his breath in my ear let me know he was still alive. We'd reached Phillipa's office. I knew it was hers because of the way in which the carpet was worn—a woman's heel had tread this, and often, a tall heel judging by the pressure points, and I'd seen her wearing stilettos at our horrid lunch. Just inside the door, her bodyguard checked the time. I could hear the snap of his phone as he locked it.

This one would be a bit more complicated.

Two and a half minutes later, I'd put the unconscious bodyguard through the window, and I had his gun trained on Phillipa Moriarty.

It wasn't particularly good to see her again. She looked much the same. Her face had a pinched, appraising look I most often associated with toddlers. "What do you want?"

We had approximately thirty seconds more before her baby brother arrived with the cavalry. The battering sound at the door had finally stopped. There was no use worrying about August—what was done was done, and anyway, I'd seen that he carried a knife in his boot.

I hoisted Watson up; his legs were beginning to go, and with an effort, he managed to straighten them. His eyelashes were fluttering. "Where is it?" I asked Phillipa.

"Where is what, exactly?"

With my other hand, I clicked the safety off my gun. "Twenty seconds. Where is the auction being held, and at what time?"

Because the halls I'd dragged Watson down, on this floor and the one below it, were filled with paintings. Paintings with quite a lot of black paint, and sad-looking young Edwardians looking at glass scarabs and their hands and microscopes and each other. This was a storage facility, but she was pleased with her wares and proud of herself, her crown jewels, these forged Hans Langenberg paintings, and what is a Moriarty if not someone who gilds their abattoir?

(Watson, when you read this, I do hope you appreciate my restraint in reserving this information until now.)

Of course they would be sold to buyers through her private network; the question was only when.

"January," she said. "The twenty-seventh. It's a pity that you aren't dead, Charlotte."

"Yes, well, we all have our crosses to bear," I said. "January is too late. You'll have one sooner."

"When?" She spat the word.

"Tomorrow."

"Why on earth should I do that?"

"Because I'll expose you. Because I'll send every last bit of information I've gathered on your operations to the government. Because, if you don't, I will have my brother hit this warehouse twenty minutes from now in a precision strike that he'll write off as a training exercise, and then, for good measure, I'll do your house. Because I'm holding a gun, you cow, and I am perfectly capable of making your death look like a suicide."

In that moment, I wasn't entirely sure I was bluffing.

"Fine," she said at length. "Where?"

I took a few steps forward. The office had concrete floors, and Watson's shoes skittered along them. "At your auction site in Prague. You still use that museum after hours? Give me the address."

She hesitated. My time was up. I could hear the feet pounding up the stairs.

Very, very carefully (as one must be in these situations), I shot out the panel of glass above her head. She screeched.

"Phillipa!" someone called below.

"You will in fact give me the address, or I'll have all of your assets frozen by the morning." I thought for a moment. "And your new orchid gardener sent on permanent vacation."

"Without your brother, you'd be toothless," she said.

"Accurate. Unfortunately for you, he's very much alive. The address. Now."

She gave it to me: it was in Prague, in Old Town, and I committed it to memory. The footsteps in the hall now. Watson moaned, low in his throat. Under his weight, I'd lost all feeling in my left shoulder.

"Return our phones," I said. She placed them on the table; I caught them both up in a hand. "Thanks. You've been a great help."

"Don't you want to know what's happened to your uncle?" she said to me. "Don't you care at all?"

I knew what had happened to Leander. I hadn't wanted to believe it. I had insisted to myself that I needed to find firm evidence. But the truth of it was I had known, bodily known—not known with my brain, and so perhaps not legitimately—but my heart had been saying it since the day we'd left Sussex. My heart! The absurdity of it.

I knew, too, that there was nothing I could do to rescue him until I could tie Lucien Moriarty to the crime. Whether or not he was guilty was beside the point.

The alternative was unthinkable.

"Tell anyone I know about this auction, tell anyone I'm coming, and I'll have you killed. No," I said, as Watson coughed, "I'll do it myself."

The door flung open behind me.

"Charlotte," August said cautiously, as the men behind him raised their guns. They both had Greystone haircuts—military, with better sideburns. Milo appreciated aesthetics.

I relaxed marginally.

"August," I said, as it's polite to greet one's friends.

"Charlotte. There's a girl on the roof. She says her name is Lena." He cleared his throat. "She says she brought the helicopter you wanted?"

eleven

IN THE BACK OF HADRIAN MORIARTY'S CAR, I HAD TEXTED
Watson some suggestions about fleeing. In the process, I'd
also discovered a number of texts from my Sherringford roommate, Lena, informing me that she had decided to do some
last-minute Christmas shopping in "a European city" and had
chosen Berlin ("Though, ew, Char, do they even have a Bar-
neys?") because she was tired of "you and Jamie dodging me.
Is it because he's still mad at Tom?"

Tom and Lena, our Sherringford roommates, were dating.
And no, Watson was not still angry at Tom, even though the
little charmless frog had spied on him throughout last semester
in exchange for cash. Tom had believed—erroneously—that
his girlfriend, the daughter of an oil tycoon, would dump him

if he didn't have the means to impress her with presents and trips and the like.

Things Lena Gupta was impressed by, in my experience with her: high-fashion jackets covered in snaps, spikes, and other metal hardware; unstudied eccentricity; things that exploded; boys who were willing to hold her bag. Things Lena had zero interest in: other people's financial backgrounds. Lena was the kind of girl that let me draw her blood for an experiment without asking a single question. Lena never asked very many questions at all. This quality, among others, made her an excellent friend.

When, outside the Moriartys' warehouse, I sent both her and my brother messages saying I might need medical assistance, Milo didn't immediately respond. Lena did. She wrote back "ok!" and a number of those smiling faces with hearts for eyes. As Watson was being pummeled, I took the few seconds needed to send her our location before I joined into the fray myself.

Lena arrived with a medevac helicopter, two nurses, a pilot, and a bug-eyed Tom with headphones on. Around her shoulders was a faux fur stole. It was beautiful. I was very happy to see her.

"We should live together again next year," I told her as we helped Watson into the cabin. August climbed in next to the pilot.

"Totally," she yelled back over the noise. "Do you think we could get a room in Carter Hall? They have private bathrooms!"

Watson was laid out on a stretcher, and though he was clearly conscious, he didn't try to speak. His jaw was swollen to the size of a grapefruit. Instead, he motioned for me to give him his phone.

Emails, he wrote, with difficulty.

"From Leander to your father? Are they on your phone?"

Yes. Read them.

I took his phone. The two nurses shooed me away. They put in IVs, shone penlights into his eyes. Tom looked over at Watson's battered face, and then buried his own face in his hands. Empathy? Delayed guilt? I raised him a quarter of a notch in my estimation.

I directed the copter to return to Greystone. There was a helipad on the roof and doctors inside the building. I wanted to avoid police involvement as much as possible, and taking Watson to a hospital in this state would certainly raise some red flags.

They would take him down to the medical bay. August would run alongside to help them through the security checkpoints. Before they left, I told the nurses to check for internal bleeding, a reminder I'm sure they appreciated.

"You're not coming?" August asked.

"No," I said. "I need three cigarettes and fifty minutes in silence. I can't have a cigarette in a hospital room, and anyway I can't think when he looks like that."

"It might be a comfort to him," he said. They were loading Watson onto a gurney.

"His comfort isn't my priority." It was number five on the

list, after all. "Give him my love, if he asks."

August blinked at me, as though I'd said something strange. I wasn't unused to that look from him. In our time together in Sussex, when he was still my tutor, he'd often do this—blink at me slowly, almost languidly, when I gave an unexpected answer to his questions. Some might have taken it as a sign of judgment. I took it to be fascination.

It never evolved past that place for him. Never into attraction, as it did for me. Still, he acted as though he had a claim on me. I wonder if he understood the nature of that claim. I was the instrument of his downfall. If he wanted to be near me, it was to ensure I didn't ruin anyone else.

"He *will* ask," August said.

"Then you'll answer. Go."

He did.

"I'll hang here," Lena said. "Don't worry, I won't talk." As usual, she understood me completely. When I looked over, she was playing Tetris on her phone.

"Charlotte," Tom said a bit awkwardly. "I—"

"No," I said. That shut him up.

I pulled a Lucky Strike from my cigarette case and lit it. Four long inhalations. My nerves lost some of their frantic hum. I missed that hum when it wasn't there, but I knew how to regain it, quickly, if I had to. I'm skilled at regulating my systems, though it's taken rather a lot of practice. Not to mention the several stints in rehab.

In the next twenty-eight minutes, I concocted, vetted, and finalized my plan. Honestly, I was pleased that August and

Watson were for the moment gone. Democratic decision-making had failed us so far, as a team (was that what we were?). Things ran more smoothly when I was their benevolent dictator.

We would go to Prague, to the art auction. I believed Phillipa when she said she'd hold it. I believed her, too, when she said she wouldn't tell anyone about our presence. She did like her orchids, after all. And these auctions were her livelihood. She would set up armed guards and hope that my goals were as childish as she believed me to be.

This wasn't to say that the auction would be safe. It wouldn't be. I simply had no doubts about our getting in.

The particulars. Something about surveillance, I thought. Something about privacy. When I'd arrived at that horrid art squat yesterday, I'd spent some time wandering through the open studios, trying to gather my thoughts. The fight I'd had with Watson had affected me more than I'd liked, and my new location wasn't very soothing.

Really, the sheer amount of blow available to me was impossible to ignore. When the second boy in ten minutes offered me a bump, I declined with enough difficulty that I was concerned I would say yes the next time.

I took myself away to a corner studio. The artist was missing, but his work was on display. It had to do with CCTV, those surveillance cameras that line both European and British street corners, and the means he'd concocted to avoid their gaze.

He had a certain display of masks I found intriguing.

I would get to that later.

The last emails, then. I spent my second cigarette reading them through.

I learned that Leander had pretended, at times, that I was his daughter. I had never pretended he was my father. Fathers were exacting and distant and cruel. Leander was none of those things. Still, I was charmed.

More importantly, my uncle doubted his theory that Nathaniel was in fact Hadrian in disguise, and I did as well. How on earth had he been teaching a class? How had he made that work? Still, if there was any truth to it, I needed to know.

I sent three texts to my brother. This time, he replied quickly. He offered resources. He approved of my plan. His final text read, *I'm sure he wishes I was his son, too.*

Well, he only said it about me, I wrote back, with some pleasure, and then I turned my phone off.

My next order of business was to confirm some minor financial details with Lena. We discussed a choice of clothing for the event, as I knew this would please her. I owed her quite a few favors at this point. We hammered out escape routes. She informed me that she'd entered my name into something called a Secret Santa back in Sherringford. The other girls on our hall were to exchange presents when we returned in January, and according to Lena, my participation was mandatory. I told her I'd contribute a book on snails. She frowned, and then shrugged in assent.

That settled, I reviewed photographs of the Moriarty family. All blond. All tall. All rather vicious looking, even August, who'd taken pains in the past to soften his appearance with that particular professorial haircut. He'd pared himself down now. That guise was gone, and what was left was spiny and sad. Watson often compared our lives to art and entertainment—*this* was like a sitcom, *that* was like a circus. If that was the case, August Moriarty had gone from living in a campus novel to playing Hamlet, Prince of Denmark. The latter was more interesting, of course, but I may have lingered over the old picture of him on the Oxford website.

Because that man—the man in the photo—was dead. He and I both knew it, and knew it was my fault. I wondered if our relationship now was a kind of shared mourning for the old August Moriarty. It's strange to grieve for your former self, and still I think it's something that any girl understands. I've shed so many skins, I hardly know what I am now—muscle, maybe, or just memory. Perhaps just the will to keep going.

When I looked up, still deep in thought, I caught Tom craning his neck to see my screen. I'm not particularly proud to say that I snarled at him.

"Char," Lena said mildly. She didn't take her eyes from her phone.

"You're disloyal," I told Tom. "You proved that with Mr. Wheatley. I swear to you that if you ever give up sensitive information again—if you ever betray Watson again—I will find a way to wear you as a hat. Stop looking at my screen."

Tom shrank back into his sweater vest.

"I'll play you in Tetris," Lena offered. He nodded shakily.

I was making quite a few threats today. It wasn't my favorite mode of operation, but it was to be expected when I was surrounded by petty criminals.

I lit my last cigarette.

Final matters. For this mission, I would need to recruit a few armed guards. Only those loyal enough to Milo that they would extend that same loyalty to me. Though I disliked working with those outside my circle—Tom, even now, was *chewing gum* as he sat across from me—I understood its necessity. I couldn't perform my role if I was preoccupied with pointing a gun. To that end, I sent one of the swarming mercenaries to find Peterson and a few others. They'd follow us to Prague.

It was settled, then. I smoked my cigarette down to its filter, coaxing my brain to slow its rapid patter. If I burned too hot for too long, I would go limp and useless—I would *sleep*—and so I had developed methods to cool myself down. Running through Latin declensions worked best. *Amo, amas, amat* was standard, if sentimental, and I did like running through the declensions for the body (*corpus* has a lovely sound), but tonight I only wanted the word for king.

Rex, regis, regi, regem, rege. I inhaled one final time. Waited a beat, then exhaled the smoke. The plurals, now, and slower. *Reges. Regum. Regibus. Reges. Regibus.* I appreciated that flip and repetition: the dative, the accusative, the ablative. It had a certain musicality. I've always loved a counterturn.

I stabbed out the cigarette. Forty-eight minutes had passed. I asked the pilot to please start up the helicopter again and kept my eyes trained on the door to the building.

"You win," Lena said.

"You know, you look cute in a flight suit," Tom was telling Lena.

Her eyes were guileless. "We need to get you one, too."

"Did yours come with Milo's chopper?"

"No," she said. "I just had it lying around."

He grinned at her. Soon, they were kissing. Noisily. I hadn't put on my protective headphones earlier, but I did now.

When the door finally opened, August and Watson came slowly through it, followed by a small number of Milo's men. Watson had an ice pack against his face. He was sporting several bandages and a limp, but I was pleased to see he still moved with his usual stubborn determination.

"Are you fit to travel?"

"Yeah," he said. I had to read his lips, with all the noise. "Nothing happened to you in that warehouse?"

"*I* happened to that warehouse."

He smiled, and then he winced in pain.

"Try not to move your face," I advised. "Do you remember what I said, about Prague?"

"About us going there?" Watson said it with some difficulty.

I nodded. The pilot was motioning for us to hurry up. He'd take us to the airport, and we'd hop on Lena's father's company jet. Commercial travel wouldn't do, not this time. We were a strange group of people, and I didn't want us to be conspicuous.

That would come later.

"What's the plan, Holmes?"

The stirring in my blood when he asked me that question. Nothing in the world could replace it.

"Well," I told him, "I have a mask for you to wear."

I'D HEARD IT SAID BEFORE THAT PRAGUE WAS A FAIRY-TALE city. Watson repeated it now as we made our slow progression in from the airport. Steepled roofs, pastel buildings, cobbled roads and switchbacks. An astronomical clock that stood stories high in a public square. I'd been there once before with Milo when we were children. Our Aunt Araminta had decided we needed "culturing." I think she may have mistaken us for bacteria.

"It *is* a fairy-tale city," Watson insisted. "Look at those doors." Our cab was descending a bumpy brick road, and every few feet we passed one of them. Medieval-looking metal doors, reinforced with spiny rows of hammered-in nails. "I wonder what's behind them."

"On this street? Souvenir shops." I disliked it when the term "fairy-tale" was bandied about. Most often it was used to mean "whimsical." This is inaccurate. In fairy tales, the forest swallows you up like a dinner. Your parents wrap you in a cloak and set you loose in the dark. Everything happens in threes, and only the oldest child survives. As a younger sister, I particularly resented that last implication.

"We can buy you a commemorative shot glass, if you'd like," I told him.

He rolled his eyes, but I could tell he was pleased. "Where are we staying?"

"Somewhere far away from all this madness. Someplace sensible."

"Define sensible." The nurses had stuffed him with enough painkillers that he was able to talk without pain. He was, it seemed, taking advantage of that fact.

"My brother found us a bedsit flat near the auction house."

"A bedsit."

"It was quite expensive."

"Holmes, we'll be on top of each other."

"It doesn't have any windows, either, so it's entirely safe."

"No windows?" He flung an arm toward the window for emphasis. "The city's all lit up like a storybook. Tomorrow is Christmas Eve. We're in *Prague*. And you rented us a studio apartment without windows?"

I frowned. "I think it was originally a maintenance closet."

It was only the two of us in this car; Lena and Tom had gone on ahead to their hotel. Though we'd flown in together, we'd arrive at the auction separately. For his part, August said he'd find his own place to sleep. He was aware that Watson and I had fought, and I imagine he was giving us the chance to kiss and make up.

"I hate you," Watson said to me, emphatically. "What is it with you and closets?"

"They're often quite clean. And if they aren't, one can usually find cleaning supplies in them."

"Holmes—"

"Actually, I booked us a room in an Art Deco hotel," I said, and moments later our car pulled into its circle drive. I'd always prided myself on my timing.

"Hats on," I said, handing him his, "and sunglasses. Let them think we're film stars." I wanted no chance of our being seen.

"You're awful," he said, laughing. "I can't believe you made me think—"

"You just had yourself beaten unconscious. I thought we might as well get you a comfortable bed." Watson had laughed. His eyes had crinkled at the corners. Hours ago I thought he might have been dead. "There's also a view of the river," I said, and like a miracle, he laughed again.

Oftentimes, I withhold information from Watson for this very reason. He resents this, I think. My "magic tricks." I don't know if he's understood yet who the reveals are really for.

Inside, the desk clerk raised an eyebrow at Watson's battered face. "Lawn-mowing accident," I told her, and she averted her eyes.

"Wouldn't there be blades if it'd been a lawn-mowing accident?" he asked in the elevator. "Wouldn't I be, like, sliced open?"

"It could have been a riding mower. You could have fallen off it."

"Yes," he said. "Please continue stripping my heroic act of all its heroics."

"You did throw him to the ground," I allowed. "Before he knocked you out, of course."

The doors on our hall were all appropriately medieval. Hammered nails, stained glass, that sort of thing. When we found ours, Watson smiled to himself, and let us in.

We talked that night. It wasn't so different from these sorts of talks when we'd had them before—*I want this,* and *What you want isn't possible,* and *What's left for us, then, to be to each other?* I always felt as though he wanted us to reach a solution, as though he and I were a mathematical proof that simply needed to be balanced. For a very long time, I thought he considered *me* to be the problem, and then I worried he thought that I was the solution. I'm neither. I'm a teenage girl. He is my boy best friend. We would be everything to each other until we couldn't. The room had two beds, but we slept on opposite sides of the same one, and if I woke in the middle of the night in his arms, I can tell you that he slept through it.

He slept through it, too, when I disentangled myself from him and went to sit alone on the bathroom floor until the screaming in my head subsided. *I am in control,* I reminded myself. *I am in control.* I took fourteen breaths. I thought about the kit I had hidden away in my bag for emergencies, and then I forced myself to stop thinking about it. *I am in control of this,* I repeated, and felt better, and then I got back into Watson's bed.

I had never wanted him to see me vulnerable. But what if showing vulnerability was a decision I myself made?

"Wake up."

He stirred the smallest amount.

"Wake up," I said again. "I need you to answer a question."

This time, he sat up. His face was a mottled wreck. Eyes blackened, lips cut and bruised. Empirically, I knew that he needed sleep to heal, and if this wasn't so important, I would never have woken him up. I wasn't my great-great-great-grandfather. There was no pleasure to be had in ordering him into danger, in waking him before dawn.

I preferred to watch Jamie Watson sleep, because if he slept and I was watching, he was safe. I would rather Watson be at home, doing research and reading novels, because one prefers to have their heart locked safely in their chest. When I loved August Moriarty, it was that I recognized myself in him and saw that self redeemed. He and I were so alike in how we were raised, in how we saw the world, and he culled what he needed from that childhood and he resisted the rest with his whole self. He thought of others first. He read indiscriminately, traveled the world, listened to me when I spoke as though I wasn't an experiment or a wind-up doll, but a person, a complete one, with the contradictions that all people had. I wanted to *be* him, me, when I never wanted to be anyone else. If I wanted to be with him, it was because of that.

And Watson? If August was my counterpoint, my mirror, Jamie was the only escape from myself I'd ever found. When I was beside him, I understood who I was. I spoke to him, and I liked the words I said. I spoke to him, and the words he said back surprised me. Sharpened me. If August reflected me, Jamie showed me myself made better. He was loyal and kind, stalwart, like the knights from the old tales, and yes, he was handsome, even with a bruised face and a furrowed brow, miles away from the place we met or from the places we called home.

"What is it?" His voice was thick with sleep.

"Do you want this?" I asked him. I'd asked it once before, when I wanted to gauge how much distance I'd have to put between us if he did.

"I think so," he said. "Only—do you?"

I took off my clothes. I'd been wearing pajamas, so it wasn't a particularly slow reveal, or a seductive one. He watched me with shadowed eyes. When I reached for the hem of his shirt, he stopped me. *I'll do it,* his face said, and with a grimace, he lifted it over his head. His torso was a wreck, battered purples and reds, and from the way he moved his shoulders, like an old, tired boxer, it was clear that the painkillers he'd been given had worn off in the night.

"Do you want this?" he asked me, with effort.

"I do," I said, and hated my voice for breaking. "Can we—can we get under the blankets?"

I lay down first, and he did next, gingerly, pulling the blankets over our heads like we were children. I had the insane urge to laugh, not because he was in pain but because I was, too. I hadn't known my own motives until then. I was always so good with logic, causality. *If, then. If, then.*

If we were both broken. Then.

After what would happen in the next few days, after I made the decisions I would have to make to get Leander back, to save my family from themselves—there was a chance that he'd never want anything to do with me. Otherwise, maybe, I would have waited for this. A few more months. Another year. See if I was able to heal any further. But I couldn't wait.

And the fact of it was that I wanted him.

With the back of his hand, he traced the line of my jaw, then down my neck, and I stiffened when his fingers touched my collarbone. His skin was warm. His breath was hot. He had far more experience than me, and I thought, again, as I always did, of the last time anyone touched me this way, Dobson's thick fingers unbuttoning my uniform blouse, and I'd wanted to say something, anything, but I'd taken enough opiates that the wires had been reconnected wrong, my hands too heavy, and—

Watson stopped. He watched me, my face, and when I nodded, he gathered me up in his arms and kissed me, slowly, and we talked through it until it was over.

I suppose I could recite the literal progression of events, but I find that I have some small reserves of modesty. We didn't have protection; we didn't have sex. We did other things. *Dicere quae puduit, scribere jussit amor*—I may, for some time, think about his beautiful arms. They are lovely, like those of a statue I once saw when I was a girl, in a museum, somewhere, back when I hadn't yet cried in my best friend's bed, in a hotel in Prague at dawn.

WHEN WE WOKE, WE DRESSED QUICKLY, AS WE HAD THINGS to do.

We spent the next day holed up, fine-tuning my plan. That is to say, I told Watson the particulars and coached him on his dialogue, until he rewrote it all in a fit of pique. The two of us had never worked in tandem like this before, not purposely. It turned out we were rather good at it.

This took us through to lunch. I had Peterson bring the USB drive and our disguises and our props. At a certain point, Watson demanded a sandwich. I'd forgotten how often he ate. I made him ring room service for it and then insisted he answer the door with his mask on. It went as planned: the delivery boy ran screaming down the hall.

We didn't talk about kissing, or about getting back into bed. We played poker. He lost. We played euchre, and he lost, and he lost again in gin rummy, and then he beat me in old maid, and then it was time for us to go.

"Do you have the USB drive?" he asked, patting his pockets.

"Of course," I said. "Do you remember what we're doing?"

"'As Michel Foucault says in *Discipline and Punish*—'"

"Excellent." I paused. "Try to enjoy this. Today. It'll be fun, I think, for you."

Until it wasn't fun. Until he never wanted to look at me again.

"You know," he said, rubbing his eyes through the holes in his mask, "we might actually pull this one off."

I don't know why he sounded so surprised. It might be messy, awful, destructive, might end with a body count and my best friend disavowing me, but I do always pull it off in the end.

twelve

"Of course we're on the list!"

The clerk frowned down at his clipboard. "I'm so sorry, Miss—"

Charlotte Holmes ran a hand through her short black hair. The Coke-bottle glasses sitting on her nose made her eyes into huge, ridiculous saucers. "Don't *tell* me you don't see Elmira Davenport. How *dare* you. Check it again." She kept her arms bent at the elbow, palms up, and when she turned to me, she pivoted at the waist like a toy. "I can't even believe that we're being subjected to the hegemony of lists! Lists! I am an *artist*. You are making me perform myself! This is unacceptable!"

"Unacceptable," I intoned.

"I still don't see you," the man said apologetically.

"Fetch Phillipa then. There's surely been a misunderstanding." A line had grown behind us—women in fancy dresses, men in suits and long coats, all shivering against the cold. Holmes clearly wasn't budging. The line behind us grumbled. "Go on! Fetch!"

He scampered off into the auction house and returned with the piggish blond Moriarty in tow. If I squinted, I could remember seeing her in that warehouse in Berlin. I couldn't remember much from that night, to be honest. The carpet. Holmes tapping my cheek. The vicious beating of the helicopter blades. The rest was gone. For someone who played contact sports, I didn't have a very sturdy constitution.

Phillipa stopped short when she saw it was the two of us. "*Phillipa*," Holmes said. "This is a party! Quite a party! We are so excited, Kincaid and I. Such short notice for you to pull this off! Yes, very good."

"Very good," I intoned.

"Let them in," Phillipa said at length. I was sure she recognized us; it wasn't important if she did. She'd known that we'd be there.

"But madam," the clerk whispered, "they're not conforming to the dress code. I don't even know what to say about that mask—"

With a shrug, Phillipa escaped to the party. The clerk wasn't so lucky.

"Kincaid!" Holmes grinned toothily at me. "Kincaid does not wish to be seen by the *panopticon*." With her arms, she made a wild arc. "His mask pixelates his face, yes? The cameras on the street, the cameras in here—they cannot see him! He is the unsurveilled territory! This is his work—to disappear!"

"I am an artist," I intoned. "I am my own work."

She dropped her voice to a whisper. "And I wear these skinny jeans because I refuse to pretend to a class I am not."

"She is not of that class."

"I am not of the petticoat class! I am Elmira Davenport!"

"Is that—is that Elmira Davenport? Let her in!" It was the man behind us. "She does video installation. Very strange. Very compelling."

The line began to buzz. "Yes, I think I've heard of her," I heard someone say. "Didn't she paint herself purple on top of the Eiffel Tower?"

"Yes!" Like magic, Holmes produced a fistful of business cards from her pocket, and began passing them out to the crowd.

"Is your work up for auction, dear?" the man's wife asked, touching my shoulder.

"It is up for auction," I intoned.

"You'll have to wait for the very end," Holmes said with a wink, "when the best always comes," and dragged me in by the wrist, past the protesting clerk, past the small throng of men in sport coats and all the way down the end, to the lofted center hall of the museum.

A stage had been set up, with an auctioneer's podium. Seats were arranged in two cascading wings. From the looks of it, Hadrian and Phillipa's art auctions attracted a good hundred people, and most of them had managed to come out, even with such short notice.

"I've heard they have some incredible find they're auctioning off," the man next to us was saying. "It isn't even in the catalog."

His friend replied, too quiet to hear.

"No," he said. "They're on the up-and-up. These two scout the globe for a living; of course they're bringing home fabulous work that was thought to be lost. Doesn't mean it's stolen. Didn't you see Hadrian on *Art World Today*? He addressed this very subject!"

Holmes and I toured the room. She shook hands while I glowered into the distance. Everyone, it seemed, had heard of us from somewhere they couldn't really remember. Liars, all of them. It was incredible the lengths people would go to to feel like they were in the know.

As we made the rounds, we kept hearing that same echoed uncertainty about the legitimacy of Hadrian and Phillipa's catalog. Someone would say, *But all of these paintings were presumed lost,* and someone else would reassure them, too loudly, *So they must be very good at finding them.* The whole room stank of desperation, and Holmes flitted through it, tossing her bristly wig and ranting on about *art* and *the intellect* and *the soul.* She sounded like Nathaniel Ziegler on steroids, which I think was probably the point.

My throat was going dry. I still wasn't feeling like myself—to be honest, with every hour, I discovered a new part of me that hurt—and I pulled Holmes away so that I could regroup. "Are you enjoying yourself?" I asked her.

"Immensely."

"Do you see Peterson and his squad?"

"He was in line behind us outside. You didn't recognize the old man? The one who'd heard of Elmira? Or did you think I'd built a fabulous art world reputation in the last ninety minutes?"

I snorted. "That was Peterson?"

"The rest of his squad is coming. And Tom and Lena have seats in the front row. Look for the girl in fur."

"Tell me it isn't, like, actual fur."

Holmes adjusted her poncho. "Lena isn't above killing for what she wants."

We surveyed the room, shoulder to shoulder. I spotted August across the room, leaning indolently against the stage, and yanked my gaze away. I didn't want to call attention to him. "Honestly, I'm feeling pretty good about this. I'd be feeling even better if I didn't look like the Elephant Man."

"It was either that, or we covered your bruises in white stage makeup and brought you along as my mime."

I reached under my rubber mask to touch my neck. One of my "abrasions," as the nurse called them, had started to bleed again. Not that anyone would be able to tell. Only my eyes and mouth were showing. The rest of my face, and my neck down to the collarbone, was covered in a series of exaggerated pixilations, the kind of scrambling they did to naked photos when they showed them on cable TV. I was a walking censor bar.

Cameras wouldn't be able to make heads or tails of me—or that was the idea that I'd explain to anyone who asked.

"Your partner in mime?"

"Very high concept," Holmes said, mimicking Kincaid's Frankenstein's-monster delivery. "Very cutting edge."

A group of old women tottered by to claim their paddles from the auctioneer. All were dressed to the nines; one fiddled with the jeweled reindeer pin on her hat. I hadn't seen Hadrian at all yet—I was dreading that—but Phillipa was standing next to the auctioneer, smiling like a wind-up doll.

"Who *are* all these people? This is a last-minute thing on Christmas Eve. Shouldn't they be home with their families?"

Holmes gave me a pointed look. "Marketing, Watson. A small auction of select rare works from their collection? A string quartet playing Handel? Snacks? The architecturally lauded modern art museum rented out for the evening? Of course they've all come out. It smacks of exclusivity. Privilege."

"I'm still stuck on the part where you used the word 'snacks' in your argument."

"Clearly," she said, "they're hors d'oeuvres. I just didn't know if you were familiar with the term. You don't speak French, do you?"

Since last night, something between us had eased. It was more like we'd both been pulling desperately at opposite ends of the same rope, and now we'd walked to the middle to fold it up together. Last night had been . . . honestly, I wasn't even sure if it had really happened. In the middle of the night, in a city like Prague, the girl that I loved slipped into my bed. I couldn't find a way to describe it without using simple, stupid terms. It had been difficult. She was beautiful. We'd both been frustrated. She'd said my name. I never wanted to make her cry again. All I knew was that I didn't want us to fight anymore. I didn't want to try to kiss her, either. Not until I understood it—us—better. I wanted to exist in this stasis as long as we could, this place where we were tentatively getting along.

The thing was, since it was the two of us, our not-fighting looked a lot like . . . fighting.

"I took French," I reminded her. "I've taken French for years. You met me outside of French class almost every day this fall."

"I did not. Surely I'd remember that."

"You did. You *know* you did, too. You're just being difficult."

"I have an impeccable memory, Watson. Say something to me in French."

"No."

"You can't say anything to me in French. A phrase? A word?"

"I can, but I won't."

"See? My point. You can't say a word—"

"Hors d'oeuvres," I said, and snagged a pair of blintzes from a passing waiter's tray. "Do you want one?"

Beneath the wig, beneath the Coke-bottle glasses, despite every fight we'd had in the past few weeks and the ridiculous plastic mask I wore, Charlotte Holmes was looking at me like I was her violin.

It was a look she hadn't given me at all last night, and I didn't know what that meant.

"'Give my love to Watson,'" I said softly.

Her eyes didn't change. "August told you that?"

He had, as he'd muscled me through the roof access door and down to Milo's personal infirmary. I'd been laid out on an uncomfortable hospital bed—why did it always end with me in a hospital bed?—and was asked if I remembered the past few hours, where I'd been. I did. I told her to run, I told August, who put a hand on my shoulder.

She's in the helicopter. She said to give you her love. When he said it, he looked sad, and not for himself.

It took me a second to process it. *The first part doesn't make sense,* I said, *but the second is just crazy.*

He's fine, August advised the nurses. *Get him some acetaminophen and an ice pack.*

"He did tell me," I said. "Is that okay?"

She brushed her hand against mine. "It's okay," she said as the hum of voices around us quieted down. "They're taking their places. I need to go talk to the auctioneer. Find August, will you? And Tom and—oh."

Never let it be said that Lena couldn't make an entrance.

She strolled in without even looking up from her crystal-encrusted iPhone. The clerk scurried to hold the door open for her, like she was a queen. Around her shoulders, she wore a fur coat like a cape, and underneath, a top that barely covered her chest. It tied around itself, leaving a good five inches of skin bare above her painted-on leather pants. Her black hair had been dip-dyed blue and gold, and when she finally glanced up at the room, she rolled her eyes and reached out a hand for her bag.

Which was when I noticed the three bodyguards behind her. Greystone mercs in disguise. They hustled her up to her seat in the front of the room, leaving a space beside her for Tom, who, with his suit, sweaty face, and handful of auction paddles, looked exactly like a pop star's put-upon assistant.

This afternoon, Milo's techs had created a constellation of websites and Snapchats and false news references and lyric videos for YouTube for Serena, the rising EDM star. And here she was, in the flesh, looking to build the art collection in her Laurel Canyon home. She'd requested an invitation before dinner, one that the Moriartys quickly granted. Phillipa may have known Holmes and I would be here in disguise, but we wanted her to think that Serena was the real deal.

Phillipa rushed over to say hello to the pop star, Hadrian at her side. It had to be Hadrian; he was blond and tall, but moved with the hunched-over jerkiness of a crab. I watched him for a moment—Hadrian in his natural form. I looked for signs of Nathaniel. Hadrian's nose was longer. His eyebrows thinner and higher up on his forehead. All Nathaniel's warmth and openness wasn't there.

Since the Moriartys were distracted, Holmes seized the opportunity to talk to the auctioneer, slipping something small into his pocket. She took her seat again before they saw her.

A hush fell over the room. We were about to begin. A pair of armed guards took their position to either side of the stage—Moriarty men, there to stop any trouble before it began.

"Ladies and gentlemen," Hadrian cried, rushing up the stairs to the stage. His voice had the same timbre as Nathaniel's, though it sounded less . . . educated, somehow. Rougher. "Thank you so much for spending your Christmas Eve with us. We love seeing you all at our private auctions—your loyalty means ever so much. We extend these invitations selectively, and we appreciate your discretion. That said, since ours is a family affair, we understand yours is as well. This will be a far briefer showing than usual, so we can get you all back to your homes for mince pies and fruitcake."

Fruitcake? No wonder the Moriartys were all so miserable, if that was their idea of Christmas.

"Let's begin," he said, and when he stepped off the stage, he was immediately pulled aside by August Moriarty.

Things were in motion.

The auctioneer began the proceedings with a painting by Hans Langenberg. It was a clear challenge. A way to feel out our motivations. As it was announced, Phillipa craned her neck to stare at Holmes, who shrugged back at her with a smile.

"A work from the same era as *The Last of August*," the auctioneer said. A screen behind the painting listed "facts" about the piece. "Notice the brushwork. The use of ecru, here in the corners. The faces of the two boys are turned from the viewer's eyes, but we can tell, even at this angle, that the artist has chosen not to detail their features. But the girl between them has those striking brows and red mouth. See the wild expression on her face, that the painter has suggested with only a few lines? The map in her hand? This is an exquisite work. We'll open bidding at one hundred thousand."

There was a small flurry of discussion, and paddles began going up in the air: numbers 103, 282, 78. In the front row, Tom leaned in to whisper a question in Lena's ear. She nodded without looking up from her phone. Eagerly, he stuck their paddle, 505, in the air. The price went up. 505 went up, too, every time, and soon the other numbers, one by one, began to drop out of the running.

I should have been paying attention to the auction, not to August and Hadrian off to the side, their heads together, arguing in fierce whispers. Twice, Hadrian turned to look at me over his shoulder and was wrenched back by his brother. We'd never spoken, not while he wasn't in disguise, and so the intense hatred in his eyes startled me. It looked so personal.

I'd been having fun until that moment—a tense sort of fun, but fun all the same. It was shocking to me, that this was fun at all, that this was even happening to me—that I was about to take down some elite art auction in the Czech Republic on Christmas Eve. What jerked me back down was the realization that Hadrian clearly wanted to dismember me. I didn't want to imagine how he felt about Charlotte Holmes.

Right then, glaring at me, he didn't look a thing like Nathaniel. For the millionth time, I wondered if Leander was wrong.

I wondered if Leander was still alive.

Slowly, I moved closer until I could hear the edges of their conversation.

August was trying to refocus his brother's attention. "Look at me," he hissed. "If you're claiming all this madness is about me, about my 'death,' then you'll bloody well look at *me* when we're talking."

"Nine hundred thousand," the auctioneer was calling. Lena tapped Tom's shoulder, and he raised paddle 505 again. On the stage, Phillipa's greedy smile grew. "Sold," he crowed, "to 505! Our next work is also by Hans Langenberg. . . ."

The Moriartys were mocking us. One by one, they hauled up their faked Langenberg paintings, and auctioned them off for hundreds of thousands of dollars. Even Hadrian, still in the throes of his conversation with August, kept turning to grin at his sister. The guards standing with semiautomatics to the sides of the stage would keep Holmes and me from making any obvious move on their life. If we tried, we'd forfeit our own.

Three paintings. Five paintings. Six. The auctions went up, and Lena, in her disguise, won them. Every single time. The Moriartys would have confirmed her banking information ahead of time when they'd accepted her request to join. They felt certain about these sales. About that money.

Underneath my mask, I was starting to sweat. I knew we were nearing the end.

"And *The Thought of a Pocketwatch* goes to number 505," the auctioneer said as the painting was hauled off the stage. The crowd began to grumble amongst themselves. I couldn't blame them. They were, for the most part, older, conservative art aficionados who came out on Christmas Eve in pursuit of new work, only to be outbid by a teenage pop star who wouldn't stop cracking her gum.

"That's the last one," I heard Hadrian say to August. He put a hand on his brother's shoulder. "I'll wish them all goodnight, and then we can finish our conversation."

August smiled thinly. "Yes," he said. "Do."

Before Hadrian could take more than a step, the auctioneer cleared his throat. "We have a final piece to present, one that isn't in your catalogs."

The room fell silent. Phillipa started toward the auctioneer, her smile frozen on her face.

Holmes beat both of them to the punch. "Ah, yes!" she said, standing from her seating in the back of the room, stretching her arms out to her sides. "Yes, I am very excited for this!"

"It's Elmira Davenport," Peterson said in a loud whisper. "I wonder if it's one of her early pieces!"

The man next to him nodded sagely. "Davenport really is the future of video art."

"I've always said so," said his wife.

She must've sensed that she was losing control of the situation, because Phillipa reached out and grabbed the auctioneer by the arm, hard. "Miss Davenport," she said, in a carrying voice. "Surely we can fit your work into our next showing—"

"Let her show it now!" called Peterson.

"Yes!" another voice called. "None of us are taking home anything! Give us a chance!"

Tom turned to Lena and said loudly, "You're not interested in video art, are you?"

"I hate it," she said in a dull voice.

"She hates it!" someone repeated, and then the room began to buzz. The museum's high walls of the room gathered their voices and looped it on itself; it sounded almost like a swarm of bees was descending from the ceiling. On the stage, Phillipa bit her lip so hard it turned white. August held Hadrian in place with a firm hand, and while the armed guards looked across the room at each other—I was watching—they made no movement toward their weapons.

Into that anticipation, Holmes and I climbed up onto the stage.

The auctioneer backed away from the podium, letting Holmes step up in his place. "Hello, all! Yes, this is Elmira Davenport. That is my name. That said, I feel that you should call me whatever it is that you want to call me. Identity is so stifling! It is a construct!"

"A pernicious construct," I intoned.

"Identity is slippery. We go by many names! Our many selves have different wants! Today, I am in Prague, away from my family on a day meant to be with family—and am I family without them?"

"She is not."

"I am not!"

"She is not family without family," I intoned.

"Today I am here by chance. I heard about this auction and decided, yes, I will show you a piece to illustrate who I am. Who you are. Who *we all are*, underneath our wrappings. Kincaid beside me, he hides from the cameras! He hides his face from your faces! What is a face?"

She paused there, looking distantly over the audience's heads. They stared up at her, enraptured, or pretending to be.

"Ah," she said with the solemnity of a sage. "No one knows what a face is. I have my theories. A face produces voice. A voice carries sound. In that sound, we find ourselves *prisoners*. Now I show you a piece that says, *faces. Family. Identity. Prisoners!* All these things."

I nodded. "This is a piece about all these things."

The screen behind the easel went dark. Moments later, the whole echoing room followed. There was a shuffling. Some gasps. On the stage, a small scuffle, and the moments stretched into each other until the black-and-white video finally began to play.

It was surveillance footage. The outside of a warehouse, as seen from above. A giant man wiped off his hands on his pants. He straightened, stared into the distance. Then he bent and, with a visible heaved breath, hoisted the limp body lying at his feet up and over his shoulder.

It was my body, but the audience didn't need to know that. My identity wasn't important to this story.

Static crackled from invisible speakers, set somewhere behind the stage. From them, a girl's voice threaded out, broken sounding, desperate. "What exactly do you hope to accomplish here?" she asked. "You can't hope to hold us for more than a few hours."

The man dipped his head. "I'm sorry," he said. "Where should I put the boy?"

"Be careful with him," the girl said, stepping into frame. I wondered what the audience made of her—she was slight, swaying in her boots, in her tiny dress. "Please. He's my— Be careful."

At that, the giant said something inaudible, and carried the body away.

It was just the girl in the frame now. She wrapped her arms around herself. "I suppose you'll want our phones," she said.

A pause, where a response should be. The girl was speaking to someone who wasn't in the picture.

"I'm just trying to help you to be thorough," she said, and pulled hers out of her bra, dangling it from her fingers. "Here, you can have it."

(In the audience, a young man's reedy voice: "Don't you love the composition of this shot?" Holmes shifted her weight next to me.)

"No. I won't bring it to you," the girl said. "What makes you think I'll be a party to my own destruction?"

"Past events have suggested it," the voice responded, barely audible. A woman's voice, but the speaker was still off-screen. "I'm happy to help you in any way I can. You're welcome to try to run, if you want. See how far you can get. Go on, we can time you."

"You must be waiting for more guards," the girl said. "You have a pistol in your pocket, but you're too chickenshit to try to threaten me with it, even though I'm unarmed."

An incomprehensible reply.

The girl took a step forward, then another. "Why are you doing this?"

"Stop moving," the voice said.

"No!" she cried. "Where are you *taking* him?"

"Are you blind? He's in the warehouse. Where you'll be. We have business to discuss—" You could see her now, the back of her black-and-white head, blond and curled.

"Is this worth it? You abduct my uncle, lock him away God knows where, all so that you can continue selling your forged paintings?" (A gasp from the audience, a series of coughs.) "How much are you making off of them? Is it enough blood money for you? Where is my uncle? He'll blow this up! He's a detective! We'll take this to the media! I swear it!"

She gave her speech clearly. She enunciated her consonants. She stated facts that were pure exposition, and she said each word with a clarity of emotion that was meant for a Broadway production. I turned to her—the *now* her, the one beside me—and grinned, even though she couldn't see it under my mask. Holmes, my patron saint of trapdoors and failsafes, of always remembering to pour the foundation so that, later, if you needed to, you could build a brilliant house on top.

It was her show, after all.

In the video, Phillipa took a staggering step forward, and when she turned her head, her face was clearly visible. "You should ask *yourself* where your uncle is," she said, like some leering villain, and the audience began to stir. Someone stood and said, "Is this fake? Was this staged?" The rustle of chairs pushed back, paddles dropped to the floor.

The video kept rolling. "Do you think you're such a genius?" Phillipa said. "What if I told you he was right under your nose the whole time?"

"Oh God," past-Holmes said, with a gasp loud enough to be picked up by the bug in her coat. That was how she'd gotten the audio, she'd told me; the Moriartys had hacked into the bug in her shoe, the one that Milo had put there to track her movements. She'd had one of the Greystone techs break into the Moriarty servers to look for audio she could use for her "installation." *The security footage was their own,* she'd said. *We found it when we broke in to get the recording. They'll kick themselves over that one.* "How could you? How—"

"Finally," Phillipa said, as guards swarmed in to grab the girl and frog-march her out of the frame. "Took you long enough."

The sound of a door slamming, then the video cut off. A low-pitched static snuffle.

Silence.

When the lights came back up, three things happened in quick succession.

One: The audience of grandmothers and grandfathers and genteel sons and daughters rioted. There wasn't any other word for it. A man picked up his chair and threw it at the stage, and then the woman beside him followed, and then another, another, like children throwing bricks at a glass window to see it shatter. The elderly women I'd seen walk by earlier, the ones with the jeweled reindeer pins and fancy Christmas hats, turned like synchronized dancers to run for the door. The clerk held it open. I had to give him credit—he wore the same impassive expression he did when the night began.

Two: The Greystone guard who had been holding Phillipa Moriarty to the side of the stage, one hand over her mouth, was sent staggering backward when she threw an elbow into his face. I ran to help the guard up, who waved me off— Phillipa was running, arms pumping, toward the winding marble stairs to the museum proper. The sign above her head said SCULPTURE WING. I pulled off my plastic mask and made to follow her. Tom and Lena and the rest of the Greystone guards followed suit. I made it off the stage and three more feet when I skidded to a stop, but they sprinted on ahead, tearing up the stairs, shouting her name.

Three: Hadrian Moriarty ripped off Charlotte Holmes's wig and glasses and put a gun to her head.

"Go help my sister," he told his own guards, and they took off up the stairs. "As for you, girl," he said, "you wanted to see your uncle? I'll send you there, then," and he pushed the mouth of the gun hard into her temple. Holmes's face went white. She didn't flinch, didn't make a sound. Only her colorless eyes moved, darting back and forth like she was reading lines from a book I couldn't see.

"You know as well as I do that Leander is alive," August said, stalking out from the shadows. A knife glittered in one fist. "So please, stop making canned threats and be a *person*, Hadrian."

"He's alive?" I asked August, not taking my eyes from Hadrian. "You're sure of it."

"I'm sure of it. Factually sure."

"Which means you have to be involved," I said. Hadrian's gun still had the safety on. His other hand was wrapped around her throat. "How?"

"I'm dead, Jamie—"

"Will you stop acting like you're the goddamn star of a goddamn tragedy, and *answer my question.*"

August took a slow step toward his brother. "This summer, Hadrian saw me at a punk show here in Berlin. I was in deep cover. It was the first time I'd gone out alone since—since everything happened." He jerked his head. "Word got back to my brother, but I only found out that night. I met up with Nathaniel. Or I guess I should say, with Hadrian."

"You're posing as a *teacher*," I said to Hadrian. It came out as a sneer. "You're disgusting."

At that, he ground the gun into Holmes's head. I clenched my fists. "You don't know a single blessed thing about me, *Simon.*"

"So August helped you."

While Hadrian was preoccupied with me, his brother had moved even closer. "No. Of course not. I found out that Nathaniel had been letting my brother pose as him for his meetings with Leander. For those nights at the underground pool, where Hadrian trolls for new art. Nathaniel Ziegler is a real person. He teaches during the day, has friends, an apartment in a crappy part of the city. But he's been letting my brother moonlight as him. Apparently Milo's intelligence made that possible. That, and my brother's money."

"And I'm sure that made it easier to convince Nathaniel to recruit his students to forge paintings for him to sell."

"All but the Langenbergs. Those Hadrian did himself."

"I'm sure you're so proud," I spat.

"Yes, well." He gripped his knife. "As usual, I'm thrilled to be part of my family."

"And you knew Leander was alive. Do you know where he is?"

August hesitated. "No," he said.

"This is all beautiful, really," Hadrian said calmly, "but I'd like to get on with it." At that, Holmes shut her eyes. Her mouth moved, almost like she was counting.

"What do you want?" I asked him.

"It's simple." He cocked the safety off his pistol. "I want her dead. She spent the night wrecking my livelihood, my reputation. My reputation is *everything*. Did you see how much she was enjoying herself? Yesterday, she put my bodyguard in the hospital. She crushed his windpipe. She *killed* you, August. You have no future. You have *nothing*, now. She's a child that thinks she can play with adults, and she needs to understand that this isn't a game." He dug his fingers into the flesh of her throat, and Holmes gagged. "Lucien and I might disagree on our methods, but our goal is the same. We want her punished. My brother wants to draw this out. I want it over. Now."

I had no weapon. No plan. I wanted Milo then, desperately—where was he? Why was he in Thailand? Since when had we gone from solving the case ourselves, from our dorm room, to relying on his resources? We were in Europe. In *Europe*, and alone. How had this happened? And August, gripping that blade like he knew how to use it—that was a lie, too. Even now, he held it up in front of him like it was a candle, or a prayer. So much for geniuses. So much for getting out of this alive.

August put the knife to his own throat.

"Hadrian," he said calmly. "Drop the gun."

His brother stared back at him. They looked so much alike—the nose, the square jaw. A pair of mirrors on either side of a black-haired girl. Only the eyes were different. August's were suffused with such bitter melancholy that, looking at him now, I didn't doubt his intentions.

"Stop pretending," Hadrian said, "that you care about what happens to her. What are you even doing?"

With a steady hand, August pressed the knife harder into his skin. A red stitch of blood sprang up on either side of its blade.

Hadrian's brows furrowed. "What the hell are you—"

"She killed me," he said. The blood trickled down his neck, a strange echo of what leaked, even now, from my own cuts. Involuntarily, I touched my own throat. "You keep saying it. Lucien *screamed* it, the night the police came to her house to haul us away. My brother took the fall for me—went to jail for a few months for selling coke, but sure, who's counting—and because of that I'm in hiding. Forever. I'd worked my ass off for years to get to where I was. I persuaded people to believe in me, despite my name. They expected me to be a monster. They expected me to be like *you*.

"And now"—August laughed wildly, a high-pitched sound that must've moved his throat, because the knife cut in still deeper—"what does it matter? I have nothing. You saved my life and then you cast me out, and I live in Milo Holmes's gilded tower. I'm in the wreckage of it all. All I have left are my ethics. Do you know how I do it? Live my life? All I think about is, what would Lucien do? And then I do the opposite. Spy on Milo's mercenary operation? Of course he would. Poison Charlotte's parents just to watch her agonize? He'd do that, too. Tell this Watson kid to stick around so that I could mess with his head, use him to get to *her*? No. I warned him. I stole one of Milo's cars and drove him around and orchestrated a bloody massive scheme to try to convince him to go home. What would Lucien do? Plot this teenage girl's death because she was a drug addict and lost and confused and no one ever loved her and she lashed out at me when I couldn't give her what she wanted?" His voice quickened. "Lucien hates her for that. And, despite everything else, despite everything I do, I guess I'm a failure because I hate her for that too. I hate her. I *hate* her. And I don't hate her at all." A deep breath. "I refuse to let myself see her as anything but what she is. She's a lost girl, and I was a lost boy for all those years too, growing up, and you used to know what you were, Hadrian, you used to go to plays with me and stay up late reading *A Wrinkle in Time* and you'd make things out of clay and we'd bake them in the oven when Mum wasn't around to complain about the smell, and some of them cracked, but you make *beautiful* art—"

"Shut up," Hadrian said.

"Even those Langenberg paintings—I know your handiwork, Hadrian. They're beautiful—"

"Stop," he said, begging. "Just stop—"

"You were my older brother. I looked up to you. I don't anymore," August said. "You say you want to kill her for me. But if you do it, if you kill her, I swear to God I'll end myself, too. It's all the same to me. You've made sure of it."

I was aware of my body, then, my useless limbs, how heavy and damaged they were, how slow I'd be to stop either of them. Behind the stage, up in the wings, there was shouting, like maybe Tom and Lena and the Greystone mercs had caught Phillipa after all. They'd be bringing her back down, their guns in tow, and with every pistol pointed at everyone else, this could only get more complicated.

Throughout all of this, through August's confession, the blade to his neck, Holmes's eyes hadn't once focused on him. They weren't focused on me, either. They were shut, as gently as though she was sleeping.

"Charlotte!" Lena called from an upper balcony. "We caught her! We caught her! I think I gave her a black eye!"

In front of me, Holmes took a ragged breath. She opened her eyes. In one smooth motion, she grabbed Hadrian's arm, the one with the gun, and wrenched it away from her while she slammed the back of her head into his face. Hadrian Moriarty yelled, staggering backward, and she disarmed him, neatly, with a single hand.

His pistol went off into the floor.

A pause, where no one really knew what to do, and then Charlotte Holmes dove down on top of him, pressing his nose down into the marble ground, pinning his arms behind his back.

"August," she said over her shoulder. "If you're done trying to kill yourself, will you please fetch me some handcuffs?"

thirteen

WE FLEW, ALL OF US TOGETHER, BACK TO ENGLAND ON one of Milo's military-grade planes. Me and Holmes and August and a pair of Moriartys in chains. Not to mention the armed guards, still nameless and interchangeable, all staring at Hadrian and Phillipa like they were rabid dogs about to slip their leashes.

"Mr. Holmes has requested that we watch them closely until he arrives to claim them," a soldier said, when I asked what was going to happen next.

"Are they under arrest? Proper arrest? Like, going to jail?"

Holmes shrugged. "Does it matter?" she said. "We'll dispose of them one way or another. Sussex first, though, please."

"When will Milo get here?" I asked.

"He's on his way now," she said. "He has information about Lucien that he needs to tell me in person."

August stared down at his hands. "Can you take the two of them somewhere else?" he asked quietly, and the soldiers hauled his brother and sister to the back of the plane and out of view.

We'd left Tom and Lena at the Prague airport. They were about to catch a flight back to Chicago to spend Christmas with Tom's family. A compromise, Tom told me, for having spent so much of his break bumming around Europe with Lena.

"And your parents agreed to let you be away all this time?" I asked. We were at the curbside drop-off. Holmes and Lena were inside, arranging for the faux-Langenberg paintings to be delivered back to Germany. It was Christmas Day; everything but the airport was closed.

He nodded at me, hands in his pockets. "Her family's paying for it all, you know? My parents figured it might be my best chance to do some traveling. They can't afford any of this stuff. Even after I got suspended, they thought . . . well, why pass up an opportunity?"

So they weren't the parents of the year. I was beginning to understand Tom a bit more. "Was it worth it? I mean, did you and Lena have fun?"

To my surprise, Tom shook his head. "I kind of miss them. My family. After all the crap that happened this semester, I thought I wanted to escape them . . . but like, Lena and I went to all these fancy restaurants and crazy stores where they make you *tea* while she tried on dresses and yeah, it was all interesting, but I kind of miss my couch. And my TV. And then this stuff with you and Charlotte?"

"Yeah?" I pulled my hat down further around my ears. Without that plastic mask, I felt self-conscious in public, especially now that my bruises were beginning to turn green around the edges. I looked like a piece of rotting meat. August had a bandage around his neck. Holmes wasn't speaking to anyone except Lena, and then only in dark whispers. I didn't need Tom to tell me that the last few days had been hard.

"Dude, just . . . you need to get yourself out, now. Like, guns? Soldiers for hire? A whole family of weirdos trying to kill your girlfriend? You're not married to her, and I really *like* Charlotte, I think she's interesting and, honestly, really scary, but I kind of think that if you keep following her around, you're going to wind up dead."

"August's taken care of it," I said.

Tom shrugged. "Maybe. If so, it's a hell of an anticlimax, isn't it?"

Before I could respond, Holmes and Lena came through the sliding doors in their dark jackets and hats. Lena slipped her gloved hand into Tom's back pocket. "Ready?" she asked.

"Let me know if the Germans don't reimburse you for the cost of those paintings," Holmes said to her. "The Moriartys had some nerve, auctioning every last one of them off. I think you have a complete set. I don't think my surveillance videos would be permissible in court, but we do have enough evidence to at least lean on the government to write you a check."

"It'll be fine," Lena said. "I kind of like the paintings, anyway. I might put one in our room this spring."

Holmes nodded tightly. "If they give you trouble," she said, "tell them to shine a flashlight onto the canvases to look for cat hair."

"Cat hair?"

"Hadrian's trouser cuffs were coated in it. White," she said, "so I assume it's one of those wretched longhaired Persians. Hans Langenberg famously died alone. It was weeks before they found him. Since I haven't read anything about his face being eaten—"

I wondered how long she'd been sitting on *that* information.

"No cats. Got it. I'll tell them, if they ask." Lena leaned in to kiss her roommate on the cheek, leaving a smudge of red where her lips had been. "Bye, guys. Merry Christmas. See you back at school!"

Holmes smiled briefly. "Go on, you'll miss your flight."

We met August at the airstrip. The Greystone plane was there waiting for us, and he was too, standing at the foot of the stairs with windswept hair and exhausted eyes. He looked like a photograph of himself rather than the real thing.

We all nodded to each other, too tired to say much. When we boarded and took our seats, Holmes huddled up against me. She tugged my arm down around her shoulders. Through the layers of sweaters and scarves and coats, I could still feel her shivering, and so I held on to her more tightly.

She'd almost died. We both had. I still wasn't sure why we were alive, where her brother was, why we were headed back to Sussex at all. Her mother was still in a coma. Leander was still lost. We'd pulled off a feat back in Prague, to be sure, but had things veered off one inch to the left or the right, the three of us would all be in refrigerated drawers. I was still processing it there in the museum lobby, my mask in my hands, when Holmes looked down at a handcuffed Hadrian Moriarty and said grimly, "I suppose there's no delaying it further. We need to go home."

"Go, then," August had said.

"No," she'd told him. "You're coming with."

She'd refused to answer further questions. I was done trying to ask them.

The Moriartys were brought in, and then brought to the back. The plane took off. We looked at each other.

"So what now, for you?" I asked August.

He shrugged. "I don't know," he said. "I think—I think maybe I've been lying to myself, a little bit."

"Really, now," Holmes said.

"No sarcasm from you." He said it with a half smile. "I disappeared because my parents wanted me to. Really, I took that job working in your house in the first place because they wanted me to—and I took that job from your brother at Greystone because I was so determined to try to bring an end to this war. A lot of good that did. But tonight's shown that I don't have to do it anymore."

"Greystone?" I asked.

"Any of it," he said. "Make peace. Offer up my life. Now, I might . . . go back to my academic work, in maths. Take on a persona. A new one, you know, build it up from the ground. I could forge some records, or maybe I could even do my DPhil again—it might be nice to take my time, this time—and get a teaching job somewhere. I hear Hong Kong has a nice expat scene. Maybe I'll go there."

I snorted. "It's not a big deal to do your doctorate again?"

"What would you rather do, Jamie? Data entry for the rest of your natural life?" He grinned. "Even if that's your calling, you'll be safe. My brother Lucien won't touch you. Not if he knows he'd be ending my life, too."

"I don't know if we can count on that."

August shrugged. "Forgive me if I don't feel the need to reassure you of your safety. It's not like you think it's important. I kidnapped you and told you to go home, warned you about the dangers of your situation, and all you did was double down."

I stared at him. Even after hearing him tell Hadrian, after hearing him say it now, I still couldn't quite believe him. "That, instead of telling me, *Hey, maybe you're in danger, Jamie.* Which would've been too easy. Or un-psychopathic."

To my surprise, August looked over at Holmes. "I was raised to solve problems in a particular way." His voice was clipped and rough, a simulation of hers. "Generally, I ignore my education. There, it seemed apt. I keep my promises, Charlotte."

Holmes scoffed. "You were serious. You were serious about killing yourself to save us."

"I was serious about that."

"Hong Kong," I echoed. I tried to imagine it. The August from the photos, from the research I'd done. With a professorial beard and a briefcase and a whole bunch of papers to grade. Somewhere out of reach, somewhere far away from all of this.

I couldn't hold on to the image. It didn't seem possible, that you could walk away from this burning wreck with a brand-new name and no scars but the scratch on your neck.

"Well, good luck with that," Holmes said, leaning back into my coat.

"Stop being a child, Charlotte," he said.

"I'm not being a child. I'm being realistic. How can you believe that your brother isn't a complete monomaniac? That he has compunctions? You think he won't hunt you down for sport?" She barked a laugh. "You'd use the name Felix. You'd teach at an English-speaking university. I could find you within ten minutes. Lucien? Within seconds."

"This isn't about me," he said formally. "It's about you. You're hurt that I said those things. I understand, you know. It can be difficult."

"*Difficult?*"

"Actions have consequences—"

"Don't you trot out that patronizing bullshit with me, August, I can't stand it—"

He threw up his hands.

"—I thought of you as the last good one. Of all of us. I thought you'd *forgiven* me."

"How could I? How could I possibly, when—" August

cleared his throat. "You know where Leander is." It wasn't a question.

"Why do you think we're going back to Sussex?"

"How? How long have you known?"

"No." She peered at him over my arm. "First show your work."

That expression crept across August's face again, the one I'd seen him smother so many times before. This time, he didn't try to mask it. Bit by bit, it played out, the look of a man who's torched his own house only to fall in love with the flames. He hated himself, anyone could tell that—the bandage around his neck was still stained red—but I don't think he hated Charlotte Holmes as much as he claimed. I think it was something else completely.

Did he want to be her? Did he want to be with her? It didn't matter now. This was the tail end, the epilogue. After what he'd said to us in Prague, I couldn't imagine our paths would run together much longer.

August leaned forward in his seat, his hands steepled before him. "You haven't had any urgency on this matter since we've arrived. All the tools in the world to track down your uncle, and instead, you play back the same voicemail, again and again, not picking it apart for analysis but listening to it like you're mourning for him? My brother and sister were at your disposal. At your *mercy*. You held them at gunpoint, and then at an auction that you demanded they hold, and instead of extracting information from them, by force, about your uncle's whereabouts—don't give me that look, I know precisely how bloodthirsty you are—you show a cute little surveillance video that implicates them in his disappearance and then you buy up all the Langenberg paintings, one two three? There's no hard evidence there. It's bad detective work, plain and simple. You're solving this *sloppily*, Charlotte, with money and borrowed power, and you're going to use Milo—who, unlike you, has a moral code underneath all that expediency—to put them in whatever black box you put Bryony in. It's like you're trying to race to some end before the howling wolves catch you, and that would make sense if you feared for Leander's life, but you don't. And now you're saying he's been in England the whole time? I don't know what you're doing, but why are you dragging me along?"

I wasn't holding her anymore. I was blank, in shock, trying quickly to catch up. No. That was a lie, and I knew it. But there had been something wrong with the way Holmes had gone about all of this from the moment we'd touched down in Berlin, and all my exhausted heart could do was hope that August had come to the wrong conclusions.

"My brother is meeting us there," Holmes said. "We need to speak to my father, and then we all need to go. Immediately. All three of us."

She turned from him, burying her face in the cloth of my coat. August pulled a notebook from his pocket; he turned it over in his hands. And me? I felt so thoroughly betrayed, so abandoned, that I hardly knew what to think. She was holding on to me like she thought it was the last time I'd let her.

And if she's kept all this from me, maybe it should be, I

thought, and stared out the darkened window, waiting for the first lights of London to appear.

We took a cab to the train, and the train down to Eastbourne, and a black car from the station up to her family's estate. There was snow on the ground, a dusting of it that turned and turned in the wind. We weren't speaking to each other. None of us. I didn't know what to say to August, especially now, and I didn't try. As for Holmes, she'd disappeared into her magician's trunk and swallowed the key. There wouldn't be any prying her out, not until the big reveal.

I thought I knew what it might be. I hoped I was wrong.

The house came into view at the end of the drive, and beside me, I heard August draw a sharp breath. He hadn't been back here since the night he had Lucien deliver his latest shipment of coke. This was the last place he'd been August Moriarty.

It didn't seem to register for Holmes. She sat between us, hands folded in her lap. Her jaw was set. "You need to decide what we do with Hadrian and Phillipa," she said to August.

"I thought you'd made that Milo's call."

"Greystone is keeping them subdued. I want you to decide what happens next."

"Can't we ask Milo his opinion?"

Without looking, Holmes pointed out the window. "He isn't here," she said. "Ours are the only tracks in the drive. Things are about to happen very quickly. Make a decision. Or else I will."

August sighed. "It's difficult, Charlotte. That's my brother. My sister. I don't know."

"Dammit, August, Milo will *have them killed*. That's what happened to Bryony. All right? What do you want? Make a decision!"

The car began to turn down onto the long drive, but Holmes told the driver to stop. August sat stunned and unspeaking.

Holmes took a breath. "Fine," she said, measured again, and leaned over me to pull the door handle. "I'll do it my way. The way I've wanted to all along. God help me—

"Watson, get out."

"What are you—"

She pushed me, and I stumbled out onto the gravel on my hands and knees. Holmes followed, and before she slammed the door on August's face, I heard her say, "You always sit back and let someone else be the monster. Hadrian. Lucien. Me, as a matter of fact, but it stops now. Let's go."

I knelt there, on the ground, in disbelief. I'd never seen her do anything that cruel. Never, at least, to me. Even now, she was stepping over me, wrapping her scarf more tightly around her throat, and instead of heading down the drive, she took off down the salted path that cut through her house's backyard. Careful, even in her haste, to keep from leaving footsteps in the snow.

Behind me, August clambered out of the car and offered me a hand up. "Do we follow her?" he asked.

I was brushing the gravel off of my knees. "What do you think?"

We weren't as careful as she'd been not to leave footprints, though I tried. Even now the light was fading, at four o'clock in the afternoon, and behind us and down the cliffs to the sea, the water raged against the rocky shore. Holmes didn't once glance back at us. She moved quickly through the grounds, head down, keeping to the stands of bare trees and bushes, until she reached the house. The woodpile was there, the one I'd worked with Leander, my ax still standing upright in its fallen log.

It didn't interest her, not in the slightest. The basement windows did, low to the ground, and Holmes was pulling a metal pick out from the inside pocket of her coat. She studied its sharpened edge for a moment before jamming it into the top of the window frame, pulling it free from its hinges. I was at her heels, then, and she handed it up to me.

"You didn't tell Milo about this access point?" August asked, behind me.

"If he's worth his salt, twelve alarms are going off at Greystone right now." She dusted off her hands. "Come on."

Down into a storage room, all rakes and hoes and storage bins, and through the door into a room that looked like it'd been used as a training ring. For combat, maybe, or for something else, but there was a dirt ring in the middle of the floor lined with tape. On the walls were knives and wooden staffs, a set of fencing foils, a pistol with the orange plastic ring around its mouth that meant it was a toy. Did Alistair use it when training his daughter to disarm an enemy? Black ribbons hung from a pipe, thick enough to be blindfolds, and below that were coils of rope, a wooden chair with its seat cut out. I didn't look too closely. After all my wild curiosity, the years I spent as a boy dreaming of the training I could get from the Holmes family in spying and deduction, how I could be transformed into a weapon at their hands, and here it was, the proof. When I'd asked him for training, my father had given me spy novels to read, but Alistair and Emma had put their children through their paces until they gleamed like blades.

The basement smelled like cedar chips and mold. A set of stairs led up to the main level. Already Holmes was at the door at the far end of the room. She tried the knob once, twice, then pulled out her pick again and got to her knees.

"This door isn't ever locked," she said to herself, as if in confirmation.

The door was reinforced with steel bars. The lock was the old-fashioned kind, with a large keyhole you could peer through. I was reminded of the doors I'd liked so much in Prague. What had Holmes said were behind them? Tourist shops? I peered up at the doorframe.

"It's wired," I told her, pointing up. "There must be a key-pad on the other side, some kind of alarm system."

"On the far side?" August asked. "I know this house. The only entrance into that room is from this door."

"What's inside?" I asked him, but he looked away.

Holmes moved the pick to the left, then the right, and paused. "The silent alarm is about to sound. If we haven't been detected already, we will be now. I don't want commentary on what you see. I don't want judgment. I want you to follow me in and then we move out."

She looked ill. Pale, drawn, her eyes flat as coins.

And with that last confirmation, I let myself think it, make it into words, the thing I'd known since we boarded that flight back to England but hadn't wanted to believe. Leander was being kept in this house. In this room. I didn't know why (though I had my suspicions) or what the consequences were of springing him free, but as Holmes picked the lock, humming that strange, tuneless melody under her breath—even now, she was a creature of habit—I tried not to think about what would happen next. After.

If he was still alive in there.

A click. A creak. Holmes charged in before me on her long legs, August muscling past me to follow, and all I saw, at first, were their coats as I pushed in after them. There was a low buzz in the air, like the vibration of a phone going off in a pocket, but amplified, something hanging between these cinder-block walls. This lightless room.

It was coming from a generator, and the generator was powering a series of beeping machines, something that whirred and something that beeped and something else that had clear plastic tubes and wires that wound up from its base and over to the hospital bed where Leander was lying, in a blue cotton gown, his hair lank and greasy like it hadn't been washed since we'd left. A tube taped to his mouth, as if to feed him. An IV tower next to him hung with bags that didn't hold saline and blood. I knew what saline and blood looked like. I'd been in the hospital enough myself. The room was scattered with crutches, a wheelchair, what looked like a Persian rug. It was a makeshift hospital.

This was enough to stop me dead, more so than if the room had been set up for torture or interrogation—though, now that I looked more closely, I thought I saw the metal hardware for hooks and chains still attached to the walls and the ceiling—the idea that Leander had been here, underneath everything, sedated to be kept out of the way of whatever plan was in play.

Except that he wasn't sedated. He was awake. And Emma Holmes hovered over him in a mask and a lab coat, a scalpel in one latex-gloved hand.

Then she reached over and yanked the cord from the security camera in the corner.

Instinctively, I searched my pockets for a weapon; next to me, August did the same, coming up with nothing but the stained knife he'd pulled out in the museum in Prague.

Charlotte Holmes rushed over and flung herself into her mother's arms.

"Lottie," she said, one arm around her daughter, the other pulling off her mask. "Excellent timing. He's fine to travel. We have about four minutes. Move."

UNDER EMMA'S SWIFT DIRECTION, AUGUST HELPED HER remove the IVs. I took socks and a sweater from the suitcase in the corner—Leander's—and helped him into them, taking care to lean in closely to his ear to whisper, "Is she hurting you?"

"She isn't," he said, his voice strangely strong. "He is."

Alistair? August? The latter was putting an arm under his legs now to help turn him off the bed and put him into the wheelchair.

"Get off me," Leander said, and stood. "I'm fine."

"Where is Dr. Michaels?" Holmes was asking her mother. "Where is she being kept?"

"In my room," Emma said. "Your brother had a camera put there—is he secure? Leander, are you ready to go?" I was shocked to hear her speak to him with such gentleness.

"Fastest way out," I said. "The window we came in?"

"Done." Emma Holmes was pulling things from the suitcase—a pair of passports, an envelope, scarves and gloves and a hat—and stuffing them into the pockets of her lab coat. "Go," she said. "I'll follow."

We ran. Leander kept pace behind us, moving far too quickly for a man who looked as debilitatingly ill as he did. The window was just ahead, but there were footsteps, now, above our heads, the scuffle-run of someone moving too quickly for grace.

August hoisted himself up out of the window. "Here," he said to me, "help him up."

"Oh, for God's sake," Leander said. "Come on, Charlotte. Move."

I grasped her waist and lifted her high enough that August could pull her out onto the snowy ground. Leander went next; I made a cradle with my hands and boosted him up and out.

Footsteps on the stair, a different set of footsteps behind

me. Emma had her arms full of files; wordlessly, she handed me half the stack, and we passed them up to Holmes until her mother's arms were free, and then I lifted her up to the window and pushed her out, my arms aching, my bruises pulling painfully against my skin, and just as August reached down both hands to drag me out of the basement, a voice behind me said my name.

I didn't have to look to know it was Alistair Holmes. He said my name again, louder, a shout now, "*James Watson,*" like there wasn't a difference between me or my father at all, like we were all interchangeable, these idiot Watson men who were beaten up and outsmarted by the enemy, kidnapped and shoved out of cars by their friends, men who left their own families behind to find themselves in the thick of a family feud that would leave a trail of bodies by the time this was all over.

"Jamie," Alistair said again, approaching me with his hands out, entreating. "You don't know what you're doing. Lucien's made threats. He presented them through Hadrian. He'll know. He needs to see Leander sick in that hospital bed. He needs to see my wife debilitated in her room, unable to work. He needs to see us at his mercy."

"What are you even talking about? That isn't even what I saw—"

"Idiot boy. The cameras aren't omniscient. I sedated the 'doctor' he sent, Gretchen Michaels, dressed her like my wife and put her in Emma's bed. I locked up Leander, like he demanded, but I had Emma tend to him. He's fine. Wholly fine. This is—"

"Jamie," August hissed. "Come on."

But I was so close to understanding. Alistair was drawing closer to me, his eyes wild, and I said, "It's crazy. What this is is crazy. Why did Mrs. Holmes help Leander escape? How long were you going to keep this up?"

"Hadrian and Phillipa are here, aren't they." There was steel in his voice. *"Aren't they*, child."

"What are you planning—"

Alistair Holmes lunged for me.

"Now," August said, and I grabbed for his hands. As he pulled me out of the window, Alistair Holmes grabbed at my leg.

I kicked him in the face, and he staggered backward.

There was no time to process what I'd just done. There wasn't any up or down anymore, any right path to take. August replaced the window, and Holmes was there with a piece of wood from the pile and a hammer. I held the board while she hammered it into place.

I gripped her shoulders. "Your father—"

"Not important," she said, shaking off my hands. "The car's out front. Help her—I don't know about the Greystone guards, if they're still on our side—"

Holmes's mother was conferring with Leander. "I'm about to give you something that will make you very sick. In actuality. You understand that."

His mouth twisted. "I understand."

"Remember," she said. "There isn't any antidote. This will get worse before it gets better. You'll speak to the police. You'll have them run tests at the hospital. You'll implicate Hadrian and Phillipa. And then you'll recover, and disappear. My suggestion is you go to America. Go see James." She lifted an eyebrow in my direction.

"Of course," I told him. "My father can help. And there's nothing—nothing you can give him to help? Was he poisoned, as you were?"

"There's nothing he can take," she said. "I'm a chemist, Jamie. I mixed this myself. I *tested* it on myself until it became too dangerous to continue. There's a Dr. Gretchen Michaels comatose in my bedroom. Hadrian sent her here to oversee this whole operation, and she stayed long enough that I had to put Leander under for a night—but the next day, I slipped her enough of this compound to put her into a coma. She looks enough like me to fool Milo's cameras, to fool anyone watching his feeds. I didn't need him to worry. I didn't need anyone else to know."

"Listen," Holmes said. "I know you're tired, but—"

"Don't you *dare* patronize me, Charlotte," Leander said. "Not now."

"I know what you've been through," she said, taking his arm. It was almost as though she were pleading with herself. "I couldn't come before now. I needed to know how to pin it on Hadrian and Phillipa—I brought them here, even, but I couldn't have it be my father's fault—"

Emma stared at her daughter. "Your father's fault?"

"You're sick," Holmes said quietly. "You're not working. We'd lose the house. I heard the fights you were having, about money. Through the vents. I heard you shouting at each other.

I assumed—" She ducked her head. "I assumed Father was keeping him somewhere until he agreed to give us the money to ensure we'd be okay. There wasn't a digital record of Leander leaving, not one I could believe. There was a faint echo to his message—that sound you only get in a room with concrete walls. I know every inch of this house. I was made to explore it, blindfolded, so many times, and I . . . he hadn't left. I knew that he was there. When you eliminate all other options—"

"Don't you dare quote Sherlock Holmes. You—you've been trying to frame them," I said in a rush. "Hadrian and Phillipa. All this time—you were trying to draw them in close enough to *frame* them for something you thought your father did."

Holmes turned to her mother. "He wasn't—I wasn't—"

"Lottie," her mother said. "It wasn't your father. It wasn't about money. It was about you. It's always been because of you. Do you understand? There isn't *time* for this. Here."

She pulled a vial from her pocket and gave it to Leander. After a long, bowstrung moment, he bit off the cap and drank its contents down. Emma turned from us, her phone to her ear. "Yes? Yes, I'm requesting police assistance—" She walked toward the house, out of earshot.

No one moved. Above our heads, the moon hung heavy in the sky. Clouds raced across it, hastened by the wind. Was it shouting that I heard from inside the house? Was it just the ocean against the cliffs?

"Alistair just chased me out of the basement," I told them. "I had to—I kicked at him, to get out. He was coming for me—"

Beside me, August threw a hand up over his mouth. He

was laughing. Silently, horribly, his eyes squeezed shut. "You're all such *monsters*," he said. "Monsters, all of you! Trying to pin this on my family, trying to make us out to be worse than we are, and look at this horror you've built with your own hands."

"No," Leander said, wrapping his jacket more tightly around himself. "Don't pretend you don't know how this started. Not when Lucien Moriarty can say two words to his brother on the phone, and Alistair Holmes is given the option to either turn both Charlotte and all of his ill-gotten holdings, his paintings, his offshore bank accounts, *everything* over to the police—Lucien has the information, it would be a matter of minutes to bring it to the authorities—or to keep me in his basement until his brother and sister wrap up their Langenberg operation, safely, without my putting them away. Lucien wants this to go nuclear. He wants to bring all of us down. When he spoke to Hadrian and found out that August was still alive—when he heard word from his spies that August was working for *Milo*—"

"Oh God," I said.

"Well," Leander said. "It's all the same. Everyone has another face. Hadrian and Phillipa are in custody?"

Holmes nodded, her expression unreadable.

"And I'll be the evidence to hang them with. I'll be the poisoned, wronged party. Poison—all it took was a single dose in Emma's tea, administered by the man who takes out the trash, and the whole world goes to hell. Well, I know my place in it. I'll be used, and then it'll be over." Leander turned and spat onto the snowy ground. "And after this, I'm done with it."

I took a step forward before I'd really processed what he'd said. "Done with it?"

Leander swept out an arm. "All this—what is any of it for? Did you hear the Moriarty boy? Monsters. It takes the son of professional sadists to call us what we are. And you follow along in her thrall. I thought—I thought, somehow, that Charlotte would find a way to transcend it. But even now she's putting blood before justice. Her and her mother both. I find myself wanting to thank you, Emma, for tending to me instead of just throwing me into a cage . . . but is that Stockholm syndrome?" He swept a shaking hand over his hair. "God only knows. I want out."

"Wait—" August stepped between us, his back to me. From this angle, he looked exactly like his brother. The close-cropped blond hair. The dark clothes. The slight hunch of the shoulders, like a man always looking up at the guillotine. "I'm sorry—I'm sorry for what I said. It doesn't have to be the truth. This doesn't have to be the end of all of us. I'd had the same plan, you know, to run—but what if we both stayed? Built a bridge between our families? It was my plan to begin with, and it failed, but we could find a way to make it work. There are sane men on both sides. There has to be a way for us all to work this—" He reached a hand out to Leander, touched his chest.

The smallest sound. Like a can being opened, or the click of a door shutting behind you. Like your mother shutting off the light when you were ready to go to sleep. I couldn't place it. Couldn't tell where it came from. I didn't connect it with the way that August dropped, suddenly, to his knees, and then fell in a slow dive face-first onto the ground.

While Leander and I were staring dumbly down at August in the snow—even now, a dark halo was gathering around his hair—Holmes was tracking the shooter. "There," she snarled, pointing at a cluster of trees across the field, and took off unerringly, an arrow loosed from a bow.

I followed her. I didn't know what else to do. Had I just seen August shot down? Had Hadrian or Phillipa escaped to do it, or was it someone else—was it Alistair? He'd gone sprawling when I kicked him, but he'd had enough time to recover. Had he decided to cut his losses and start killing any Moriarty he could get within his crosshairs? *Money,* I thought, *and keeping up this old monolith of a house, and all the things you're willing to give up to keep it—*

August. Holmes's biggest mistake. Our saving grace with a knife to his neck. Hamlet, prince of goddamn Denmark. Shot dead on the Holmeses' back lawn.

The copse of trees was right before us. "I see you," Holmes said, her coat flapping behind her as she skidded to a stop. "Come down. Come down." Her voice broke on the edge of the last word. "Come down and *face me.*"

With a rustle of branches, a man dropped down to the snow. He held a rifle in one hand, a scope affixed to the top. His collar was turned up against the cold. "Lottie," Milo said shakily. "Is Hadrian still alive?"

"You—what did you do?"

"I put Hadrian down," he said, his eyes wild. "I came here

as quickly as I could, Lottie, I have something to tell you—something—"

"Milo, *what have you done?*"

Her brother shook his head, as if to clear it. "My team told me he'd escaped from his holding cell on the plane. I saw him threatening our uncle. I put him down. Lottie, you need to know something about Lucien—"

As gently as my hammering heart would let me, I said, "You've made a mistake."

He frowned, as though that'd never been said to him before. "What mistake? Is Leander all right? I admit I took a risky shot, but I'm fairly sure that I saw—"

Charlotte Holmes put her hands to her face. She was crying. "Milo," she said. "Milo. Milo, no. No, you didn't."

In the distance, a car started up. There was yelling, someone crying out, *Don't touch me, don't touch me,* and then wheels on loose gravel. When I turned to look, a lone figure, a man, was standing in front of the Holmeses' dark estate. Like someone locked out of their home, or a drifter looking for a place to spend the night.

Emma was gone. Hadrian and Phillipa—where were they?

"I—" Milo was shaking. He held the gun out in front of him. "Is August—and Hadrian—God, Lottie, I can't do this anymore. Lucien disappeared. He disappeared. There's no footage, no intel, no . . . *I can't keep doing this.* How could I, and succeed?"

The master of the universe, asking us this question.

Holmes wrenched the rifle from his hands. Without

looking down, she stripped the gun of its clip and dropped it all on the ground.

"Leander's *done*," she said. "August is *dead*. Is this it for you, too? Are you leaving the two of us here to pick up this mess?"

"It's your mess," Milo said. "Isn't it time you did?"

I was only half-hearing it, what they were saying. In the distance, the ocean raged louder. The cold bit at my hands. August Moriarty was spread-eagled, and it wasn't a dream, I could see the outline of his coat in the snow. I couldn't look at them, either of them, Holmes or Holmes, two faces of the same terrible god staring out in opposite directions. Passing their judgments. Firing their guns. And the figure in front of the house—he was gone, the field empty now, and the ocean was deafening.

But it wasn't the ocean. It was sirens, a cacophony of sirens, and by the time the red and blue lights reached the top of the drive, Charlotte Holmes and I were alone.

EPILOGUE

FROM: Felix M ‹ fm.18.96@dmail.com ›
TO: James Watson Jr. ‹ j.watson2@dmail.com ›
SUBJECT LINE: Sorry to spoil your holiday

Dear Jamie,
Well, here we go. Trying this out. One of those time-delay
email tools. This should arrive around the New Year, after
you're safely home. I don't want a fight. I don't want to talk
about this in person. So I'm taking the coward's way out.

Most likely, we won't see each other again. That isn't
any judgment on you; please don't take it that way. (I know
you're taking it that way. Stop.) But I'm realizing that mine

313

isn't any kind of life, not even for a man that's dead. Sitting in this cell of a room in Prague isn't helping matters, I'm sure, but it's more than that. I need out. The auction tonight will happen, and whatever awful thing Charlotte's been brewing will happen, and you'll be the collateral damage, one way or another.

How could you look at a girl like that and trust her with anything other than your life?

That isn't me being flippant, understand. I imagine she'd do anything to keep you alive. But giving her your heart is like handing a glass figurine to a child. She'll flip it over, peer through it like a lens. Shake it to see if it makes a sound. In the end, it will slip her hands and shatter. In the end, it's your fault. You were the one who gave it to her.

I imagine you're thinking, *August and his terrible metaphors.* I do know you're better with words than I am. I see you scribbling in that journal, trying to put down a version of you and her that makes some sense. A story you can tell with confidence. I know what it's like, trying to make a myth out of your life while you're living it. But this isn't a story. It isn't a history. It isn't anything other than a horrible gamble, and Jamie, I know my older brother, and you tangling yourself up in someone else's business won't get you anything but dead.

And if you find yourself reading this and thinking, *Moriarty is being horribly condescending, you're not my dad*, etc., then think of this as a letter I should've written myself, years ago.

Think of yourself as another version of me. And if that makes you angry, too . . . then just think of yourself, full stop.

If you can't do that, run.

Happy New Year, Jamie,

August

ACKNOWLEDGMENTS

THANK YOU, THANK YOU, THANK YOU TO MY INCREDIBLE editor, Alex Arnold, in whose hands Jamie and Charlotte are always made better. Thanks too to Katherine Tegen and everyone at Katherine Tegen Books, especially Rosanne Romanello and Alana Whitman. You are all wonderful beyond my wildest dreams—deerstalker parties, boundless support and encouragement, and matching release-day lipstick? Yes, sign me up, forever.

Endless thanks to Lana Popovic, my agent and friend, who is always there for me, always, with wit and humor and help. Thanks too to Terra Chalberg and everyone else at Chalberg and Sussman for their work on Charlotte Holmes here and abroad.

Thank you to Kit Williamson for all the time and effort and love he's put into this project, from the book trailer to the late-night phone calls to every detailed, smart reading. I love you, oldest friend.

Thank you to Emily Temple, for Berlin and Prague and the world's fastest read and critique of one hundred pages ever.

Sister mine: let's go find an ATM and then get some naan pizza.

Thank you to Emily Henry and Kathy MacMillan, my amazing readers and friends, without whom this mystery would be a giant tangle of string. Thanks to Rebecca Dunham, my mentor. Love and emojis to Chloe Benjamin, Becky Hazelton, Corey Van Landingham, and, again, Emily Temple. One day we will have a girl gang name, but for now, just call us Group Text.

Love to my family, especially my parents. I hope you know how wonderful you are. Thank you for your excitement.

Thanks, and apologies, to Sir Arthur Conan Doyle.

And thank you to my husband, Chase. May we have many more years of love and ridiculous banter. Elmira Davenport, of course, is for you.

In *The Case for Jamie*, Charlotte and Jamie finally face their longtime enemy—and their true feelings for each other.

READ ON FOR AN EXCERPT . . .

one

IT WAS JANUARY IN CONNECTICUT, AND THE SNOW HADN'T stopped falling in what felt like forever. It gathered in the window wells, in the hollows between the bricks of the rebuilt sciences building. It hung from the boughs of trees, tucked itself up in the root systems below. I shook it from my wool cap before every class, ruffled it out of my hair, pulled it from my socks. Underneath, my feet were rubbed red. I found it everywhere, snow that never seemed to fully melt, that lingered on my backpack and my blazer and, on the worst days, my eyebrows, melting down my face in the warmth of first period like it was sweat, like I was guilty of something.

When I got back to my room, I took to laying out my parka like a body on the spare bed, so that the snow could drip somewhere other than into the carpet. I was tired of having wet feet. A wet spare mattress seemed less important. But as the winter stretched on, it was hard not to see a metaphor in that pathetic almost-man, especially on those nights that I couldn't sleep.

But I was done finding metaphors everywhere.

Maybe I should start here: there aren't a lot of benefits to being framed for murder. Once I would've told you that meeting Charlotte Holmes was the only good thing that came out of that mess. But that was my former self speaking, the one who mythologized that girl until I couldn't see the person beneath the story I'd made up.

If I couldn't see her for what she was, what she'd been all along, then I'd had trouble seeing myself clearly as well. It's not an uncommon delusion, the one I had. The Great Big Destiny delusion. That your life is a story that twists and turns its way up to a narrative precipice, a climax, the moment where you'll make the hard decision, defeat the villain, finally prove yourself worthy. Leave some kind of mark on the world.

Maybe it started when I read my great-great-great-grandfather's story about Sherlock Holmes going over the Reichenbach Falls, after finally vanquishing the evil Professor Moriarty. A great sacrifice made by a great man—to defeat great evil, Holmes had to give himself. I studied "The Final Problem" like I'd studied all the others, using those tales to cobble together an instruction manual for adventure and duty and friendship, the way any kid looks for models, and then I'd clung to those ideas for years longer than I'd should've.

Because there aren't any textbook villains out there. There aren't any heroes. There was Sherlock Holmes, who faked his own death and reappeared three years later like nothing had happened, expecting to be welcomed with open arms. There were selfish people, and there were those of us who yoked ourselves to them out of a misplaced sense of loyalty.

I knew now that it was stupid, the way I'd obsessed so much over the past—not just my own ancestry, but over the recent past, the months I'd spent with my own Holmes. I'd lost too much time over it. Over her. I was done. I was changing. Butterflies, chrysalises—whatever. I was building one. I was going to emerge from it a more realistic Jamie Watson.

AT FIRST, IT WAS HARD TO STICK TO THE PLAN. WHEN I'D gotten back to Sherringford from the Holmeses' estate, I'd found myself more than once on the fourth floor of the sciences building without any real memory of taking myself there. In the end, it didn't matter. I could have knocked on the door of 442 as long as I wanted. I wouldn't have gotten an answer.

It didn't take long for me to decide that moping wasn't doing me any good. I decided I had to take stock. On paper. Instead of making a story out of it, the way I'd done in the past, I'd be objective. What had happened to me since the day Lee Dobson turned up dead in his room? What were the facts?

The bad: dead friends; dead enemies; utter betrayal; widespread suspicion; heartbreak; concussions; kidnappings; my nose broken so many times that I was beginning to look like a two-bit boxer. (Or like a librarian who'd been violently mugged.)

The good?

My father and I were on speaking terms, now. I was beating him at cell phone Scrabble.

As for my mother—well, not a lot of good there, either. She'd called the other night to tell me she was dating someone new. *It's nothing serious, Jamie,* she'd said, but the hesitancy in her voice suggested that, in fact, it was. That she was afraid I'd bite back with the same resentment I had for my father, way back when I was a child, when he'd met and married Abigail, my stepmother.

"Even if it is serious," I'd said to my mom. "Especially if it is. I'm happy for you."

"Okay." A pause, then: "He's Welsh. Very kind. I told him you were a writer, and he said he'd like to read some of your stories. He doesn't know how dark they are, but I imagine he'd like them anyway."

Those stories that I wrote, the ones that were all about my own life. They weren't stories at all, and my mother knew it. She just couldn't bring herself to say it aloud.

Weirdly enough, that was the last straw—not the list of pros and cons, but the realization that the months I'd been friends with Charlotte Holmes were so dark my mother was handing out content warnings.

Ten minutes in the headmistress's office, pleading my case, and I was packing my things to move down a floor in Michener Hall. I'd used the whole wrongfully-accused-of-murder thing to wrangle myself a single room. That excuse was a year old, but it still held water. It got me what I wanted. No more roommate to stare at me while I cried. No more anyone at all. Just me, alone, so I could rebuild my life into one I actually wanted to be living.

So time passed, as time tends to do.

It was January again in Connecticut, and it wouldn't stop snowing. I didn't care. I had a literary magazine to edit, drills for the spring rugby season, hours of homework every night. I had friends, new ones, who didn't demand all my time and patience and unearned trust.

It was my final semester at Sherringford. I hadn't seen Charlotte Holmes in a year.

No one had.

"I saved your spot," Elizabeth said, pulling her bag off the chair beside her. "Did you bring—"

"Here," I said, pulling a can of Diet Coke out of my backpack. The dining hall had done away with soda last year (and the all-day cereal bar, a loss we were all publicly mourning), but my girlfriend neatly sidestepped the rules by keeping a six-pack of soda in my room's mini-fridge at all times.

"Thanks." She popped the top and poured it into a waiting glass of ice.

"Where is everyone?" I asked, because our lunch table was empty.

"Lena is still microwaving her tofu. She's trying this soy sauce–honey thing this time; it smelled awful. Tom's therapist had to reschedule his session, so he's there, but he should be almost done. Mariella's still in line with her friend Anna—she

5

might sit with us today—and I don't know where your rugby bros are."

I grimaced. "I saw them over by the bread. I think they're carbo-loading."

"Gettin' huge," Elizabeth said, in a credible imitation of Randall.

This was an old joke; I knew my line. "Huge."

"Huuuuge."

"Yuuuuge."

We snickered. It was part of the routine. She got back to her burger; I got back to my burger. Our friends showed up, one by one, and when Tom finally arrived, he patted me on the back and then stole a fistful of my fries. I raised an eyebrow at him, the how-was-therapy eyebrow, and he shrugged back that it was fine.

"Are you okay?" Elizabeth asked. In my darker moments, I thought it was her favorite question.

"I'm fine."

She nodded, looking back down at her book. Then looked back up. "Are you sure? Because you sound a little—"

"No," I said, too quickly, then forced a smile. "No. I'm fine."

It was like a dance I knew all the steps to, one I could perform upside down, backward, on a sinking cruise ship that was also on fire. In the fall we ate on the quad; in the spring, the steps outside the cafeteria. It was winter, so we'd claimed our usual table inside by the hot bar, and I listened to the low hum of the lights keeping the food warm. Mariella and Tom went over their odds of getting into their choice of college early decision. They were supposed to hear this week (Tom, University of Michigan; Mariella, Yale), and they couldn't talk about anything else. Lena was texting someone under the table, eating her tofu with her free hand, while Randall and Kittredge compared bruises from practice. Kittredge was sure someone was digging holes into the rugby field at night. Randall was sure that Kittredge was just a clumsy asshole. Elizabeth, as always, was reading a novel next to her tray, deaf to everyone else as she turned the pages in her own Elizabeth-world. I never knew what went on in there. I didn't think there was enough time before graduation for me to find out.

More than anyone else I knew, Elizabeth was competent. Frighteningly competent. If her uniform pants came back from the tailor an inch too long, she'd teach herself how to hem and fix them herself. If she wanted to take both Shakespeare and Dance II, and they were scheduled for the same time, she'd have an independent study in *Romeo and Juliet* Through Irish Step Dancing approved by the end of the day.

If the boy she'd had a crush on came back to school heartsick and bitter, she'd wait a semester for him to get over himself before she asked him out. *Go with me to homecoming?* the note slipped in my mailbox had said, this past fall. *I promise not to choke on a diamond this time.*

I'd accepted. I really wasn't all that sure why, at the time—though I wasn't still mourning my and Holmes's notrelationship, I hadn't been looking at girls. Mostly, I'd been studying. It was as boring as it sounded, but if I didn't bring up my grades, there wasn't any possibility of me getting into college anywhere, much less where I wanted to go.

Dobson's murder won't excuse your grades forever, you know, the guidance counselor had said. *Though it'll make for a really compelling college essay!*

So I studied. I played rugby, both seasons, in hopes that if my grades still weren't good enough, some dream college somewhere was looking for a wiry English halfback. I took Elizabeth to homecoming out of a sense of duty—that plastic diamond down her throat was more or less my fault, even if I hadn't put it there myself—and to my surprise, I'd had a better time with her than I'd had with anyone in months.

It hadn't surprised Elizabeth. "You have a type, you know," she'd said, laughing under the dance floor lights. Her blond hair was in long, ribbon-like curls, and she had this bright necklace that swung as we danced, and when she laughed, she did it with her whole body, and I liked her. I really liked her.

I had the strange sense that I was taking an old chapter of my life and writing over it until the text beneath was gone.

"What's that?" I asked. I wasn't really sure I wanted to hear the answer. Already, with the music, the smoke machine—I had one foot in this year and one foot in the last.

But she'd grinned at me, wickedly. It was a different kind of wicked than what I was used to. Wicked without secrets. Wicked without danger. It was the smile of a smart girl who was coming into her own, who knew she was about to get the thing she wanted.

"You like girls who don't take any of your shit," she'd said, and kissed me.

She was right. I liked girls who pushed back; I liked girls with thoughtful eyes. Elizabeth had both, and even if sometimes I got the sense that I was an item on her checklist that she had successfully crossed off (*date boy you crushed on freshman year*), well—

Well, it was more my own bullshit than anything I got from her. Because, as usual, I was staring out the bright-lit window, thinking about my essay for AP Euro, my problem set for calculus, about the million other balls I had up in the air—and more than that, convincing myself that I did need to think about them, that I needed to make myself care.

Then someone dropped a tray behind me with a sharp pop and a clatter, and I was back there again.

Me on a lawn in Sussex, August Moriarty at my feet, blood on all that snow. Police sirens edging closer. Charlotte Holmes's white, chapped lips. Those last few seconds. That other life.

"I'll be right back," I said, but no one was listening, not even Elizabeth, lost in her book. At least I made it to the bathroom before I started to dry heave.

One of the lacrosse starters was in there washing his hands. "Brutal," I heard him say over my retching. By the time I came out of the stall, I was alone.

I braced myself against the sink, staring at the drain, the fissured ceramic around it. The last time this had happened to me, it'd been a slammed car door, and that time the nausea had been followed hard by rage. Horrible, mind-bending rage, at Charlotte for making assumptions; at her brother, Milo, for gunning a man down and getting away with it; at August

Moriarty, who'd told me, two weeks too late, to run—

My phone pinged. *Elizabeth,* I imagined, as I fished it out. Checking on me. It wasn't a bad thought.

But it wasn't Elizabeth. It wasn't any number I knew.

You're not safe here.

That feeling, like someone hit Play on a movie I'd forgotten I was watching. A horror movie. About my life.

Who is this? I wrote back, and then, horrified, *Is that you? Holmes?,* and then I called the number once, twice, a third time, and by then they'd shut the phone off.

Leave a message, it said. I stood there, stunned, until I realized I'd let it record a few seconds of my breathing. Hurriedly, I ended the call.

I made it back to our lunch table somehow, my head crackling with dehydration and fear. Elizabeth was still reading. Randall was eating his third chicken sandwich. Mariella and Kittredge and that Anna girl were bitching again about the cereal bar, and there was a whole ecosystem here, a landscape that functioned fine without me.

Why would I put any of this on them? What did I want to do, go back to being some kind of victim? Even Elizabeth, the person I'd usually turn to, couldn't help me here. She'd dealt with enough because of me.

No. I squared my shoulders. I finished my burger.

I kept one hand on my phone, just in case.

"Jamie," Lena was saying.

I shook my head.

"Jamie," Lena repeated, frowning a little, "your father's

here." I was dully surprised to see him hovering over our table.

Elizabeth smiled up at him. "He's been like this all day," she said. "Off in dream land." I didn't point out that she'd been ignoring all of us in favor of *Jane Eyre*.

I put on a smile as best I could. "Ha, yeah, you know. Lots of, uh, school things. Schoolwork."

Across the table, Lena and Tom exchanged a significant glance.

"It's true," I said, and my voice shook a little. "Uh, Dad. What's up?"

"Family emergency," he said, sticking his hands in his pockets. "I've already signed you off campus. Go on, grab your bag."

Oh God, I thought. This again. Plus, I wasn't sure if my legs would hold me if I stood. "Can't. French class. We have a quiz."

Tom frowned. "But that was yester—"

I kicked him, weakly, under the table.

"Family emergency," my father said again. "Up! Come along!"

I ticked it off on my fingers. "AP English. Physics. I have a presentation. Stop looking at me like that."

"Jamie. Leander's waiting in the car."

A surge of relief. Leander was one of the only people I could be around when I was like this, all shaky and strange. I knew as well as my father did that Leander was his trump card, and that I'd lost this round. I packed up my things, ignoring Lena's stage-wink across the table.

"See you tonight," Elizabeth said, already back in her book. But then, she was used to this by now.

"I actually do have a presentation in physics tomorrow, you know," I told my father as we left the cafeteria.

He clapped a hand on my shoulder. "Of course you do. But that's hardly important, is it?"

READ THEM ALL!

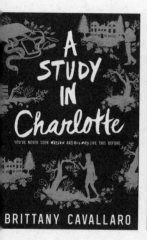

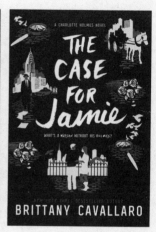

You've never seen Watson and Holmes
like this before!

JOIN THE

Epic Reads

COMMUNITY

THE ULTIMATE YA DESTINATION

◀ **DISCOVER** ▶
your next favorite read

◀ **MEET** ▶
new authors to love

◀ **WIN** ▶
free books

◀ **SHARE** ▶
infographics, playlists, quizzes, and more

◀ **WATCH** ▶
the latest videos

www.epicreads.com